Please return / renew this item
by the last date shown.
Books may also be renewed by
phone or the Internet.

Tel: 01204 332384

www.bolton.gov.uk/libraries

Black Hills Gold

Since the signing of the Laramie Treaty six years earlier, the tribes of the Plains have followed their nomadic lifestyle within the boundaries of the lands set aside for their use. The dwindling herds of buffalo and deer, which provide the staple requirements of their existence, are a growing source of discontent, but as long as the Americans, the *wasicun*, stay out of the tribal lands the tenuous peace is maintained.

One word, however, uttered at a riverside meeting with 'Yellowstone' Kelly, raises Wes Gray's concern that that peace might soon be broken, that white men might breach the borders of the Great Sioux Reservation and bring with them the turmoil of war. And the object of their trespass: to gain that for which men will risk all: gold.

Black Hills Gold

Will DuRey

A Black Horse Western

ROBERT HALE

© Will DuRey 2017
First published in Great Britain 2017

ISBN 978-0-7198-2547-7

The Crowood Press
The Stable Block
Crowood Lane
Ramsbury
Marlborough
Wiltshire SN8 2HR

www.bhwesterns.com

Robert Hale is an imprint
of The Crowood Press

Typeset by
Derek Doyle & Associates, Shaw Heath
Printed and bound in Great Britain by
CPI Group (UK) Ltd, Croydon, CR0 4YY

ONE

The foraging grizzly was going about its business less than thirty yards downhill, searching the undergrowth for marmot or tree-squirrel or any other creature that would feed its appetite. Fortunately for the buckskin-clad man, the slight breeze was coming up from the river, and the nervous snicker of his pack horse had prevented him from blundering into range of the grizzly's vision. Now he stood behind a large tree with his hands over the muzzle of both of his animals, keeping them calm and quiet.

The sight of the bear so early in the year surprised Wes Gray. Females would be in hibernation with their cubs for at least another month, but even males were rarely seen this early in spring. If this one's winter sleep had been disturbed then it was likely to be easily angered, so Wes remained hidden while the bear continued to hunt for food. They were unpredictable creatures at the best of times, and even though their gait seemed ponderous when moving slowly, it belied the speed and power they could generate when launching an attack. Although the one he was watching didn't have the bulk it would attain later in the year, Wes wasn't anxious to tackle it. He figured it still weighed over four hundred pounds, and if it caught the scent of the horses, was capable of swiping him aside before killing one of them for a meal that would be more satisfying than a dozen small vermin could provide.

Wes Gray's life had been littered with such moments of sudden, imminent danger, and like the bear and every other wild creature, he'd come to depend upon his innate instincts. They had preserved his life on many occasions.

From youth, with neither place to call home nor folks to call family, Weston Gray had travelled the uncharted country west of the Missouri, living the arduous life of a trapper and earning a paltry living from the pelts he sold – but by the time he was twenty-five, due to his association with the last of the mountain men and the tribes-people through whose land he wandered, he had gained a knowledge of the country that few others possessed. He had crossed prairie land, climbed mountains, dwelt in forests and navigated rivers that few white men even knew existed.

Often he had made a temporary home with a

tribe of Sioux or Arapaho people, joining in their summer hunt or sharing their winter deprivations, and learning that their primitive lifestyle required an understanding of their role in the natural world, how they affected and were affected by their surroundings and the changes wrought by the seasons. Wes had been a quick learner, soon able to predict changes in the weather as easily as he could identify the best types of rock for making arrow-heads, tools and weapons. The tribesmen taught him their language, both their spoken tongue and the sign language that was common to all the tribes that wandered the Plains. In addition, he soon came to recognize the habits of other creatures and how to interpret the message in any abnormal behaviour, and he became aware of those plants and trees that bore fruit he could eat, or had seeds, leaves, roots or sap that he could crush and pulverize for medicinal purposes.

He fought the enemies of those among whom he chose to live, danced at their ceremonies and told tales around their fires until he became accepted by the elders and was allowed to speak as an equal at their village council. The Sioux called him *Wiyaka Wakan*, which is Medicine Feather, and on more than one occasion he had spoken on their behalf at treaty meetings with the American military. Among the nomadic tribes of the Plains, 'Medicine Feather' became a name as much feared as it was honoured, while that of 'Wes Gray' aroused similar emotions among the white Americans.

After the War Between the States, Wes's knowledge of the land west of the Missouri prompted his friend, Major Caleb Dodge, to hire him as chief scout for the wagon train he was leading to California. Such a journey appealed to Wes, and each year after that he and Caleb had led settlers west, either to California or Oregon.

An annual routine had been established, one that was almost as fixed as a grizzly's need for winter sleep, or the springtime return of the grey goose to the valleys along the upper Missouri. The journey west extended from late spring to late autumn, and when it was completed he'd make his way to the Wind River country, to the Arapaho village that was the winter home of his wife, Little Feather – and there he'd spend the cold months trapping beaver, whose pelts he would sell when he returned east.

In spring, when the days warmed and the tribe moved towards the buffalo trails, Wes went with them, the first stage in returning to the towns of his own people where the next wagon train would be assembling. Usually, when the summer village was established, he would pack his pelts into a canoe and continue his journey alone, following the tributaries that led him to the great Missouri and onward to Council Bluffs. With the rivers in full flood he was able to complete the journey in less than half the time it would take on horseback – but this year it was different. Buffalo had been sighted while the Arapaho were still well west of their regular haunt, and the headmen had had no hesitation in establishing a village in the first suitable location.

Even though it was early for a herd to be so far north, it was essential to hunt them while they were within close proximity – there was no guarantee that the scouts would discover another herd before they returned to their winter home in the Wind river country. Those vast herds that had previously roamed the prairies had been reduced to a scattering. A fashion for buffalo coats, and a slaughter policy ordained by those railroad magnates determined to get top dollar when they sold their trackside holdings to settlers, had wreaked unimaginable destruction upon the herds, and their disappearance added to the plight of all the tribes of the Plains. The buffalo were their staple of life, providing food, clothing, tools, weapons and ornaments. So the sighting of a herd couldn't be ignored.

In order to provide for Little Feather and her parents while he was away from the village, Wes had joined the hunt alongside the other warriors. Much of the meat would be dried and taken back to the Wind River country to supplement their winter diet, and some of it would be mixed with fat and berries, then pounded into cakes of pemmican, some of which Wes had brought with him to sustain him on his journey.

Because the Arapaho had erected their tepees along the Powder River, Wes had forsaken his usual route to Council Bluffs. The Powder flowed north into the Yellowstone before joining the Missouri at the Fort Union Trading Post. Instead he'd loaded his packs on a pony, which trailed behind him as he followed an easterly route through the Black Hills. He expected to find a Sioux village along the Cheyenne or White river, which flowed directly into the Missouri many miles downstream from Fort Union.

Suddenly the bear halted, lifted its head and looked around as though alerted by some in-bred alarm, a primeval notion that a threat to the dominion of its territory was close at hand. For a full minute it remained still, then, rising on its hind legs, slowly turned its head to allow its gaze to sweep the heavily timbered downhill slope for the presence of danger. Its ears flicked to catch unexpected sounds, and its nose twitched in search of olfactory messages. Unable to detect any proof for its concern, it dropped back on to its front paws with surprising delicacy. Before recommencing the search for food, however, it turned its attention uphill, studying the upper slope with intensity. Satisfied, it emitted a throaty grunt then headed down towards the stream below.

Among the ponderosa pines, Wes Gray watched

the big animal as it lumbered away, its great bulk swaying from side to side with every stride. He remounted and set a course that would take him well away from the grizzly's route.

Rarely did he venture into these Black Hills, the sacred *Paha Sapa* that was the heart of the territory defined as the Great Sioux Reservation by the Laramie Treaty of 1868. This vast range of hills and prairie had been set aside to enable the tribes-people to pursue their traditional lifestyle, because Washington deemed it wild and uninhabitable land. Most Americans, *wasicun*, were forbidden to enter the Reservation, but *Wiyaka Wakan* was one of the few tolerated. Not only had he spoken on their behalf at meetings, but he had also taken a Sioux wife. *Apo Hopa* lived in his cabin on a V-shaped chunk of land where the Mildwater Creek met the South Platte, and as with Little Feather of the Arapaho, his marriage had a deeper purpose than an expression of their feelings for each other. In the West there were no rules that guaranteed survival. Strangers were regarded with suspicion by white and red men alike. Actions that threatened a society's accepted behaviour were usually punished with pain and death. To be accepted into a strange community meant adopting their ways, recognizing their laws, observing their religion. Taking a wife was a symbol to the entire village that his relation-ship with them was permanent: their needs were his needs, their enemies his enemies, their struggles his struggles.

Even so, the Black Hills were the Sioux Holy Ground, and Wes was careful not to risk causing offence. The majority of Sioux warriors accepted him as a friend, but there were those who were less affable, and he wasn't prepared to antagonize them unnecessarily.

But it was an abundant land, teeming with game that supported the life pattern of the nomadic hunter tribes. The low mounds of the foothills were green, lush with vegetation where white-tailed and mule deer, pronghorn and Bighorn sheep grazed. For Wes, who had travelled the continent east to west and north to south, it was a place without equal. Assailed by the pleasant scent that arose from the numerous stands of mountain mahogany and blossoming juniper, Wes experienced a moment of contentment, a warmth unrelated to the morning sun, and a hope that this Eden would last forever.

His horse lifted its head and snuffled in the way it had when it smelled water. As he reached the crest of a hill he found himself above a valley through which a rising river flowed swiftly with spring thaw. Its course twisted in spectacular fashion, disappearing eventually behind the high, distant tree-lined hills. Although the heights were raggedly rocky, the river's banks were wide, green and flat, dotted here and there with shade-spreading alder and willow trees.

To his left, Wes espied a collection of high tepees, but the sound of drums had alerted him to the presence of the village before breasting the rise. He rode along the ridge, getting closer to the village before riding down to the valley. In addition to the sound of drums, the high, reedy sound of primitive flutes could be heard, an indication that the villagers were gathered together for a ceremony or celebration. For a moment, Wes was reluctant to ride into the village: butting into their festivity might be the wrong thing to do. He didn't want to offend these people, as he was hoping to trade his horses with them for a canoe. He reined to a halt and counted more than fifty tepees; most were the homes of Minneconjou families, the remainder were daubed with the markings of Hunkpapa people.

The centre of the village was a scene of great activity. A wide ring had been formed by people moving rhythmically to the beat of the drums. A procession consisting of a dozen men and women in various costumes and disguises paraded within the circle. Their leader was a young man, barely more than a youth, who carried a folded length of deerskin that he showed to the bystanders. Wes recognized the skin – he had seen such artefacts among other tribes, the characters drawn on them depicting the history of the village. The importance of the ceremony was marked by the inclusion of this relic, a fact acknowledged by the women in the assembly who gave voice to their tremolo song when it passed by.

Four maidens followed the leader. The first carried a bow, the sign of war; the next bore a pipe, the sign of peace; the third carried the white eagle feather of wisdom; and the last held a flowering branch which signified a bountiful and healthy tribe.

Four warriors walked behind the maidens, each painted head to toe a different colour – white, red, yellow and black – and leading a matching horse – white, sorrel, buckskin and black. They represented the four portions of the world – north, east, south and west – and only a leader whose medicine was powerful would invoke those spirits in a ceremony.

At the end of the parade were warriors covered with buffalo skins or wearing antlers or the pelts of other creatures, an acknowledgement of the Lakota belief that every living thing was important to maintain their own existence. The hoop of their world, the circle of life, could not be maintained without them.

Clearly for the village it was an important occasion that had been planned in advance. As he had time enough to reach Council Bluffs before the wagons rolled west, Wes tactfully chose to set aside any notion of riding into the village until the ceremony was completed. He was preparing to dismount when a movement on the river bank almost directly below caught his eye. A man was inspecting a canoe, getting ready to put it in the water, but he had ceased his labour at the appearance of Wes on the hillside. Like Wes, he was a white man, a *wasicun*, and he kept his eyes on Wes as the scout rode down through the trees.

He was tall, with long dark hair that was as unkempt as that of any Sioux brave. Crossing from the man's right shoulder to disappear behind his left hip was a well-filled cartridge belt, ammunition for the rifle he was holding in readiness. His dark eyes had a piercing quality to them, as though he was accustomed to fixing his gaze on one location for a long time. When he recognized the new arrival he placed his rifle in the canoe, then in thoughtful manner, like a scholar or man of learning giving study to a troublesome problem, rubbed the back of his hand over his long moustaches.

Wes knew this to be nothing more than a mannerism, an unconscious act with no more significance to the thoughts in the other's head than spitting in camp-fire embers to watch them splutter – but like every move that the man made, it was performed with slow deliberation, nothing hurried or sudden that might startle any creature in the vicinity.

'Wes,' he called, greeting the oncoming rider.

'Luther.' Wes stepped down and joined the other

at the waterside.

It had been more than two years since the men had last met, each with a pack of pelts for sale, haggling prices in an Omaha trading post. Luther Kelly was a handsome man and half a dozen years younger than Wes. Since leaving the army in 1868 he had gained a reputation as a trapper, Indian fighter, army scout and explorer, surviving, often alone, in the northern territories, earning for himself the soubriquet 'Yellowstone' because he knew the land around that river better than any other white man alive. 'Yellowstone' Kelly had learned much about the habits of the nomadic tribes-people and had developed some sympathy for them, but Wes knew that Luther Kelly's sympathies rested with the army.

The lack of pelts and goods in Luther's canoe surprised Wes. It seemed to be too early in the year for the young trapper to have sold his haul downriver and already to be heading back to his cabin in the hills, but nonetheless he commented on the fact.

'That's a light load in your canoe,' he said. 'Have you traded your pelts here, with the Sioux?'

'No,' Luther told him, 'They're holding one of their medicine ceremonies from which wasicun are banished. Seems we might interfere with their mystic messages.'

'You were told to leave?' Wes asked.

'Didn't even get into the village. Their headman, Black Buffalo, came here to talk to me. Seems they've been preparing for the ceremony for some days and didn't want my presence to spoil the purification rituals that had already been performed.'

Luther Kelly tried to keep the cynicism out of his voice, but Wes knew the importance of a holy dance to the participants, and that the smallest deviation from the requirements for its enactment could lessen, even destroy, the power of its revelations. Wes had known many Sioux who had experienced medicine dreams – holy men, wise men, warriors and women – and had never had cause to doubt that any one of them had experienced the revelation they described. Some had claimed to have flown with eagles or run with deer, had spoken with buffalo or sat with the Great Spirit, but they all had one thing in common, and their dream had nothing to do with personal gain: its interpretation was always concerned with the effect on the village, the tribe or the entire Sioux nation.

Although Luther seemed irritated by his exclusion from the village, Wes had no such concerns. Like every other society they had their ways, the mores that governed their lives. Wes was content to respect their wishes and stay out of the village until the ceremony was ended. He turned his attention to Luther and his empty canoe, wanting to know if he'd already been downriver to sell his pelts.

'I'm here as a messenger for the army,' Kelly told him. 'I've been all over these hills to let the tribes know that a Washington delegation is coming up the Missouri to talk to them.'

'Talk about what? I haven't heard of any trouble.'

'Terms of the treaty.' Luther Kelly examined his canoe for damage in preparation for putting it back in the water.

'As far as I know the terms haven't been broken. The warriors might have roamed beyond the reservation boundary, but only when hunting. They don't trouble travellers on the trails or do damage to the railroad.'

'Didn't say they did,' Luther answered, lifting his head and fixing the other with a look of such frankness that Wes was gripped immediately with a sense of foreboding.

'There must be some reason.'

'Guess so,' Luther said, holding Wes's gaze as though the reason was too obvious to need putting into words.

'So what is it?'

'Washington doesn't inform me of their plans and purposes, Wes. I've just been sent to pass around word that a delegation wants to meet representatives of all the tribes at Five Squaws Meadow.'

'That's all you've told the village chiefs?'

'That, and the fact that it's important that they attend. There will be gifts for them.'

A snort from Wes expressed his disapproval, knowing that the gifts would be more useless glass beads and mirrors. 'Come on, Luther, tell me what it's all about.'

Yellowstone eyed the other with a certain amount of cynicism, as though it wasn't possible that the other could be in the dark about the government's plans, but he also knew that Wes Gray was a plain-talking man who wouldn't waste time denying something he knew. 'You haven't heard the rumours?' he asked.

'What rumours?'

'Gold.'

Wes repeated the word. 'A new gold strike?' Kelly nodded, and pushed the canoe into the water. 'Where?' Wes asked.

'The Black Hills, Wes. They say there's gold in the Black Hills.'

For a moment, Wes was too stunned to speak. The Sioux would never surrender the sacred Black Hills. If the government were hoping to take it from the tribes-people it wouldn't be achieved with glass beads, blankets or even dollar bills: blood would be the price. 'How do they know there's gold there? Who's been there to take samples?'

'Like I say, Wes, rumours, but there must be some foundation to them if the government are prepared to negotiate for them.'

'It'll mean war if they try to move the Sioux out

of this region.'

'That's what I told Senator Goodwin.'

'Who is he?'

'The leader of the delegation. One-time soldier but now a politician from Colorado.'

'I knew a Colonel Goodwin during the war,' Wes mused aloud. 'Jeremiah Goodwin.'

'Same man,' said Luther Kelly. 'He's down river on board the *Far West* with the rest of the delegation. I'm on my way to join them. I'm to act as interpreter at the meeting.'

'When will it take place?' Wes wanted to know.

'Five days,' Luther told him as he pushed away from the shore. He pointed to the east, along the course of the river, and shouted, 'Five Squaws Meadow!' then was caught up in a rush of water and swiftly carried downstream.

TWO

By the time the ceremonial drums had stopped beating, Wes had removed the trappings from his animals, watered them at the river, then tethered them where the grass was lush and abundant. He was boiling coffee when a Minneconjou warrior with whom he'd hunted on previous occasions, rode up. His name was Tall Horse, and they greeted each other as old friends. According to Tall Horse, the youth who had performed the medicine dance, Yellow Hawk, was favoured by the Great Spirit.

'One day he will become a great leader of his people,' Tall Horse told Wes. 'His visions are strong, and the elders of the tribe listen to his words. The ceremony was necessary to allow the Great Spirit *Wakan Tanka* to talk to him. The People are afraid that the buffalo will not return again.'

Wes Gray had no words of encouragement to offer, but Tall Horse was speaking again, inviting him into the village and a meeting with their chief, Black Buffalo. The stony facial expression and guttural utterances often made it difficult to judge the true tenor of Lakota conversation, whether friend or foe, but Wes suspected that there was more purpose behind the proposed meeting with Black Buffalo than the simple act of courtesy that was required by both parties when a traveller arrived in a village.

Wes carried some shells from the Pacific shores that his Arapaho family had acquired by trade with some Nez Perce they'd met along the Snake the previous summer. He took them to the Sioux village, shared them out among the women to be used as jewellery or decoration on the next dresses they made. In return he got to dip his fingers in several food pots, finding bits of venison and buffalo meat which were preferable to the rabbit and pemmican that had been his main sustenance since leaving the Arapaho. There was a happy atmosphere in the camp, due, Wes supposed, to the ceremony that had been enacted that day. The children were playing noisy games, the women were chattering and smiling, and the men were lying on the ground smoking and waiting for the food that was being prepared for them. Wes recognized several of the warriors and older men, and stopped to speak to them as he made a haphazard tour of the village towards the tepee of Black Buffalo, which was situated in the centre.

In keeping with the other men, Black Buffalo sat outside his tepee, ostensibly watching his wives at work, but his pale, watery eyes had seen the white man's arrival and had followed his progress through the village. Despite the warmth of the day he had a blanket wrapped around his shoulders, which seemed to be a burden difficult to bear – its weight seemed to be forcing his torso forwards, lowering it into a tight angle over his crossed legs. His hunched shoulders gave him the appearance of a small man, and the two feathers that touched his left shoulder seemed to hang in sadness from the bone ornament that kept them fixed in his hair. His unsmiling face was creased with countless wrinkles, reminding Wes of many curmudgeonly old men he'd seen sitting on verandas in towns and cities he'd visited all across the country.

'*Hau*,' said Wes, raising his hand in traditional greeting.

'*Hau*,' replied Black Buffalo. The chief didn't stand, but gestured for his visitor to squat with him. 'Tall Horse spoke of your arrival. It is a good time. The wisdom of *Wiyaka Wakan* is talked about in lodges all across the Lakota nation. Tonight a pipe will be passed around our council circle and we will listen to his voice.'

In the late afternoon, the council of village

elders, war chiefs and holy men formed a half-circle in front of Black Buffalo's home. Arraigned behind was every man, woman and child who wanted to listen to the debate of their chosen decision makers. Wes Gray, whom they called *Wiyaka Wakan*, mingled with the villagers. Unless invited, those congregated behind the council were not permitted to speak.

When he addressed the gathering, Black Buffalo no longer bore the wizened appearance of an ancient. The lines on his face were still apparent, but they gave the impression of being etched by wisdom and experience rather than weariness and worry. No longer was he the humble, almost menial character who had earlier greeted Wes. Now he stood tall and proud, a true leader of his people. He wore a fringed and painted buckskin shirt, and a colourful feather bonnet that reached almost to his ankles. His deep, guttural voice was strong.

The message brought by Luther Kelly wasn't the reason for the council – indeed, it became clear to Wes that news of the meeting at Five Squaws Meadow had reached the village long before Yellowstone Kelly had found them. However, when Black Buffalo spoke of it, it was generally accepted that the purpose of the delegation from Washington was linked to the matter that was their current cause for concern.

There were white men in the Black Hills who

should not be there. This territory had been set aside for the Sioux, and the terms of the Treaty of 1868 declared that no white man would be allowed to enter without their consent. The problem that faced Black Buffalo was knowing what to do about it. Although some of the war chiefs were in favour of driving away the interlopers, scaring them with a show of force, Black Buffalo spoke against it. He was quick to point out that if the Sioux attacked the white men, even though they were on Sioux territory, then the Sioux, too, would be breaking the terms of the treaty. Those who had put their mark to the paper had agreed that the Bluecoats would mete out punishment to everyone who violated the law. It was one of the terms of the treaty opposed by many of the tribes-people, whose continued distrust of the *wasicun* gave rise to a doubt that punishment for their transgressions would not be matched by those imposed upon white people. That opinion was expressed by several of the council members, and, they argued, if the present invaders weren't chased away it would encourage more white people to come. If that happened, then hunting grounds would be lost to the Sioux and the sacred *Paha Sapa* taken from them.

Black Buffalo was gripped with the same thoughts, but he feared the reprisals that his people would face if those who had invaded his land were killed. He remembered the outrage at the *Washita* when the village of his Cheyenne friend Black Kettle had been destroyed by the Bluecoats. Defenceless women and children had been killed, their homes destroyed and their ponies slaughtered. Afoot and destitute, those who survived had been condemned to starve or surrender. Black Buffalo didn't want such a fate to befall his own people.

Black Buffalo used the approaching gathering at Five Squaws Meadow as a means of delaying any action against the white invaders. He would attend that meeting, he told the council, and tell the delegates that the Sioux didn't want those men on their land. If the Great Father in Washington wanted the Sioux to obey the words of the Treaty, then he must make his own people obey them, too. To honour the treaty the Bluecoats must drive all other white men off the Reservation.

Wes Gray had no doubt that the white men currently in the Black Hills were prospectors searching for gold. Although he had an appointment in Council Bluffs he had time enough to seek out and talk to the miners who had penetrated the Reservation land. His intercession could be a benefit to both parties, avoiding as it would a direct confrontation between the miners and the Sioux. In the past, such confrontations had led to misunderstandings and violence. By undertaking the task, his willingness to speak on their behalf would strengthen his reputation among the Sioux, and if they heeded his warning, the miners might get out of the country with their hair still on their heads.

The council raised no objection to the plan, but several members voiced the opinion that this was the *wasicuns'* last opportunity to get off the Reservation alive. Other tribes making their way to the meeting at Five Squaws Meadow would soon be in the Black Hills. Among them were the *Ogallalah* people led by *Tashunka Witco*: Crazy Horse would consider it his right to kill any American he discovered on the Reservation. It would be his way of proving to the Commissioners that the Sioux weren't prepared to lose any more land; it would also be the first step to another confrontation with the government.

Next morning, Wes Gray and Tall Horse rode deeper into the hill country. Tall Horse had agreed to guide him to the creeks where prospectors were known to be working. It was a warm, late spring day, so despite the eagerness of the animals they travelled at little more than walking pace; even though their destination wasn't the distant high peaks dense with ponderosa pine, this lower terrain would still make demands on the stamina of the horses.

For now, the ground beneath the hoofs was gentle and springy, and as they made their way through the low foothills Wes found himself enthralled once again by the majestic landscape and the abundance of game that lived upon it. It was idyllic, and the thought flashed through his mind that the Sioux should be left in peace here to pursue their way of life. But it was gone in a moment, chilled by the recollection of a single word that had been uttered by Luther Kelly: gold. A sudden shadow seemed to be cast across the ground.

It was mid-morning when they arrived on the banks of a narrow creek through which a slim stream of water swiftly flowed. There was no one in sight, but the noises that reached them from further upstream provided a clear indication that other humans were in the vicinity. Wes and Tall Horse turned their animals in that direction and rode slowly along the ridge. The scattering of alder trees and willows along the route was enough to conceal their approach from the two men standing calf-deep in water. While the Sioux warrior remained concealed among the trees, Wes Gray nudged his pony forward and slowly descended to the water's edge.

His approach unobserved, Wes was almost at the panners' shoulders when he spoke. His voice was low, but still it startled them. One man, big-boned but lacking flesh, gaunt almost, his clothing wrapped around and tied with belt and rope as though taken from some other, dropped his riddle as he turned abruptly to face Wes. His eyes were wide as though in expectation of danger. The second man, whose thick nose, dark eyes and dull reddish hair matched the other's, was a younger version. His hand moved towards the pistol that was holstered high on his right hip.

'Leave it,' ordered Wes. His rifle, withdrawn from its boot as he descended from the high ridge, lay across his thighs.

The younger prospector paused; an initial assessment of the new arrival told him it would be foolish to do anything else. Even though the newcomer's wide-brimmed hat relieved him of the suspicion that he was in mortal danger, that they weren't under threat of an Indian attack, the long feather that was fixed to the hatband, the fringed buckskin shirt, soft moccasins and tight necklace of colourful stones at his throat hinted at the possibility that their visitor was more Sioux than white man. In addition, the painted pony on which the newcomer sat had neither saddle nor leather bridle.

For a moment, no one spoke. Wes Gray surveyed the two men, then looked around to the place where two mules had been tethered. The packs with their assortment of basic tools and equipment had been unloaded and propped beneath a tree. Rifles rested against the packs.

'Who are you?' Wes asked.

'Tom McKendrick,' the older man stated. 'This is

my son, Jos.'

'What are you doing here?'

'Looking for gold.'

'What makes you think you'll find it here?'

'Everyone knows there's gold around here.'

'You know somebody who's taken a sack-full out of these hills?'

'Heck no, but it's here all right. It's been reported in every newspaper from New York to San Francisco.'

Wes studied the faces that were turned towards him. Now that they'd overcome their initial nervous reaction to his appearance, obstinacy showed in their expressions. Wes figured it was the same sort of obstinacy that had driven others on to forge new frontiers, trek west and work land that lacked a willingness to yield a crop. Just people who wanted to succeed and were prepared to face adversity to do so. In this instance, however, they were in the wrong.

'You shouldn't be here,' he told them. 'This land is part of the Great Sioux Reservation. Without their permission to be here, you're trespassing.'

'Reckon you're trespassing, too.'

Wes shook his head. 'They know me. I'm welcome to pass through.'

'Mister,' Tom McKendrick said, 'we've been here nearly four weeks and we haven't seen one Indian in that time.'

'The Sioux know you're here. They've been watching you since you first arrived. Just because you haven't seen them doesn't mean they haven't seen you. Take my advice, Mr McKendrick, get out of these hills.'

The prospectors exchanged a glance: the thought that the man on the pony wanted them to leave so that he could get the gold for himself passed between them. 'We'll leave as soon we've got all the gold our mules can carry,' Tom McKendrick declared.

'You'll never get across the river with it,' Wes told him. 'You might get away with trespassing but not with theft.'

'Theft!'

'I told you, this land belongs to the Sioux. Don't know of any place in the world where taking gold that doesn't belong to you isn't regarded as stealing.'

'Mark Owenfield tells it differently. He says the Sioux can't keep us away, that all this territory belongs to the United States of America, and if we want to prospect in these hills then any gold we find is ours.'

'Six years ago the government signed a treaty at Fort Laramie, which granted this land to the Sioux.' The phrase *absolute and undisturbed use* from the Articles of the Treaty had always stuck in Wes Gray's mind, and although it sounded too pompous to

31

utter aloud, it carried for him an inviolable intent on the government's behalf. 'You are breaking the law of the United States of America by being here, and will be punished if discovered by the army.'

Tom McKendrick's response was dismissive of that warning. 'We'll take our chances. According to Mark Owenfield it's the army's duty to protect us. The Sioux will get their wings clipped at a powwow that's fixed to take place further up the Missouri, and then we'll be able to clean these hills of every nugget.'

Wes wasn't sure what troubled him most: the fact that the prospectors knew about the meeting at Five Squaws Meadow, or the assumption that it would culminate in a reduction of the Sioux's power. Clearly, McKendrick and the other gold seekers had known about the meeting before the message reached Black Buffalo's village, but while it was true that the message Luther Kelly had carried from village to village would have been discussed among the tribes-people, no one would have spoken of it to *wasicun* invaders. Moreover, whoever had passed on the news of the impending meeting had attached to it a purpose of which, if true, Black Buffalo and his fellow chiefs were unaware. If the government thought they could talk the Sioux into allowing gold seekers access to the Black Hills then they either overestimated their negotiating skills or underestimated the determination of the tribes to hang on to their way of life. If the miners continued their hunt for gold they would be killed, and if soldiers entered the Black Hills there would be war.

'How many men are prospecting around here?' Wes asked.

'A handful. We've got a base in a creek around the other side of that hill. Camping together provides a bit of security.'

'And this Mark Owenfield you spoke about, is he camped there?'

Tom McKendrick guffawed at the suggestion. 'No. He's not a prospector. Some kind of politician back in Washington or New York. His articles appear in all the eastern newspapers.'

'Is that how you know about the delegation coming up the Missouri?'

'Jake Preston brought that news.'

'Is he a gold-seeker?'

'Reckon so, although for the moment he seems content to concentrate on setting up a base camp. But he assures us that after Washington's representatives have had their meeting with the Sioux we'll be free to find gold wherever it lies.'

'I think I need to talk to Mr Preston. Where will I find him?'

Wes had been directed to a canyon that had probably been cleaved through the layers of granite, magma, limestone and sandstone before any man had ever walked that land. To reach it he could follow the route recommended by the McKendricks, who refused to quit their work in the creek. But instead of staying at the foot of the hills and skirting the base of the craggy faces, he rode back to the summit, rejoined Tall Horse, and crossed the high ground in the belief that they would be able to reconnoitre the camp before making their presence known to those in occupation.

Like many of his people, Tall Horse was a taciturn man, but often their silence expressed their thoughts as eloquently as words. So it was on this occasion as they looked down on the location of the miners' camp. They had left their ponies on the rim before carefully descending the hillside until, unseen, they were only twenty feet above the canyon floor. By this time, Wes was already aware of Tall Horse's silent displeasure. His deep, dark eyes were surveying the scene below as though he were gazing upon the body of a favourite relative.

It was a box canyon where water spilled over the high rugged hillside into a stream below. Tall Horse's anger had been triggered by the line of canvas shelters that had been erected along its bank. Wes stopped counting at twenty; this was a substantial camp, not isolated prospectors but a group organized and determined to succeed in their mission. If there was gold in these hills they meant to have it.

It was clear that Tall Horse had not expected to see so many *wasicun* in the hills, but their number was only a part of the problem. The gold seekers had been more industrious than just running stream water through a sieve. Trees had been felled, their trunks hewn into sections then piled into the ground, forming a compound around the mouth of a cave. It was fashioned in the style of those army forts that had been constructed and objected to all along the west-bound routes. Although these walls were no more than six feet high, they still represented some form of fortification – but more importantly they bespoke permanency, as though the miners were establishing a base, a settlement.

Tall Horse moved, impatient to carry news of this discovery back to his village, but Wes restrained him. Using signs he told him to wait and watch while he rode down to speak with the men in the camp below.

Wes swung away from the point where he'd left Tall Horse, and approached the line of tents as though he'd been following the course of the stream for some distance. He progressed slowly, at walking pace so that those in the camp would get a good look at him before he reached their compound. In like manner to the McKendricks whom Wes had encountered earlier, a couple of men were working in the stream. At the sound of his approach they ceased their toil, straightened their backs in sudden, nervous fashion, then silently watched as he passed by with eyes fixed on the crowd that was forming a hundred yards ahead.

A tall man was pushing his way through the gathering as Wes arrived within twenty yards of the piled timber walls, summoned, Wes suspected, because he was the leader of the group. He was jacketless and hatless, the blue shirt he wore almost crisply clean. His fine, fair hair was lifting in the mild breeze. He was clean, almost pink; nothing about him declared that he had ever panned for gold. A quick glance around the assembly convinced Wes that very few of the men, perhaps half-a-dozen, bore the grimy, haggard appearance of those desperate men who trailed the nation's hills for the elusive, precious rocks.

Some of the men who were forming a barricade in front of him were carrying rifles, but Wes had his own lying across his knees in the same manner it had been when he'd confronted Tom McKendrick and his son. They regarded him with open suspicion, mainly because of the pony he sat astride. It bore tribal markings, and although their meaning was indecipherable to the men of the camp, their origin was, nonetheless, unmistakable.

The tall, fair-haired man hadn't brought a rifle, and the pistol, high on his right hip, remained in its holster – but Wes wasn't fooled into attributing this to a friendly welcome. It was an expression of the other man's belief that he had enough cover from those around him to deem unnecessary the need to issue his own threats. 'Who are you?' he asked, his voice strong and implicit of an eastern education.

'My name is Wes Gray, and you, Mr Preston, shouldn't be in these hills.'

Jake Preston was surprised that the newcomer knew his name, but did his best to prevent it showing on his face. What did trouble him was the murmur that drifted to him from one of the men standing near at hand: 'Medicine Feather.'

'You speaking on behalf of the Sioux?'

Wes paused a moment before answering, turned in the saddle to look at the line of tents behind him, then forward to cast his eyes over the palisade that lay ahead. 'Reckon I'm speaking on behalf of the government, too.'

Jake Preston allowed a grin to stretch his mouth. He looked around at those closest to him, attempting to ridicule Wes's words, confident that he was the one in charge of this situation. 'I'm not sure how you figure that. You got some badge of authority that gives you the right to speak for Washington?'

'No, no badge, just a good memory.'

Preston dipped his head to the left, a questioning gesture. 'You'll have to explain that to me, Mr Gray.'

'Six years ago I was in Fort Laramie when representatives of our government and the tribes of the

Plains put their names to a treaty that designated this land for the specific use of the Lakota people. The government solemnly agree,' Wes quoted, 'that no person will ever be permitted to pass over, settle upon or reside in this territory.' There were caveats, of course, to allow government business to be conducted, but Wes didn't speak of those, gold seeking didn't fall into any of those categories. It was true that at that time he'd been acting on behalf of the Arapaho people but the words in the Treaty had been applicable to all the sections of land that had, that day, been marked on the maps. Now, he spoke again, pointing at the timber walls as he did so. 'Those must be pulled down,' he told them and, if you want to continue living, you must get across the Missouri as quickly as you can.'

Since reaching them, little noise had come from the men facing Wes. Theirs had been an awkward silence, happy to leave the talking to their leader but poised to react as necessary to any signal he might give. Now, the few words uttered by Wes Gray seemed to have replaced the silence of expectancy to one of defeat. Wes had spoken softly, but those who heard him didn't doubt the truth of what he said: they were breaking the law, and they wouldn't survive if the Sioux attacked.

It took a long moment for Jake Preston to react. When he did his smirk was intended to dismiss the gravity of the buckskin-clad scout's remarks, and to re-establish his own authority over the men. 'There's gold here. That makes the Treaty worthless.'

It was Wes's turn to question the right of the other man to make such a pronouncement. 'Any gold on this land belongs to the Sioux. Not even the government can take it without negotiations. I don't recommend ignoring either the law or the tribes. Leave this place or you'll all be dead within a week.'

'Are you threatening us?'

'I'm advising you. Your deaths might raise a few eyebrows back east and the Sioux might have to find answers to a few awkward questions, but like every other American, they have the right to protect their land. Dismantle this camp and ride away now before it's too late.'

A man to the left of Jake Preston, a gruff, broadshouldered man who had retained a meaningful grip on his rifle throughout the conversation, spoke up. 'Do you intend telling the Sioux we're here?'

'No.'

'Then there's no reason to suppose we can't find gold and be out of here with it before we're discovered.'

'You're already discovered,' Wes told him.

'We haven't seen one Sioux brave all the time we've been here.'

'Perhaps not, but they know you are here. Besides, the Sioux aren't the only ones you need to hide from. When the army learns that you've broken the terms of the agreement they'll arrest you and put you in prison.'

Another man joined in. He had a sullen expression that matched those of half-starved Confederate prisoners Wes had seen at the end of the war. His chin was dark with stubble and his eyes sunken beneath heavy black brows. 'Do you mean to tell the army?' he asked.

'You're breaking the law,' Wes told him. 'I have no other choice if you won't go voluntarily.'

The man jerked his rifle round so that it was pointing at Wes's chest.

'I wouldn't do that,' Wes told him. 'I'm not alone. I told you the Sioux know you are here. They are watching us from the hillside. If you shoot me you'll be slaughtered.'

Many heads turned in the direction that Wes had indicated, but nothing moved and after the passing of a few moments the voices of the more sceptical began to suggest that the presence of warriors was merely a ruse, a poker player's bluff that needed calling.

'You want me to prove it?' Wes said, then raised his left hand above his head, and lowered it in a swift, slashing motion.

Instantly, an arrow hissed through air and thudded into the trunk of a nearby tree. Before the first had stopped trembling, a second arrow smacked into the ground at Jake Preston's feet, then close behind, a third embedded itself into another tree. Wes was impressed with Tall Horse's accuracy, and also the speed with which he'd been able to release three arrows. It was clear that the men were convinced they were under the threat of more than one bow. Wes nudged his pony so that it began to back away from the group he'd faced.

'I can't give you better advice,' he told them, 'or another warning. Destroy this camp and leave these hills immediately, or face either the Sioux or the army.'

As he turned the pony and began to ride away from that place he was followed by the voice of Jake Preston. 'The army aren't coming to arrest us,' he yelled. 'It's the Sioux who will be driven out of these hills.'

THREE

The gathering of gold hunters watched Wes Gray's departure until he'd swung out of sight up the slope that took him away from the stream. The stocky man at Jake Preston's side hefted his rifle as though anxious to drill a bullet into the receding broad, buckskin-clad back. His scowl bore testament to his evil intent, but any desire to act upon his rancour was stilled by a quiet word of restraint. Jake Preston was no less eager to retaliate against Wes Gray's interference, but this was not the time to do it. His caution wasn't entirely based on the supposition that they were still under the bows of Sioux warriors: it was clear that their visitor's words had unsettled most of the handful of genuine prospectors, and allowing them to witness his death could backfire on him. One of the miners, a tall, bearded, broad-shouldered man was talking, regaling everyone with information concerning the identity of the departing man and his reputation.

'That's the man they call Medicine Feather,' he announced. 'Saw him a couple of times when I was soldiering along the Oregon Trail. More than one officer held the opinion that he knew more about the ways of the Indians than any man alive. When he spoke, they listened.'

'What are you saying, Charlie Petersen, that we should pack our gear and get out of here?' The speaker was the stocky man standing shoulder-to-shoulder with Jake Preston. His name was Sol Carter. He scowled at Charlie Petersen. 'I came here for gold, and I don't reckon I'll be scared away by another man's words.'

Voices mumbled, several supporting the second speaker, but a few who were more cautious and more familiar with Wes Gray's renown, were less enthusiastic.

'I don't reckon we ought to ignore a warning from Wes Gray,' one man said.

Another pointed at the arrows sticking in the tree trunks. 'He wasn't bluffing about the Sioux,' he said. 'They know we're here. If they attacked in force we wouldn't stand a chance.'

Sol Carter argued again. 'The words of an Indian lover haven't changed anything. We knew that this was Sioux territory when we quit Fort Union. I reckon this Medicine Feather just wants the gold for himself. Means to clean up before the army clear the way for every gold-seeker on the continent.'

Charlie Petersen scoffed at the idea. 'Reckon Wes Gray's made enough visits to California and Oregon to dig for gold if he wanted to. It's not his way. He came here to help us, to warn us. He wouldn't have done that if he didn't think we were in danger.'

'It's the Sioux who are in danger,' said Sol Carter. 'When the army get here they'll push them right out of these hills.'

'Wes Gray said that we were the ones the army would be pushing, and that chimes with the attitude of Colonel Black at Fort Union. If he'd had more soldiers we wouldn't have got this far into the reservation. Perhaps the soldiers will arrest us.'

'Yeah! Well, we agreed to stick together when we crossed the Missouri and I'm not going back without a bag full of gold.'

'No one's found gold yet,' Charlie Petersen observed, 'so perhaps those newspaper stories are nothing but a waste of ink. And don't forget that we haven't seen any soldiers either. Those claims that the army would be obliged to protect us look like hot air, too. Gold is gold, but if the Sioux come calling it won't even buy us a proper Christian burial.'

A number of voices echoed Charlie's words.

'I think I speak for the majority here,' he continued, 'when I say we should take Wes Gray's advice and get back to Fort Union.'

Sol Carter scorned Charlie Petersen and those who were willing to quit the workings, accusing them of cowardice, running scared because of the words of one half-wild man. His taunts were backed up by the jeers of those others who were eager to continue prospecting for gold. There was a moment when the argument might have developed into violence, those in favour of quitting the site angrily squaring up to their detractors. No one reached for a gun but picks and shovels were wielded threateningly.

Jake Preston wasn't unduly concerned at the prospect of a few broken heads – miners were forever arguing and fighting, it went hand in glove with barren weeks scratching at rocks or wading in water and finding nothing but dirt and pebbles. However, he didn't want them to abandon the site. He'd spent a lot of time in Fort Union assuring them that the Colonel's dictate against entering the Reservation was nothing more than a token acknowledgement of the terms of the Laramie Treaty. He'd convinced them that they would not be deserted by the army, that soldiers would protect them if the Sioux threatened to attack. Now he raised his arms and yelled for silence.

He addressed Charlie Petersen and his supporters. 'I understand your concerns,' he told them. 'Someone rides in with a message of doom and it becomes difficult to shake it out of your mind. But he's wrong.'

'Wes Gray hasn't survived in this country by being wrong,' Charlie responded.

'Perhaps not, but nobody's right all the time, and on this occasion I don't think Mr Gray knows all the facts.' He waited a moment to allow the mutterings to cease. Wes Gray, he told himself, might speak the truth, but delivering it with blunt statements was no way to win over a crowd. Compared to the oratorical ability of politicians and lawyers such as Mark Owenfield, Jake Preston was a novice, but he reckoned he had the edge on a half-savage mountain man.

'Men,' he said, 'I don't know how long Wes Gray has been in these hills or living with the Sioux, but I reckon he is unaware of the delegation that is currently steaming up the Missouri. That delegation is the key to your safety. Peace is guaranteed until the negotiations are completed. No one will put them in jeopardy by a senseless outbreak of violence.' He paused again, looked around at the faces that were turned towards him, noted their attention.

'When I was in Washington I spoke to Mark Owenfield' – he paused again, momentarily, but long enough for the name to register with every listener, noting the respect that he gained by his association with a man of such importance – 'and he assured me that those commissioned with the task of negotiating with the Indians must succeed in their mission. If the government wants the gold, then it stands to reason that the army will protect the men digging it out of the ground.'

It was an uneasy silence that greeted the end of Jake Preston's little speech. Charley Petersen fidgeted – it wasn't that he agreed with what he'd heard, rather that he couldn't summon up a logical argument against it.

Jake Preston recognized the other's hesitation and spoke again. 'I can understand your concern,' he said. 'Of course the Sioux are going to be angry if they think their land will be taken from them, but they haven't caused any trouble yet, and I don't reckon they will unless the negotiations break down. What I'm suggesting is that you remain here until the meeting at Five Squaws Meadow is over. If all goes the way the government expects, then we've got a head start on all those prospectors who will flood into this area.'

'And if it doesn't?' someone asked.

'The army knows you're here. They won't leave you at the mercy of the Sioux. They'll be obliged to seek you out and escort you across the Missouri.'

Jake Preston's words weren't greeted with unstinting acclaim, but even among those most eager to get out of the Black Hills there was a grudging acknowledgement of the logic of his argument. A consensus was reached that they would remain until they knew the outcome of the talks between the tribes and the delegation. That resolve was hardened a short while later when Tom and Jos McKendrick returned to the camp. They had seen the departing figure of Wes Gray high above the riverside trail, and their report that he had had only one Sioux companion irked those who had believed themselves surrounded by warriors. It presented an opportunity for Jake Preston to press home his argument that their presence wasn't generally known by the Sioux, and that Wes Gray's interference was based on his own desire for gold. Unable to conjure up a meaningful response, Charlie Petersen quit the assembly, his mind still occupied with the belief that they couldn't afford to stint their efforts to make their camp impregnable.

With a grin of satisfaction, Jake Preston watched Charlie Petersen resume his activity. Petersen was the sort of man capable of persuading others, and now that he had abandoned the argument to leave the Black Hills it was unlikely that any other voice would be raised in protest. Not that it mattered, since the terms of the treaty had been breached, and that could only hasten the legitimate opening of the Sioux reservation to all gold seekers.

For himself, Jake Preston couldn't get back to the Missouri quickly enough. Even though he'd been well paid to get this camp established, he'd only come this deep into Sioux territory on the assurance that that there would be few warriors here until the winter camps were abandoned and the tribes came on to the hunting grounds to await the migrating buffalo herds. Now, as the land warmed with the onset of spring, the risk of encountering war-like bands had become imminent, and despite what he'd told the prospectors, he knew that the warning that had been issued by Wes Gray wasn't an idle threat. The prospectors thought he was returning to Fort Union, which was close to Five Squaws Meadow, but his destination was in the opposite direction, south to the station on the Missouri, above the mouth of the White River, where the *Far West* would take on fuel for the remainder of its journey to the pow-wow site.

Jake Preston wasn't alone when he departed the miners' camp. His companions were Sol Carter and the Watkin brothers, George and Henry. They were barely out of sight of the camp before Jake called a halt and issued orders. It had been a lucky coincidence that he'd been at the camp when Wes Gray arrived, and though the visit had unsettled them, he'd been able to persuade the men to stay. But he wasn't a man who tolerated interference with his plans, and that visit had almost been enough to scupper his work. Everything could still be ruined if Wes Gray spoke to the miners again, and it was imperative that he didn't return to the camp site. He spoke to Sol Carter.

'The pair won't expect anyone to follow them, so

they won't be travelling fast,' Jake reasoned. 'Take George with you, and make sure that squaw-man doesn't meddle again.'

Sol grinned. He had no explanation for the animosity he felt for Wes Gray, but he'd wanted to put a bullet in him from the very first moment they'd looked at each other. He slapped his hand against the rifle that was kept in the boot attached to his saddle, implying that the deed was already done.

'We'll meet up at the wood station,' Jake added as the others turned their mounts off the trail. He and Henry Watkin watched them climb up the hillside to strike the ridge along which the McKendricks had seen Wes Gray and Tall Horse riding.

Jake Preston's assumption that Wes and Tall Horse would be travelling without haste was correct. For a while they'd ridden in silence, each engaged with his own thoughts, the rights and wrongs of the intrusion by the gold-seekers and, more especially, the likely outcome of their trespass. It was Tall Horse who spoke first, his words free of preamble, their sentiment unambiguous.

'The Ogallalah are camped less than two days from here.'

Wes understood the other's meaning. The warlike Ogallalah warriors would not tolerate the presence of the miners in the Black Hills. They would be incensed by the stockade that was being constructed, affronted by its military-like appearance and its premise that the *wasicun* were settling in Sioux territory.

'Is Crazy Horse with them?'

'I do not know, but he will be coming for the pow-wow at Five Squaws Meadow.'

Wes gave his companion a quizzical look. It was well known that Tashunka Witco avoided all meetings with Americans.

Tall Horse explained that although the Ogallalah warrior wouldn't be at Five Squaws Meadow, he would be camped nearby eager to hear the details of the conference. 'He will send Little Big Man or Touch The Clouds to be his eyes and ears.'

For Wes, of course, the more pressing matter was the safety of the prospectors. If they ignored his warning and remained in the Black Hills then the extent of their lives was no greater than the time it took Crazy Horse to find them. And how many more deaths would then follow?

For an instant, it seemed to Wes that the smack of a bullet in a nearby tree and the crack from the rifle that had fired it had been engendered by his thoughts, but he shook himself free of that misconception at the sound of a second shot that was accompanied by a cry of agony from Tall Horse. The tall Sioux had arched backwards and was in imminent danger of falling from his pony, but either instinct or determination guided his movement and he slumped forwards on to the animal's neck. With Tall Horse gripping its mane, the pony sprang forwards, but came to a halt after a couple of paces.

Wes drew his revolver, looked in the direction of the shots and was able to see the tell-tale wisps of smoke rising from behind some boulders further up the hillside. He urged his horse forwards, stretching forwards as he did so, in like manner to Tall Horse, so that he reduced the target for those who had fired at them. More shots flew in his direction but they passed over or behind him, cutting through the place he'd occupied only moments earlier. Stretching out his right arm he fired two shots. His efforts lacked accuracy, but he hadn't expected to hit anyone – the sole motive for firing was to deter his attackers long enough to grasp the head rope of Tall Horse's pony and pull it forwards – if it remained still then the Sioux warrior would be a sitting target.

A groan escaped Tall Horse, but he retained his grip on his animal's mane. There was an ugly hole in his back and smears of red around it where blood had spurted. Wes Gray noted the injury but there was no opportunity to examine it. Staying low, he urged his own horse forwards and yanked on the rope of the other animal, hoping that it wouldn't resist his command. It didn't, and they rode down the slope seeking the cover of the trees on the lower reaches. They were pursued by a volley of shots that hummed overhead or flattened against the rocks and trees through which they rode. Wes was keen to return gunfire, but his first priority was to find a place of safety for his companion.

Without further injury they reached the cover they sought, but Wes knew that their assailants would come after them. Although the gunfire had ceased, Wes wasn't prepared to believe that the fight was over. Whatever reason lay behind the ambush, it was clear that the intention was to kill both Tall Horse and himself, and it was usual for men to see such a mission through to fulfilment. Although anxious to stop so he could tend Tall Horse's wound, Wes rode on, determined to find some place that would provide him with some advantage against his unknown enemies. The matter, however, was taken out of his hands by a sturdy oak: the horses bumped into each other as they swerved around the thick trunk, and the jolt unseated Tall Horse, who fell heavily to the ground.

Swiftly, Wes dismounted and reached his companion's side. The warrior was barely conscious. There wasn't an exit wound, and it was clear that the bullet had hit something vital inside. Tall Horse's breathing was shallow, and his eyes had dulled as though unable to catch the light of day. In addition, thick, dark blood was dribbling from the corner of his mouth, denoting the seriousness of the injury.

Wes pulled him into a hollow to keep him from the sight of their pursuers, and began covering him with branches and foliage which he quickly gathered. Tall Horse drifted in and out of silent consciousness, each state lasting little more than moments. Sometimes his eyes were fixed on Wes Gray as though aware of the purpose of his labour, but mostly he showed no interest in the activity around him. Once he coughed, and a gout of blood shot out of his mouth and over his chin.

It was at that moment that Wes heard the sound of an approaching horse. His attackers had covered the ground more quickly than he'd expected. They had come without caution, determined to catch their quarry before they got clear of the hill country. He pushed his own horse into a thicket, hiding it from the immediate sight of the oncoming riders, and slapped the rump of Tall Horse's pony so that it jumped forwards and ran away through the trees, causing a distraction, Wes hoped, that would lure away the men on his trail. With a final glance at the dying Sioux warrior, he moved back among the greenery where he'd left his horse. Gun in hand, he awaited the men who had ambushed him. He'd counted two wisps of smoke from rifle barrels but there could be more.

George Watkin came cautiously into view, following the route of his quarry but peering ahead as though expecting at any moment to be in a position to throw his rifle to his shoulder and fire the shot that would end the pursuit. He was a red-haired man with a long nose, and narrow, slit-like eyes. The grey jacket he wore over an open-necked blue shirt was dusty from travel, but was free of the dirt and grime that usually clung to the clothing of prospectors. His face, too, although etched with the lines of a man who had lived with hardship and danger, showed neither the expression of excited expectation that marked those setting out on a search for riches, nor the craziness of years of distrustful lonesomeness. And the way he carried his rifle made it clear that he was accustomed to its use. Whatever he had hunted in the past, it hadn't been gold in the ground.

When he was level with the place where Wes Gray waited, he slowed the pace of his horse until it was almost at a standstill. He raised his rifle higher, not yet sighting along the barrel but keenly watching something ahead that had grabbed his attention, anticipating an imminent need for his firearm. He paused, then, as though suddenly aware that he had allowed himself to be fixated by what he could see ahead, and cast looks to right and left, seeking assurance that he hadn't ridden into a trap. Nothing moved, not so much as a leaf stirred. He touched his horse's flanks with his heels, and it went gingerly forwards again.

As he watched from the bushes, Wes Gray attributed the rider's behaviour to only one thing: Tall Horse's pony, he supposed, had not run far, and was idly grazing a short distance ahead. However, until the gunman was past, he remained hidden. Observing the way the man behaved indicated to Wes that he was alone. His companion would be searching a different part of the hillside, but would be close enough to respond to the sound of gunshots. Wes allowed his ambusher to ride by, then withdrew his knife.

Carefully he emerged from the bushes, his eyes fixed initially on the receding figure, but gradually lifting to the crest where Tall Horse's pony innocently grazed. Wes stepped away from the cover of the foliage that had hidden him, and began to move quickly and silently forwards. He had to act without hesitation because now, if he were seen, he was exposed to the guns of his enemies. If the rider ahead turned, he had an uninterrupted line of fire: it was imperative for Wes to strike first.

The slow gait of the rider's horse meant that Wes was able to close the gap that had been created in a handful of strides. The stealth of his attack was such that the rider was unaware of his danger until Wes was merely two strides behind, and would probably have remained that way until the scout had sprung on to the horse's haunches and encircled his throat with his arm – one fierce thrust of the knife would have ended the rider's life before he was even aware he was under attack.

But it didn't happen, because from higher up the hillside a voice yelled a warning and a rifle shot crackled from among the trees. It screamed past the horse's hindquarters, only missing Wes because he'd made the leap that carried him on to the animal's back.

George Watkin, recognizing the voice high to his left, reacted instantly to its urgency. Twisting in the saddle he caught a glimpse of the movement behind him, but by the time he'd swung his rifle in that direction Wes Gray had vaulted on to the back of his horse and was too close for the long gun to be effective. Still, he tried to use the barrel as a club, hoping to strike Wes with sufficient force to knock him to the ground, which would provide him with a clear killing shot. But the lack of space between them made it difficult for him to use his rifle effectively, and he was further hampered by the need to keep a grip on Wes Gray's right wrist to prevent the blade of the big hunting knife he held slitting him from throat to groin.

Wes Gray's initial strategy had been thwarted by the warning shout, and instead of being able to press home his attack it became necessary to ward off the blows from the rifle. Within a moment, he'd grabbed the end of the barrel and twisted it in an effort to wrestle it from the other's grip. It was pointing uselessly at the sky when George pulled the trigger. The bullet flew harmlessly among the high branches of the nearby trees, but the rifle jerked in Wes Gray's grip, and he felt the heat of the explosion as it travelled along the barrel.

The position of the men astride the horse made it an unfair fight, but Wes had no thoughts of mercy for his opponent. George Watkin had ambushed him, and had tried to kill him without warning, so death was the only true justice.

George Watkin knew he was fighting for his life, and clung tenaciously to the stock of his rifle – but he was beginning to doubt his ability to win the contest. In addition, he was also becoming wary of losing his grip on Wes's knife hand. The sun's light glinted intermittently on the broad blade, and the prospect of it slicing through his flesh filled him with dread. With a fearsome yell he launched a final effort for victory, hauling his shoulders forwards in an effort to dislodge Wes Gray from the horse's back.

Because he was a strong man, the move was partially successful. The power that George Watkin had been able to generate surprised Wes momentarily, but he was an experienced fighter and even though he slipped from his position behind the other man, he still retained his grip on the rifle. The outcome was that both men fell to the ground. The force of their landing caused them to roll apart and when they got to their feet neither man had retained a grip on the rifle. It had skidded across the hard rock and had disappeared from sight beyond the lip of land, clattering sporadically on its downhill descent. George Watkin's hand dropped to the butt of the pistol that was holstered on his right thigh, while Wes, who still held his knife, launched himself full length at his enemy.

The yell of warning that Sol Carter had given had been more a shout of surprise when he'd seen the buckskin-clad figure running like a preying cougar in the wake of George Watkin's horse. He'd gathered his senses quickly and fired a shot at the pursuer, but once the man had bounded on to the back of the animal he was too close to George to risk another shot. So Sol had spurred his horse downhill to aid his companion. Rifle in hand, he approached, watching the two men who were struggling on the ground close to the edge where the ground fell away. It seemed that neither was in possession of a weapon. They were slugging at each other with their fists, and using feet, knees and elbows in order to incapacitate the other, and at that moment it was impossible for Sol to get a clear shot at Wes.

Eventually, when the fighters had regained their feet, an opportunity arose. Blows were exchanged, which culminated in George Watkin folding over a punch delivered to the pit of his stomach – and with his ally doubled over, Sol had a clear shot at Wes's chest and head. He raised his rifle and fired – but at that moment Wes had pulled his adversary upright to finish the fight with a blow to the jaw. The bullet struck George in the back, and propelled him forwards with an impetus that was sufficient to carry both men over the edge of the hill.

Sol Carter dismounted and ran to the point where they had fallen from sight. Almost a hundred feet below, his body broken and bloody across two boulders, George Watkin stared back at him with unseeing eyes. At first Sol couldn't see Wes Gray, but he attributed that to the rocks, undergrowth and shadows so far below. Then a movement caught his eye – something was drifting to the bottom of the gorge. It was a hat with a long feather affixed to its band, the hat that Wes Gray had been wearing moments earlier. Sol Carter grinned: mission accomplished: Medicine Feather was dead.

FOUR

When George Watkin suddenly crashed against him, Wes Gray staggered backwards. Automatically his arms reached out to hold up the falling body, and his legs sought a stance that would brace him against the full weight of the impact. It wasn't until he stretched his right leg back that he became aware of how close to the lip of the hill the struggle had taken him. There was no firm ground behind and he went over the edge. Under the mass of George Watkin's body, he was almost winded when his shoulders and back thudded against the hard rock hillside. He felt the minor pains of burns and bumps as his body jarred and slid along the route of a slithering descent. The fear of being trapped by his opponent's weight was both real and momentary – but in fact, rather than putting him in greater danger, it probably saved his life. Pressing on him as it did, the body on top kept him pinned to the ground when the natural mechanics of the first impact should have caused his legs to lift, flip over his head and hurl him into the space beyond. Indeed, that was George Watkin's fate, and if Sol Carter's bullet hadn't killed him outright, then the sickening crunch that announced the end of his plunge was testimony to the fact that the rocks below had finished the job.

The moment he felt the load moving clear of his body, Wes Gray tried to put a brake on the speed of his descent by dragging his heels and scrabbling at the surface with his hands in a desperate attempt to find something that would hold his weight. Neither effort yielded success. Although moccasins were ideal footwear for swift and stealthy movement through forests and over rocky hillsides, they couldn't provide the purchase necessary to slow his current progress, and while his hands filled with dirt and stones it was all loose rubble that offered no assistance at all.

Fleetingly, below and to his left, a hardy plant sprouting from a ragged crevice offered some hope – but it was at the very limit of his reach, and he was past it with only two tiny twigs between his fingers to hint at the lifeline it might have been. The incident also brought home to Wes the velocity of his plunge – he was falling almost more quickly than he could react to his thoughts. But not quite, because no sooner had that opportunity slipped by than he realized he was approaching an outcrop. If he went over, he would be launched into the chasm and certain death.

Somehow he turned on to his stomach, hugging the ground even though it was scratching and tearing at his skin – but his foot came into contact with a small rock which, even though it jumped loose, miraculously blunted his speed and slewed him to his right. That rock was followed by others, some of which also came loose – but he bounced over others and was able to grab at them to hasten his deceleration. Even so, he went over the bulge but was able to keep his hands and body in contact with the hillside.

He fell another five feet, then hit a ledge, but because it wasn't much wider than the span of his feet he wasn't able to balance there. He slipped off, scraping his legs and belly on the rough edge – but his hands slapped on the flattish surface, and he was at last able to arrest his fall to the rocks below. He knew he wasn't clear of danger, and that only the strength of his upstretched arms was keeping him alive – and even if he managed to haul himself back on to the ledge from which he was hanging, his chances of survival were slim. He figured he'd fallen twenty-five feet, and he wasn't yet able to judge the difficulty of the climb back to the crest. Looking up, he noted the overhanging outcrop and knew that that wouldn't be easy to manoeuvre.

For several moments he dangled on the hillside, his eyes seeking handholds above, while he blindly searched for footholds that would provide some leverage for an upward push. The aids he found were minimal – a lump for his right foot to push against, and a jutting sharp rock eighteen inches above the shelf that he could reach and grip – not much, but he needed to use anything that was available to its full extent. His arms were beginning to feel the strain, and he determined to make his move – but at the very moment he raised his right foot and tensed his toes against the helpful lump, loose stones, dust and shingle showered down from above.

Wes froze, pressed himself more tightly into the hillside, and waited. The sound of scuffling feet carried down to him, then a grumbling curse as the man looking over the edge saw the spread-eagled body of George Watkin below. A few more small, loose stones tumbled over the bulging outcrop and rained into the valley before Wes heard the sound of a departing horse. The man who had killed his own ally, who had meant to kill Wes, had gone, his job, he assumed, completed. Wes had not recognized the man he'd fought, the one who now lay dead below his feet, but the other one he did know: he'd been at the miner's camp, standing beside Jake Preston, ready even then, Wes recalled, to put a bullet in him even though his visit had been for their benefit, to warn them of the danger of dwelling in the Black Hills. When he escaped from this situation, Wes vowed, he would find that man to learn the reason for the attack. Then he would kill him.

Once he'd gained the ledge and scanned the sheer hillside above, it was clear that any upward route was laced with danger. Quite apart from the outcrop directly over his head, the remainder of the face accessible from the ledge was sheer. Wes reflected that a man would need the abilities of a Bighorn sheep to be able to scale such heights. Still, he had to try to reach the top. He started on a couple of different routes, but was unable to find sufficient hand- and footholds to get more than a few steps up the hillside. Each time he returned to the ledge, frustrated by his failure but more determined to reach the top.

Then as he began his third attempt another shower of stones and dust descended. Once again he pressed himself into the hillside to hide himself from the gaze of anyone above, but because of his attempts to climb the hillside he was no longer hidden from their view by the outcrop. He hadn't heard hoofbeats, but if his assailant had returned, and if he spotted him, then he was an open target. He waited and watched the lip of the hill above.

The face that came into sight surprised him. Tall Horse had been unconscious when he'd partially hidden him among the foliage, and Wes had doubted that the Sioux warrior would ever recover. But it was the Minneconjou who had crawled across the ground and was now peering into the void, his eyes fixed on the dead body below. Wes called to him, and when he'd got his attention, explained his predicament. He wasn't sure what his friend could do to help, or what strength he had to mount a rescue bid, because he didn't respond with either words of encouragement or any movement that could be interpreted as an active gesture of help. Indeed, for the few minutes following his apparent realization that his friend Wes Gray was still alive, he didn't move – and then he was gone, and Wes feared that he had once again lost consciousness. Wes could do nothing but wait and hope for the warrior's reappearance.

It was many more minutes before there was any further activity, by which time the restricted space on which he was forced to stand was causing his legs to cramp and ache. Fearing that Tall Horse had collapsed and was unable to assist him, he began to entertain thoughts of once more attempting to scale the hillside. He'd managed to climb about eight feet before abandoning his first attempt, but perhaps another effort would be more successful. He called out to Tall Horse in his native tongue, hoping that if the Sioux warrior could hear him he would be able to assure him that he had a plan for his rescue.

There was no reply from Tall Horse, but as Wes began to look for the first hand-holds he would use, he became aware that he was under observation from above. Two warriors looked down at him, and one had an arrow nocked to his bow-string. Wes didn't know the men, but he recalled seeing one of them in Black Buffalo's village.

'I am Wiyaka Wakan,' he told them, 'and I need your help.'

A long grass rope, thick and tightly plaited, was lowered down to Wes. It was a precarious climb, the two warriors hauling on one end while Wes, gripping the other end and using his feet to bounce and push upwards, managed to climb to the top. When he lay on the flat ground he could feel every bump, scratch and cut he'd endured on his rise to safety – but concern for these was swiftly cast aside, because nearby, Tall Horse lay unconscious. It was clear to Wes that his friend had not been instrumental in his rescue, and that he had succumbed to his injuries almost instantly.

Painted Elk, one of the warriors who had hauled Wes up from the ledge, explained how they'd interrupted their hunt to investigate the gunshots, but they only found Tall Horse when they were returning to the village, and although Tall Horse had uttered Wiyaka Wakan's name before losing consciousness, they wouldn't have found him if he hadn't called out.

Getting Tall Horse back to the village was of paramount importance to his fellow tribesmen, and Wes was happy to leave his friend to their care. His priority was to catch the man who had tried to kill him, a deed that could not go unpunished. Painted Elk and his friend had not seen any *wasicun* while they'd been in the hills, but the immediate trail was easy to pick up. What surprised Wes was that it was heading away from the miners' camp. It gave him hope that his warning had been accepted by the majority of the men, and that they were heading for safety across the Missouri by a more direct route.

Perhaps the attempt on the lives of himself and Tall Horse had been a spur of the moment decision by two of the more disgruntled miners. There would always be people aggrieved when a majority decision went against them, and who would seek revenge on those they held responsible for their defeat. Wes understood their anger, but it didn't absolve them of the consequences.

Although his hat was beyond recovery, he had retained his armaments. Despite the scuffle and fall, his pistol had remained in its holster, and he found his big blade knife and George Watkin's gun close to the point where he'd lost his footing. His horse had remained hidden among the foliage, and was rested and well fed when he climbed on to its back. He told Painted Elk that he meant to pursue the man who had tried to kill him and Tall Horse, and that he would return to the village for his packs after he'd taken full vengeance. He gave George Watkin's gun to Painted Elk, then they parted company.

Sol Carter was more than an hour ahead of Wes, and daylight was dwindling. Although anxious to catch his quarry, Wes wasn't prepared to be reckless. His pace was dictated by the terrain, and until he was out of the hill country it could be treacherous. Perhaps he would gain a little ground before darkness fell, but it wouldn't be enough to put the man under his guns. Of course, his assailant would be forced to make a night camp and if Wes pressed ahead in the darkness it was possible that he would find him before morning, but it was also possible that his horse would tread on a loose rock or misplace a hoof on perilous ground and end up lame. Being afoot wouldn't help his cause. So when darkness fell and he could see no fire glow ahead, he stopped for the night. He rolled out his blanket to sleep, intending to be in the saddle early the next morning. The way ahead was into the sun's first pink rays.

Wes came across the other's camp an hour after sun-up. It was on the low slopes and he could see the range-land stretching into the distance where the line of a dense forest could be discerned. Wes peered ahead, straining his eyes in the hope of

spying a distant rider. He thought he could see lingering dust, but that could have been raised by
mule deer or pronghorns. Until he found some
shod hoofprints he couldn't be sure in which direction the man had gone. The remains of a small fire
had been spread with a boot and had cooled
rapidly, and Wes guessed that his quarry had been
in the saddle as early as himself. He found where
the man's horse had been picketed and the tracks it
had made, and set off to follow its trail.

The first stretch across open country was an
opportunity to eat up ground between himself and
his prey. Accordingly, Wes gave the Indian pony
under him its head, and it responded gamely. As
fleet-footed as a white-tailed deer, it seemed to
bounce across the lush spring grass, covering the
miles with a rhythmical stride. Intermittently Wes
would slacken the pace, sometimes loping, sometimes walking, conserving the animal's stamina so
that the pursuit continued without stopping until it
was past noon. By the time they reached the
forested section, Wes was certain that the man
ahead was heading in the direction of the White
River. He hoped to catch him before he reached it,
because he could lose his trail if he rode any distance along the riverbed.

On reflection, Wes thought the likelihood of the
man using the river to disguise his trail was unlikely.
He had no reason to suspect he was being followed,

and had every reason to stick to fast-riding ground. His aim was surely to get off the Sioux Reservation as quickly as possible, and his plan, no doubt, was to follow the White to its confluence with the Missouri. Wes grimaced: across the Missouri the man might consider himself safe from the Sioux, but he wasn't safe from the revenge of Medicine Feather.

It was late in the afternoon when the assumptions that Wes had made concerning the man's route were proved correct. An hour earlier he'd reached the banks of the White River, where the hoofprints became easier to see. The indentations were deeper and the stride shorter, both indications that the horse was tiring in the softer ground. Moreover close inspection showed that the horse had partially pulled off a back shoe, and was perhaps in some discomfort. Scanning ahead for a sight of his quarry brought no reward, but Wes believed that he was very close to him. He pushed on at a canter, eyes, ears and nose all at work to give the first intelligence of his enemy's location.

The sound of a horse snorting its anxiety carried to Wes as he approached a bushy rise. It reared, showing its black head, pinpointing its exact location before dropping its front feet back down to the ground. A loud, coarse voice mingled with the snorting of the nervous animal, berating it, whipping it with angry words as though it had deliberately gone lame, that its failure to cover another mile was a rebellious act deserving of slaughter.

'I ought to put a bullet in your brain,' the man shouted, then more quietly, 'and I would if there wasn't a risk of it attracting unwanted attention.' He'd looked around then, as if fearful that his raised voice might resound throughout the vicinity as loudly as a gunshot. When he spoke again, explaining his reasons even though the horse had no need for them, his voice was little more than a mutter: 'Don't want any redskins to come a-running today.'

Wes, who had dismounted and crept silently through the trees, was no more than ten yards behind Sol Carter when those final words were spoken. He stepped into the clearing, softly, closing the gap until they were only fifteen feet apart. It was in his power to kill the man without warning, just as the man and his friend had tried to kill him and Tall Horse. Two or three more steps and then he could pull his head back, expose his throat to the sharp edge of his knife and watch him bleed out silently on the ground. But that wasn't Wes's style. As yet he hadn't even filled his hand with a weapon, either gun or knife. Instead he spoke, his voice soft and low, but heavy with threat.

'You tried to kill me.'

Sol Carter reacted as though a knife point had pricked against his spine. He'd been bent against the horse as though examining its hind leg, but at Wes's utterance his shoulders went back and his whole body shifted so that he was standing upright. He didn't immediately turn around. Wes guessed that Sol Carter was weighing up his options, but knew he was unlikely to risk going for his gun. The other man would assume he was already being covered by Wes's gun, so attempting to turn, draw and fire would surely be an act of suicide. Wes wanted him to believe that, because he wanted answers to his questions.

'Why?' he asked.

Sol Carter moved his head, slowly, trying to look over his shoulder, still disbelieving the thought in his head that the fall had not killed the man they called Medicine Feather. He'd dismissed the tales that had been bandied around the miners' camp as nothing more than woodsman's myths – but somehow the man who should have been lying dead alongside George Watkin had survived. It seemed impossible, but the glimpse of buckskin confirmed it as fact: it wasn't the voice of a ghost he was hearing.

'Why?' Wes asked again, his tone more urgent.

Sol Carter remained silent, choosing instead to turn his head again, seeking to validate the unlikely knowledge gathered from that first look back. The sight of the bare-headed frontiersman with his arms folded across his chest was both surprising and

encouraging. He didn't know what act of provi-
dence had saved Wes from death, but he considered
him a fool for not taking instant revenge. Sol's own
creed was strict: never give another man a chance.
Suddenly he spun to his left, his right arm cocking
and hurling at Wes's head the broken half of the
horseshoe that had been gripped in his hand. As
soon as he'd released the lump of iron, his hand
dropped to the butt of the pistol at his side. He
almost laughed – the dope had thrown away his
advantage. *He* would never be so careless.

Because he'd been facing away from him, Wes
had failed to notice the missile in his opponent's
hand, so its launch was unexpected, and for a less
alert man could have been the first blow that led to
his death. Wes Gray, however, was always alert, and
was moving to avoid its impact almost before it had
left Sol Carter's hand. Stooping, the object flew over
his head, but the act of evasion deprived him of the
vital seconds that he needed to outdraw his adversary. Instead, he converted the defensive stoop into
a forward lunge, generating enough momentum to
launch himself across the space that separated them
and crash forcefully into the other's body.

Sol hadn't got his gun clear of leather before Wes
Gray's full weight hit him in the stomach. He went
over backwards, the frontiersman on top of him,
carrying him under the legs of the horse and
crunching his back against the ground. Wes Gray's

left hand gripped Sol's right, trapping it against his side so that he was unable to use his gun. Meanwhile, he raised high the knife he'd pulled from its sheath, and glared into Sol's terror-filled eyes. There would be no other stay of execution – whatever reason the man had for attacking him would only be resolved by the death of one of them, and it wasn't going to be Wes Gray.

'I am Medicine Feather,' Wes said, 'brother of the Arapaho, friend of the Sioux!' Then he plunged the knife into the other's body, deep through to the heart.

Sol Carter died without uttering another word, only an ugly gurgle in his throat.

Wes pushed aside the body and wiped his blade clean on the grass. He spent a little while with the injured horse, removing the half shoe that was still attached to its hoof, then leading it into the water to cool it and clean the area that was cut and swollen. There were ointments that could be applied to aid the healing process, but Wes had none of those things with him. Given time, it would heal naturally, so he unsaddled it, prised off the other shoes, and set it free to forage.

Wes was heading back to the place where he'd left his own animal when he was alerted by a commotion among the trees: something was heading his way with a lack of caution that usually heralded danger.

Instantly his mind slipped back a couple of days to the sighting of the grizzly, and it occurred to him that perhaps this, too, was a hungry bear that had caught the smell of blood. The cracking of twigs and branches was growing louder – any moment the animal would be upon him. If it found him there it was possible that it would regard him as a rival for the food on offer. He had seen the damage inflicted on men by angry bears, and had no wish to become another victim – but he wasn't sure he could reach his horse before the beast broke into the clearing.

FIVE

The Sawbricks' small farm had been developed because of their need for self-sufficiency. Even so, despite its remoteness and the harsh winters that could trap them in their home for several weeks, it was a section of land that Jem, Maud and their daughter Vera had grown to love. The ground was fertile, the forest's natural harvest was bountiful, and the sweep of the great river at this point provided a majestic setting.

In addition to the solid timber house that was their home, there was also a storage barn big enough to house the cows when the weather became too severe to leave them outdoors, and a smaller building where Jem kept his plough and other equipment. There was a small crop field, a cleared pasture for the four milch cows, and an enclosure and stable for the two work horses. A chicken coop had been placed in the pasture, but the hens spent most of the day scratching around the ground outside the farmhouse door, instinctively knowing that the woods were full of predators and that as long as they gave eggs they would be protected.

Jem Sawbrick, however, had not come to this place to farm – it was the timber that had brought him here, and indeed was the only reason he was permitted to build a home along this stretch of the Missouri. Riverboats needed to burn wood to keep the paddle-wheels turning, and the government had commissioned a series of refuelling stations along the navigable length of the river. This one, on the upper reaches, was the last one before Fort Union, and being on the west bank, was on land that was part of the Great Sioux Reservation. Its existence had been negotiated by the government, and it formed one of the caveats of the Laramie Treaty.

Jake and his family had lived in this place unmolested since 1868, and would continue to do so unless the government ever had reason to revoke his concession – but there was no reason to suppose that that would be any time soon. Only conflict with the river captains was likely to put his post in jeopardy, but he had a good relationship with them, and knew that only the lack of a ready supply of firewood would put an end to that. So he kept his stockyard full.

Earlier that morning, Jem had walked the forest trail behind his small homestead, marking out the next trees to be felled. It paid to be prepared. Luther Kelly's brief visit the previous day had been to inform him of the imminent arrival of the boat *Far West*. It would be the first boat of the year, but with the arrival of spring others would soon be following in its wake, all of them tethering at his jetty to take on fuel. The number of boats on the river was few, but it was surprising how quickly his stock could be depleted.

As usual, Jem was accompanied by his daughter. From their first year in that place, Vera had tagged along whenever her father had gone into the forest. She'd been eleven then, and had made herself useful by walking at the horse's head, leading it through the timberland as it dragged the felled trunks back to the yard, where her father would hew them into logs suitable for the furnaces of the boats. Although Jem had never permitted her to wield an axe, she had, over the years, taken on more demanding tasks, and had become indispensable to her father, who had passed on his knowledge of trees and animals as they worked.

It was rugged work, wrapping the heavy chains of the dragging harness around the felled trees, working with the animals, and keeping the tools and equipment in working condition, but she enjoyed the involvement with her father's work as much as the tasks she undertook about the house and farm with her mother. She had also become adept with needle and thread, working alongside her mother to make clothing that could be sold to the people who came upriver on the steamers. Maud, alone, had made the first items, some from calico and gingham – but those fashioned from the stretched hides traded from the Sioux were the most popular. They also earned the most money, so, despite the difficulty of sewing through the tough skins, they became the greater part of the Sawbricks' merchandise.

Returning home, they paused among the last trees that edged the clearing where the cows grazed. Something had caused Jem to raise his eyes to the far bank, perhaps a movement, he wasn't sure, but he caught Vera's arm so that she remained at his side.

In fact it was the girl who spotted the riders first. Two men, still as statues, were on the distant ridge, gazing across the Missouri, the farm clearly the focus of their attention.

'Who are they?' Vera asked her father.

He shook his head. Travellers other than those on the paddle steamers were rare, especially so early in the year. Occasionally they would receive Sioux visitors, looking to trade for milk and eggs, coffee and flour. In exchange they would bring skins, moccasins and jewellery trinkets, which Vera and her mother sold on profitably to the riverboat passengers, along with their own clothing items and the wood figures that Jem carved during the long winter days. It all added to the family's income. But whoever the men across the Missouri were, they were not traders – the apparent absence of pack animals made that clear.

'Do they mean to cross?' Vera asked, the tenor of her voice reflecting the danger she foresaw for them if they ventured into the river at this point. The springtime flow had filled the course almost to the top of its banks, and was moving too quickly for either man or horse to swim. Further downstream, below the place where the White met the Missouri, there was a place where the river widened, but even that wouldn't provide an easy crossing at this time of the year. There were also crossing points further north, but the nearest was at least an hour's ride away.

Before Jem could answer his daughter, another rider hove into sight, then another and another, until finally more than a dozen were ranged alongside the initial two. They formed a ragged line, all of them studying the farm buildings. One of them had a spyglass. Jem couldn't explain to himself why he was pleased he'd stayed among the trees – it wasn't as though the men could do any harm to his family when they were separated by the mighty Missouri, but he had an uneasy feeling that he knew would persist until the men had moved on.

'Are they soldiers?' Vera asked, even though there was no evidence of a uniform, company colours or any regimentation in the way they were gathered on the ridge; but the only previous occasions that she'd seen so many riders together they had been Fort Union patrols.

'No.' There'd been talk of gold in the Black Hills before the winter had closed in, and for a moment Jem wondered if matters had advanced to the point where miners were heading for the digging grounds – but he swiftly swept the thought aside. For the same reason they couldn't be traders, they couldn't be prospectors, either: they had no equipment.

Then suddenly they were moving, heading north along the ridge, and in a few minutes they were out of sight. Jem had dismissed the notion that they were soldiers, but it seemed likely they were heading for Fort Union. He and Vera returned to the house.

An hour later Maud went outside to bring in the laundry, and her call brought her husband to the door of their home. Together they watched two riders who had emerged slowly from the cover of the distant trees. Jem knew they couldn't be part of the group he'd seen at the far side of the Missouri: not only had there been insufficient time for them to reach a crossing point, then follow the river back, but the new arrivals were coming from the interior, from the hill country that belonged to the Sioux. Although it seemed impossible for the two unexpected events of the morning to be linked, Jem was once more troubled by a feeling of unease.

While Maud bustled into the house with her hands full of gathered linen, Jem stepped down from his porch and went forward to meet the newcomers. One of the riders raised his right hand as he approached, the accepted greeting of peace and friendship in the West. He was a fair-haired man, sitting tall and straight in his saddle with just such a manner of officialdom in his bearing that Jem suspected he was a representative of the War Department sent to conduct business with tribes.

'Howdy,' said Jem, his greeting directed at both riders.

Jake Preston introduced himself and Henry Watkin, who, unlike his companion, seemed to have attracted every speck of trail dust that had been kicked up. His heavy-browed, dark eyes added to a rough, menacing mien that Jem tried to ignore. Experience had taught him that the deprivations endured by those who now had the task of negotiating with the tribes-people often left them short of social graces. Wes Gray, he reminded himself, proved that such a failing didn't automatically make a man a villain. So he tried to hide his unease when he invited the two to step down.

'We don't usually see folks so early in the year,'

Jem declared as he led the way to the house, 'and those who come through those trees usually have feathers in their hair.'

'The Sioux come here?' The concern reflected in Henry Watkin's voice surprised Jem – he sounded more like a man running from the Sioux, than one who had been negotiating with them.

'Sure,' Jem answered, 'they come to trade.' He noticed the look that passed between the newcomers, but couldn't interpret its meaning.

There was coffee on the stove when they reached the house, and the men accepted a cup. Jake Preston uttered mild compliments to Maud, while Henry Watkin stepped outside to drink his coffee on the porch.

'Don't mind Henry,' Jake said, 'he doesn't mean any offence. He's just keeping a lookout for some men we've arranged to meet here. One of them is his brother. I hope it won't inconvenience you if we hang around a-while.'

'Guess not,' Jem said. 'We're accustomed to having people about the place when the boats are working the river.' Jake Preston hadn't given an explanation for his presence in Sioux territory, so Jem put the question to him, even though asking another man to divulge his business was usually frowned upon along the frontier. 'Are you a government man, Mr Preston? Like I said, the only visitors we get who haven't travelled the river are Sioux.'

Maud's face expressed her surprise at his for-
wardness. Her husband was a good listener when
travellers stopped at their home, but he didn't
make a habit of prying into their affairs.

Jake Preston didn't seem put out by the question,
in fact he chuckled lightly, but at that moment the
door opened and Vera came into the house. She'd
been in the pasture collecting eggs from the coop,
and was wearing black trousers and a red checked
shirt that she'd made herself. Although she had a
red ribbon in her long black hair, it hung loose on
her shoulders, framing a face whose prettiness was
enhanced by bright eyes and coloured cheeks,
adornments that were the result of her healthy, contented life. Henry Watkin followed her inside, so
any question she might have had about him stayed
in her mouth. Then she saw the second man sitting
at their table.

Jake Preston's chuckle turned into a silent smile
as his eyes lingered on the girl. Then he turned to
his host and answered the question that had been
thrown at him: 'No, I'm not a government man,
although I am here to meet a government delegation that's coming upriver as we speak. They should
be here before sundown.'

That information was in keeping with what Jem
had been told by Luther Kelly, but he didn't
respond to the fair-haired man's remarks. It had
become a habit to play his cards close to his chest

when government matters were under discussion; his caution was insurance against any criticism on his part reaching the ears of those in a position to cancel his wood supply concession.

Jake Preston spoke again. 'A meeting with the Sioux chiefs has been arranged up near Fort Union.'

'You mean to speak on their behalf?'

Again, Jake Preston laughed. 'Not at all. My job is to see that the interests of the miners are not ignored.'

Even in the summer months, items of news that reached the Sawbrick farm were usually two or three weeks out of date. Their main sources were cavalry patrols out of Fort Union, river travellers bearing newspapers from St Louis or Council Bluffs, and the Sioux who had their own means of gathering information, which they sometimes shared. Often in winter, no news reached them, nor did it matter if it did. It was difficult to do anything but survive when the snow came and the temperature fell. Mutterings of gold in the Black Hills had made it to print before the last trips had been made along the river, but they had barely seemed substantial enough to tempt miners across the Missouri in sunshine.

'Are there miners in the Black Hills?' asked Jem.

'There are.'

'And you want protection for them?'

Jake Preston's response was curious to the Sawbrick family: 'I mean to make sure that all the gold up there is extracted from the ground.'

It was another hour before more horsemen arrived at the farm, and during that time Henry Watkin had grown more anxious because of the non-arrival of his brother; Jake Preston's assurances that all would be well because he was with Sol Carter did little to appease him. Sol Carter had a tough reputation, but the Watkin brothers had always judged him to be a hot-head who would one day pick a fight with the wrong man. Henry was hoping that this hadn't been the day.

Jake, meantime, had engaged Vera in conversation, had listened to her account of life on the river with such interest and expressions of amazement that any witness to the scene might have thought him ignorant of the most basic knowledge of tree-felling and farming. She showed him examples of their trade wares, the moccasins and strings of stone beads that were genuine Sioux articles, the clothes made by her mother and herself during the long winter days, and the carvings her father whittled from lumps of timber. Jem's artistic collection included buffalo, bears and elk in addition to representations of Sioux artefacts, which always attracted the attention of the river travellers. These included canoes, ceremonial pipes and miniature totem poles, which, when painted, were his most popular item.

Although Jem could not find fault with Jake Preston's behaviour in either word or action during his conversation with Vera, he was wary of the visitor's motive for engaging his daughter's attention. For some time he'd been increasingly aware of the fact that Vera was no longer the child who had run at his side when following forest trails, but the full impact of her maturity was only now apparent as she was plied with Jake Preston's flattery. Although Jem had had no reason to be troubled by anything the men had done since their arrival, something had twisted in his stomach at their first appearance, and had only tightened since.

That troubling sensation increased with the new arrivals. The group was at least twenty strong, coming downriver from the north, removing any doubt from Jem's mind that they were the same riders he'd seen on the far side of the Missouri earlier that day. His assumption that they had been heading for Fort Union had been wrong. And what was more troubling was that for Jake and Henry, their arrival was not unexpected. The pair had gone outside to greet the men, walking twenty yards from the house so that they were out of earshot of Jem and his family.

Although from their earlier chatter, Jem had got the impression that his current visitors were awaiting Henry's brother and one other man, he didn't think they could be among these new arrivals. Henry's vigilance had been directed away from the river, as though he expected his brother to be following the trail that had brought him and Jake to the farm. Even now he was throwing glances in that direction, and was becoming more and more anxious.

Jem couldn't figure out what was happening. Jake Preston had told him he was going to speak on behalf of some miners to members of a delegation coming upriver. Was that what he had said, or implied, or had Jem got that wrong, too? What he did know was that it didn't need two dozen men to deliver a message. Once again, he noted the equipment that every man carried, and none of it identified them as prospectors. The thought that they were a well-armed posse filled his mind. Maud and Vera had joined him on the stoop to witness the arrival of the riders. Jem told them to go back into the house and close the door.

Men were dismounting, there were shouts and laughs and grumbles as they got out of their saddles after a long ride. Half-a-dozen, with Jake and Henry in their midst, were making their way back towards the buildings.

Jem indicated the house. 'That's our home,' he announced. 'There isn't room for all you men in there.'

Jake Preston offered one of his thin smiles, its

insincerity as thick as it had been when talking with Vera. 'Well, we aren't here to invade your home,' he said, 'we mean to put a bit of business your way. Your lovely daughter was telling me about the goods you sell to riverboat passengers. These men are eager to see your carvings, perhaps buy something for their folk back home.'

The six men had formed a line as threatening as a firing squad, although no guns had been drawn from their holsters. Jem was a strong man, and he knew there wasn't a single man in the group who could get the best of him in a fight, but he couldn't beat twenty, perhaps not even the six he now faced. 'My stock is in the store shed,' he said, keen to keep the men out of the house and away from Maud and Vera.

'That's fine,' Jake smiled. 'These men will accompany you over there.' He moved forward, intending to step on to the porch – but Jem reached out and grabbed his arm. 'I'm just going to finish my coffee,' he said, trying to shrug off Jem's grip.

'Like I said, that's our home. It's now off. . . .'

Jem's declaration remained unfinished, as one of the newcomers stepped behind him and cracked the butt of his pistol against his head. Jem slumped unconscious to the ground. Two men dragged him to the store and dropped him on the floor.

Henry Watkin approached Jake. 'George and Sol should have been here by now,' he grumbled.

Jake Preston dismissed his concern. 'They'll be here soon. They know the boat is due to arrive this evening.' Then he went into the house.

Because of the hubbub generated by men and horses outside the house, the brief scuffle that had culminated in Jem's captivity had escaped the attention of his womenfolk. Maud pretended unconcern by tending to her chores, and Vera tried to find some place in the room where she was not subjected to Jake Preston's unsettling scrutiny. When her father's absence from the house had been long enough to be worrisome, Vera asked what had happened to him. Her first enquiry invoked an off-hand response.

'I told the men about your merchandise. I reckon they're all down at the store seeking bargains.'

Vera looked out of the window, finding an angle that gave her a view of the buildings across the yard. 'The door's closed,' she said. 'It's dark inside when the door is closed.'

Jake Preston ignored her. 'Why don't you prepare some food for the men? They've been riding since sun-up.'

Vera glared at him. Maud, concern for her husband heightened by her daughter's comments, told him that there weren't sufficient supplies to feed all those men.

'You've got hens so you've got eggs, and I can smell fresh home-baked bread. So I reckon you can find enough to feed everyone.'

It was the manner of Jake Preston's speech more than the words that startled the Sawbrick females. It was dictatorial, stripping away any belief that they held sway in their own home. Jake Preston turned a cold glare on them, and there was no longer even the pretence of a smile.

'What have you done to my husband?' asked Maud.

'I told you, he's in the store shed, and he'll come to no harm as long as you do as you're told.'

Although the colour was draining from her face, Vera defiantly threw back her shoulders and raised her chin before speaking. 'I want to see my father.' Her voice crackled tremulously, betraying her nervousness, undermining her demand.

'You'll do what you're told,' he answered. 'After the men are fed I might let you see him.'

'Is he hurt?'

'Food. Now. No more talk.'

Vera stood her ground, determined not to flinch before the man's aggression, and she would have continued to defy him but couldn't summon up the necessary words. Still, her pale face registered contempt and a challenge to his authority. Its insolence angered him and he jumped to his feet, his arm drawing back in readiness to strike her, and he would have done if Maud hadn't interfered, stepping forward to protect her daughter and pulling her to the other side of the room and through the door that led into the adjoining room where the meals were prepared.

Maud was no less concerned for the safety of her husband than her daughter, but figured that for the moment, until they knew what had happened to Jem, they would be better served by acceding to the demands of the invaders. As quietly as she was able, she conveyed that strategy to Vera. 'Prepare the food,' she said, 'and we'll get the chance to help your father while they are eating.' Maud wasn't sure she believed that herself, but for the moment she had no other message of hope to give to her daughter.

For half-an-hour the skillet was in constant use with the preparation of bacon and eggs, to which were added beans and large chunks of the recently baked bread that Jake Preston had detected. Pots of coffee were brewed, poured and drunk as the men came in teams to fill their stomachs with the Sawbricks' provisions. The only man who had any cause for dissatisfaction was Henry Watkin. His brother had still not arrived, and the fear was growing that George and Sol Carter had been caught and killed by the Sioux.

'We want to see my father now,' Vera told Jake Preston when the last of the men had finished their food.

'Sure,' he said. 'Why not. . . .'

93

The easy way he acceded to her request was wholly unexpected, and it caused her more alarm than his intention of striking her had invoked earlier.

Maud collected a cloth-covered tray from the kitchen area and made for the door. Jake stepped in front of her, grinning, and whisked away the covering material. If he'd expected to find a weapon on the tray he was disappointed: it contained nothing more than some bread on a plate, coffee in a pot and an empty mug.

'He'll be hungry,' Maud explained, 'he hasn't eaten since first light.'

Vera opened the door and stepped outside. Before following, her mother addressed Jake Preston once more. 'Why are you doing this?'

'Don't worry, we'll be gone soon enough.'

'What do you mean to do with us?'

A smile spread across Jake Preston's face, as insincere as every other smile he'd bestowed on them since his arrival. 'Nothing,' he said, 'nothing at all.'

She knew he was lying. As she and Vera made their way towards the store many faces turned in their direction, faces of ruthless men, not a single ally for her family. She saw Jake Preston make a signal to Henry Watkin, an order to go with them. It crossed her mind that he was going to kill them, and she sought a plan of escape. Her thoughts dwelt on the store's rear door: there was no reason to believe that it had been discovered by the men who had taken Jem there, so it was probably not under surveillance. If they were left alone for a few minutes there was a route behind the stable by which they might reach the trees unseen. They could hide in the woods until the men had gone.

At first the outside light lit up only the immediate triangle of the store's floor that stretched away from the partially opened door, but even that was sufficient to reveal Jem's booted feet, making it clear that he was stretched out, immobile. Maud pushed the tray into her daughter's hands, then dashed to her husband's side. If Jem was dead she didn't want Vera to make the discovery. Her immediate fear, however, was instantly relieved. As the door opened wider and daylight filled the interior, Jem moved, rolled over, and then began to sit up.

He groaned and raised a hand to his head. Blood had streamed from the place on the crown of his head that had taken the blow from the gun butt, and although it had ceased to flow, his left ear and brow were covered in its drying stickiness. Maud reached for the cloth on the tray and used that to wipe the blood away from his forehead and eyes. She knew instinctively that the blow he'd received had left him incapable of any exertion. Even if Henry Watkin wasn't standing guard, there was no possibility of an immediate escape attempt for the whole family. Her husband wasn't currently capable of fleeing under his own resources, and he was too heavy to be carried by her and her daughter.

Henry Watkin was standing in the doorway, proving to be an obstacle to the only source of light. Maud told him to move – she hoped he would go outside, but instead he came closer, although he didn't seem interested in either Jem's injury or Maud's nursing ability. He was preoccupied, wondering about his brother, which probably accounted for his being caught unawares by Maud's sudden move. She reached for the coffee pot as though intending to pour some of the hot liquid for her husband, but instead threw the contents into Henry's face. He yelled, raised his hands to his burning eyes, leaving his sidearm open to Maud's reach. She pulled the gun free and crashed it down on Henry's head, needing to hit him a second time to render him unconscious on the floor.

Vera stared at her mother in open surprise.

'Go!' said Maud, pushing her daughter towards the rear door. 'Quickly! Get to the trees and don't stop. Make your way downriver until you find someone who can help.'

'I'm not leaving you and father,' her daughter protested.

'You must. Your father can't run. Go, before someone comes to investigate.'

Her father's incapacity was clear to see, but Vera was still reluctant to go.

'I don't know what purpose has brought these men here, but they don't mean to leave any witnesses. So go, Vera. Someone must tell what has happened here!'

Voices outside the store were a warning that someone could enter at any moment, then all would be lost.

'Go!' Maud urged again, and Vera, looking at the unconscious figure sprawled on the floor, knew she had little choice.

She opened the rear door quietly and slipped outside. No one was keeping an eye on it, and she was able to dash across the space between the store and the stable unobserved. She had almost reached the trees but then her luck ran out. She hadn't seen the man who was tending his horse in the pasture, but he caught sight of her ducking between the rails that fenced off the pasture from the forest.

He raised the alarm: 'It's the girl!' and pointed in the direction she'd fled.

'Catch her!' ordered Jake Preston, and two men set off in immediate pursuit.

Vera heard the commotion behind, and knew that men were after her – but she had a start on them, and knew many of the woodland trails. She ran, and ran, and ran.

SIX

The sounds emanating from the undergrowth of the tree-lined slopes spurred Wes into action – they told of a rapid approach, and Wes knew that if it *was* the grizzly, and he was the object of its charge, he had little hope of outrunning it. A charging grizzly was a fearsome opponent. But a niggling memory reminded him that it was probably the smell of blood that had attracted the beast, so it was unlikely to ignore the carcase in favour of chasing a running man.

Wes regarded Sol Carter's body without pity: he had inflicted the great gash from which blood was now seeping, and before morning other teeth and claws would surely have ripped it apart. And if that process began immediately, if it helped to preserve his own life, then so be it. The dead were dead, and the living survived by whatever means were available. However, Wes knew that a grizzly's behaviour was unpredictable at this time of year: it might regard a running figure as a threat, and its inbred response might be to attack. It was a risk Wes wasn't prepared to take – he had no desire to be the target of a rampaging bear.

A nearby oak tree offered itself as a refuge. New leaves dressed old branches that twisted out from its sturdy trunk. The lowest branch was within his grasp and looked capable of bearing his weight, and from there he could climb beyond the grizzly's reach. Even if it saw him, it wouldn't waste time trying to shake him down when there was unresisting prey available. All he had to do was wait until it had satisfied its appetite and wandered away. But as he began to haul himself on to the lowest bough, his thoughts turned to the safety of the horses. His own was twenty-five yards away, partly hidden among a stand of elms, while the other, the lame one, still grazed near the water's edge. Once the scent of the bear filled their nostrils they would flee and he'd be left afoot many miles from Black Buffalo's village where he'd left his equipment and pelts.

It was with a degree of surprise that he observed the behaviour of those animals. Although both had become aware of the disturbance among the trees, neither had done more than turn their heads in that direction. They were interested, but unconcerned, and Wes assumed they hadn't yet picked up that tell-tale scent that would startle them into flight. He was standing now in a fork of the tree, which provided a comfortable viewing post. For a moment the possibility that he was mistaken about the identity of the approaching animal crossed his mind, but he quickly cast it aside. As the movement among the trees turned into a shape and glimpses of red could be discerned, his conviction that it was a grizzly on the rampage re-settled in his mind.

He waited, motionless, watching the place where he expected the beast to break from the trees – and when it did, he stared in surprise. It wasn't a grizzly, it wasn't any wild animal of the forest, it was a girl – and what is more, one he recognized – running and stumbling as she cast fear-filled glances behind her. She rolled a little way down the slope and scrambled for a moment or two on hands and knees as she tried to regain her feet. Her legs seemed to be almost without strength, a sign that, desperate though she was to continue running, she had little strength left in her body to do so. She was struggling for breath, unable to suck in as much air as she needed, and the exhalations were almost sobs of failure. She paused, hands on knees to ease her breathing, but a sound reached her that caused her to begin again, running down towards the river.

Wes Gray watched her, assessing by the way she turned her head first one way, then the other, that there was no direction to her flight. She was running away from what was behind her without any destination in mind, and it was clear that she was close to collapse – her mouth was open as she continually gasped for breath, and her legs were barely able to hold her upright. Wes lay along the bough he'd been standing on, and called to her.

'Vera!' He'd recognized her almost as soon as she'd emerged from the trees, knowing her instantly because of her long black hair. The Sawbrick farm had become an annual stopping point for Wes on his spring journey down the Missouri. As she'd grown, her face and figure had altered, but her hair had always been as long and shiny as it was this day. He stretched down his arm and beckoned her on.

Startled at first by the announcement of her name, and almost stepping backwards in alarm that one of her hunters had somehow got ahead of her, Vera hesitated. Then she fixed her eyes on the tree where the call had come from, and saw the figure in the fringed buckskin clothing lying along the low bough. Recognition brought about an overwhelming sense of deliverance. Her father's respect for this frontiersman had grown with his every visit to their farm, and her admiration of him had increased with each new story she heard of his

101

adventures. Even though she almost disbelieved the evidence of her own eyes, there was no other rescuer she would have preferred to Wes Gray. When he waved his arm again, she found a last spurt of energy and ran forward. Using the strength of one arm, he hoisted her up to the branch on which he lay, then got to his feet and together they stood in the fork of the tree.

Allowing her a moment to regain her breath, he let her rest her forehead against his chest. Her back was against the trunk of the tree, and by peering over her shoulder he could see the area of the forest from which she'd emerged.

'Who's after you?' he asked eventually.

She shook her head; she didn't know the identity of her pursuers, but she still found enough words: 'They mean to kill me.'

'How many?'

'Two. Perhaps more.'

Another look beyond the girl was rewarded with a glimpse of movement among the far trees. He knew that as the hunters were unaware of his presence, his buckskin clothes would make it difficult for them to see him, but they would instantly pinpoint the girl's location because of her red shirt. He cupped his hands and she used them like a step, so he could silently lift her into the denser foliage of the higher reaches of the tree. Then he waited.

There were two men, each with a revolver in his

gunbelt and carrying a rifle in a manner that indicated they intended to use it at the first opportunity. Wes regarded them with scorn. Their tracking lacked guile, and they blundered into the clearing in almost the same manner as Vera – but she had been running for her life. They looked around carelessly, as though they expected to find her sitting under a tree awaiting their arrival. That she was capable of escape was a concept not entertained by either man. They came forward apace, separated by a dozen yards, restricting the scope of their search to the open pasture of the riverbank, gazing ahead in expectation of a sight of their prey fleeing from their pursuit. So they had almost reached the oak before the unsaddled horse at the water's edge attracted the attention of the man nearest the river.

His curiosity aroused, the man veered in that direction to investigate – but he hadn't reached the animal before a shout from his companion took him in the other direction. The second man had paused on the embankment, studying something he'd discovered in the grass.

'What is it, Joe?' the man asked as he approached. As he got closer the item became less hidden by the long, lush grass: he could make out a shape and caught a flash of red, and figured Joe had caught the girl hiding in the grass.

'It's Sol Carter,' Joe announced. 'Someone's slit

him open.'

The two men looked down on the corpse. 'Indians?' asked the other man.

'Still got his hair,' Joe pointed out.

'Where's George Watkin? According to Henry they were expected to turn up together.'

'Perhaps they had a disagreement,' mused Joe.

'You think George did this?'

'Well, it wasn't the girl. Come on, let's get after her. We'll report this when we get back.'

After a moment's thought, the first man spoke again. 'There's a horse down by the river. It's been unsaddled. I'll take a look at it first, see if there's anything that gives a clue to what happened here.'

Joe grumbled, he was more interested in catching Vera. Jake Preston, he knew, wouldn't be happy if she gave them the slip. 'Don't waste time with that,' he called, but his advice was ignored.

While the men had been examining Sol Carter's body, Wes Gray had dropped to the ground. He'd landed silently and unseen on the far side of the oak, and now pressed himself against the trunk and waited for the man who was heading towards the river. He'd been able to hear enough of the exchange of words over his victim's body to know that they were part of the group who had tried to kill him. In other circumstances that might not have been reason enough to kill them, but they had chased Vera with the intention of killing her, so

104

there could be no reprieve.

The man walked straight past the place where Wes was waiting, his focus on the horse at the river's edge, with no thought that Sol Carter's killer might be close by. Wes chose not to use his gun: Vera had been unsure how many were following her, which meant that there could be other men in the vicinity. If so, he wasn't prepared to help them find him.

He struck quickly, ensuring that the oak still obscured him from Joe's view, stepping out behind the other man and using the big bone-handled knife to end his life with a bloody gurgle. The rifle slipped from the man's hands and was lost from sight in the long grass. Wes bent to wipe his knife clean on the dead man's shirt, then set his mind to the capture of his companion. If that man provided answers to his questions he might give him the opportunity to survive. As it happened, Wes didn't get that opportunity.

'Come on, Sam. Leave it until we come back,' Joe called, the sound of his voice closer than Wes had expected. As Wes rose to his feet, Joe came into sight, edging sideways, trying to get an angle that would give a sight of his companion heading for the river. He reacted to the appearance of the buckskin-clad stranger with alacrity, swinging his rifle in a tight arc and firing from the hip. The bullet clipped the tree and ricocheted over Wes Gray's shoulder. While Joe ratcheted the mechanism to eject the spent shell, Wes responded: before Joe could fire again Wes had thrown his knife, so it sank deep into his adversary's chest. As his rifle fell to the ground, Joe went over backwards, dying, clutching at the blade that was embedded in him.

Wes watched him die, then pulled his knife free and cleaned it again before returning it to its sheath. Joe's death had cut off one possible source of information, but it wasn't a loss that Wes dwelt on – he'd had no alternative but to kill the man. Vera would tell him what had happened at her home, tell him the fate of her parents, so he called to her with the news that it was safe to descend. Cautiously she reached the ground, averting her gaze from the bodies of her pursuers as best she could.

The possibility that other men might be chasing her, and that they would have been alerted to her location by the recent gunshot, prompted Wes to leave his questions until they had distanced themselves from the spot. Vera had regained some of her energy, but Wes put her on the back of his pony and led it up the embankment to the tree-line. The place he chose to rest was high on the slopes, from where he could look down on the uncovered bodies of his three victims. He wanted to know if other men were searching for Vera, but the bodies still lay undiscovered by the time he and the girl moved again. In between, Vera related the events of her day to the frontiersman; the amiable behaviour of

106

the first two visitors, which had become hostile almost as soon as the other riders arrived, and the attack on her father, and the whole family's imprisonment in their storehouse.

'How did you escape?'

'Through the rear door. I guess they didn't know it was there.'

'Why alone? Why didn't your parents flee with you?'

'Dad's injury was too severe. He couldn't even stand, so it was impossible for him to move.' She paused a moment. 'Ma thought they were going to kill us. That's why she insisted I got away. To let people know what happened.'

'But your parents were alive when you made a run for it?'

Vera nodded. 'I want to go back,' she told Wes. 'I can't leave them there to die.'

Wes couldn't account for anything that had happened over the past few days. First, in contradiction to the Laramie Treaty, he'd discovered that gold hunters had not only moved into the Black Hills, but believed they had the backing of the army to do so. Then he and Tall Horse had been ambushed by men who had been at the miners' camp. He couldn't understand the purpose behind such an attack – even if they didn't like or agree with what he'd told them, they had to know that killing them would only aggravate the Sioux into seeking revenge. Now a wood supply station had been invaded and a family terrorized. Why? 'How many men are at your farm?' he asked Vera.

'I can't be sure. More than twenty.'

'And you haven't seen any of them before?'

She shook he head. 'All I can tell you is that the man who did all the talking introduced himself as Jake Preston.'

The name took Wes by surprise. As unlikely as it had first seemed to him, the attack on the Sawbrick's home had to be linked to the miners in the Black Hills. He described Jake Preston, 'Tall. Fair haired. Clean shaven.' Vera gave a nod to each item.

Until the appearance of Vera, Wes hadn't realized he was so close to the Missouri. 'I need to take a look at your farm,' he told her.

'I'll come with you.'

'No. Stay here. With such a large body of men I might not be able to help your parents immediately.' In truth, he feared they might already be dead, but he didn't want to upset her unnecessarily. 'They might have the place too well guarded, and we'll have to wait for them to leave before we can get to them.'

Vera's stubbornness was born of fear. 'We must do something,' she said. 'My mother believes they are going to be killed. I'm coming with you.' Wes knew he couldn't afford to waste time arguing.

It had always been Jake Preston's intention to kill the family living at the riverside wood station: if successful, the dictates of the plan he was executing allowed for nothing else. He was, however, a careful man, and while there was still the possibility of something going amiss he would keep them alive: in dire circumstances they could be invaluable bargaining chips, but with nothing incriminating to pass on to the authorities that would lead to his capture. He'd adopted the name Jake Preston at Fort Union, and would abandon it the moment he recrossed the Missouri.

The daughter's escape was inconvenient, of course, but didn't cause him too much concern. There was nowhere for her to go, no one she could summon for help and no knowledge to impart if she survived. One of the men had picked up a sound that he thought had been a gunshot. Sam and Joe, it was assumed, had caught up with her, and although some men watched for their return, everyone knew that the girl wouldn't be coming home again.

Another one whose eyes were fixed on the woods was Henry Watkin, still watching for his brother. His agitation had begun to bother Jake Preston, not because he doubted Sol Carter's ability to conduct a successful ambush, but because the possibility that

109

the pair had fallen into the hands of a band of Sioux had developed in his mind and he couldn't shrug it away. Within a few hours they would be leaving this place, and no one would be waiting for George and Sol if they hadn't joined them by that time.

So it was a busy farmyard that Wes and Vera surveyed from their place among the trees. Three small fires had been lit with a handful of men around each, drinking coffee and playing cards like soldiers on patrol, emigrants crossing the continent, or drovers on a cattle drive. Other men were ranged along the boundary fence, keeping their eyes on the trees but with indifferent watchfulness, chatting and laughing as if they were gathered at a saloon bar.

Across the paddock full of grazing horses, Vera pointed to the distant building that was partially obscured by the stable. 'My parents are in there.'

Wes moved to his right, seeking a position from which he could see the whole of the back of the store. Beside the rear door, a man was sitting on the ground with a rifle across his knees. A guard was significant: Jem and Maud were still alive.

'Can we get them out?' she asked.

Wes shook his head. 'There are too many men around to attempt a rescue,' he said. 'We might have a better chance when it gets dark.'

Vera was disappointed with Wes Gray's assessment. She offered to act as a decoy, to lead the men into the woods so they would try to capture her while Wes released her parents. He dismissed the idea with barely concealed contempt.

'Patience, Vera!' he told her, 'Committing suicide won't help your parents. We must wait and watch for an opportunity that at least has some chance of success.'

Somewhat chastened, Vera remained silent for a minute. 'They used the house earlier when they had a meal. Perhaps they'll do the same again.'

'Perhaps,' Wes conceded, but added nothing more.

Half-an-hour later nothing had changed apart from the fact that the sun was lower in the sky, deepening in colour and losing some of its strength. Vera wanted to tell Wes that dusk was less than an hour away, but she figured he knew that, and the cold expression in his eyes deterred her from interrupting his thoughts with anything that wasn't critical.

In fact, Wes was mulling over the girl's suggestion that the men might go into the house for a meal. He pointed to the guard at the rear door. 'I think he's asleep,' he said. 'Of course, there might also be guards posted inside to watch over your parents, but if there comes a time when only a handful are out of doors, it might be the best chance we get.'

Eagerly Vera asked, 'What do you want me to do?'

He grinned at her. 'Nothing, yet. Let's wait and

see what happens.'

What happened took them by surprise. Only moments later three distant rifle shots spurred the men at the farm into action, their attention drawn to the river and the sight of a solitary rider on the far ridge. Jake Preston emerged from the house and fired three answering shots in the air. The rider removed his hat and waved in celebratory fashion then turned his horse and disappeared from sight. Jake Preston began issuing orders, and the men reacted instantly. The fires were kicked out, coffee pots and mugs were emptied and stashed away in forage bags. Every man grabbed his saddle, sought out and harnessed his horse, then led it out of the paddock and hitched it to those rails along which, earlier, men had been standing.

'They're leaving!' said Vera.

Wes didn't reply, just watched the activity.

With rifles in hand, two men crossed the clearing in a long-striding loping run and followed a wood-land trail fifty yards away from the place where Wes and Vera watched.

'They've gone in search of the men who chased you,' Wes said. 'Quarter of an hour to find them, quarter of an hour to get back. If we have the choice I'd rather wait until they return. Better to know where they are, than run the risk of running into them when we're trying to make our escape, especially if I have to carry your father.'

Vera was reluctant to endorse any delay, but she knew she wouldn't be able to sway Wes Gray's decisions. He would act when he chose to, when he decided he had the best possible chance of success, and if that put additional strain on her, and increased her consuming worry for the safety of her parents, then she would be forced to endure it. But it didn't still her mind, didn't prevent her from seeking another plan, or an argument that would persuade him to act immediately. So deep were her thoughts that she almost didn't hear his low muttering.

'What are they doing?'

Wes was studying the activity in the farmyard. Most of the men were now lost from sight, hidden from view behind the stable, or they had gone into either the house or one of the other buildings. Wes wasn't sure where everyone was, which greatly increased the risk of discovery if he attempted to free the Sawbricks. Four men, however, were still within his sight, each carrying a blanket-wrapped pack across his arms in a manner which suggested rifles – but the ease with which they carried them was an indication that they lacked the appropriate weight. The bundles were left on the house porch before the men went indoors. The farmyard was deserted. Even the rear door guard had roused himself from his slumber and left his post.

When Wes pointed out the lack of activity, Vera

113

felt compelled to urge action. 'We could go now!'

'We can't be sure your parents are not guarded,' Wes told her. 'There could be men inside the store-house.' Those cautionary words were uttered to check the girl's impatience, but he'd already decided he couldn't afford to wait. If the lives of Jem Sawbrick and his wife were in danger, then the imminent departure of the invaders meant there was little time left to rescue them. Crossing the clearing posed a threat: if he was seen, not only would it put his own life in danger, it would almost certainly hasten the end of those he was attempting to save. 'I'll go and investigate. You wait here and watch for the men returning from the woods.'

He was moving almost before he'd finished speaking, deceptively quick even though he was crouching down to keep low to the ground. The horses along the fence formed an effective screen between himself and the buildings, but it wasn't until he reached the stable that he realized he was not alone: Vera was fifteen yards behind, emulating his running style to the best of her ability, her eyes fixed on the face that was turned towards her. It expressed Wes's exasperation even before he spoke.

'I told you to stay back among the trees!'

For their protection, to limit sound and avoid detection, the words were whispered, but to Vera they came across as an angry hiss. 'I want to help!' she said.

'I needed you to keep watch for the men return-ing from the woods.'

'And if they came, how would I let you know if we're quarter of a mile apart?'

Acting as lookout was, of course, nothing more than an excuse to leave Vera in the woods, and it wasn't done just to keep her safe from the men who had commandeered her home, but because he needed to concentrate on the task of freeing her parents – if they were still alive. He didn't want Vera to accompany him into the storehouse if only Jem and Maud's bodies were to be found there. And even if they were alive, he had no knowledge of the conditions under which they were being held captive. There might be resistance to overcome, and he couldn't afford to be worrying about the girl's safety while fighting for his own life. Besides, the red shirt she wore made her easy to see – although that at least he could rectify: he removed his buckskin jacket and made her put it on. It was too big, of course, but it achieved its purpose, and in the now dimming light she blended into the stable timbers.

Muted sounds, men talking and laughing, reached them from beyond or within the outbuild-ings, and Wes conducted the girl to the rear of the stable. 'There's no reason for anyone to come here,' he told her, 'but stay low and keep an eye on the house. Warn me by tapping on the door if you see anyone heading in this direction, but don't let them see you. If things don't work for me in there, then get as far away as possible. Make sure you avoid the two men in the woods.' He began to move away, then stopped. 'And don't follow me inside unless I call for you.'

Swiftly, Wes crossed the space that separated the stable from the rear of the storehouse and pressed his ear against the timber door. No distinguishable sound reached him, neither voices nor evidence of activity within. After a moment he thought he detected a scratching, shuffling noise, but it ceased almost as soon as it had begun. Wes pulled his knife from its sheath, opened the door slowly, only wide enough for him to slip through the gap and step inside. A lit lamp hanging from a nail in a central support post provided a dull yellow glow which showed the layout of the barn-like building. Sacks, tubs and boxes that represented the family's provisions and sales goods were arranged along one wall, spreading out towards the centre in such manner as to form a division between the front and back of the storehouse. On the opposite side a long workbench could be seen, with saws, hammers, axes and other tools hanging in a neat line.

On the floor beside the bench lay the trussed forms of Jem and Maud Sawbrick, tied back to back. Maud's eyes were fixed on him, her initial expression of surprise changing swiftly to one of warning.

With flicks of her eyes she made to inform Wes that there was someone else within, a guard near the front door who was hidden from Wes's view by the assembly of containers in the middle of the building.

Stealthily, Wes moved forwards, knelt on the floor and used his knife to slice apart the rope that bound the Sawbricks' feet together. The sudden release startled Jem, who was as yet unaware of Wes Gray's presence. He grunted, and stretched out his legs so that his boots scraped across the floor, and that attracted the attention of the guard.

'What are you doing?' he called out. Wes, who had withdrawn behind the container wall, sensed him moving towards the prisoners.

To distract him, Maud asked for a drink of water. He ignored her, and, happy to attribute the noises he'd heard to her discomfort, began to turn away from where they lay. But then at the last moment, the loose piece of rope caught his eye, and he stopped to take a closer look – and then noticed the untied feet.

'How did that happen?' he asked. Instinctively his right hand reached for his gun, but he wasn't wearing a gunbelt – indeed, apart from some fringed trousers and a feather stuck in a band around his head, he wasn't wearing anything. He twisted at the waist, reacting to the movement behind him as Wes, standing upright, shifted his weight. His mouth opened to yell for assistance, but Wes clamped his left hand over it with such force that the man staggered two steps backwards and tripped over the legs of his captors. He went down, and Wes lost his grip on the man's face as he, too, tumbled to the ground.

By this time the guard had seen the big hunting knife in Wes Gray's hand, and he searched around for a weapon to defend himself with. There were plenty in the storehouse – one of Jem's tree-felling axes was within his grasp. Springing to his feet, he grabbed the long axe handle and stepped towards the frontiersman.

Wes, too, moved quickly, leaning forward so that his head was on a level with the other's chest, his knife gripped in his right hand. If the guard shouted for help, then they were all doomed, but the leering grin that had spread across his face sent the message that he believed the axe gave him an unbeatable advantage.

To provide the maximum arc and generate the maximum power, the guard held the axe with both hands at the very end of the handle. He hefted the weapon, suggesting to Wes the damage it would do to his body.

In response, Wes spoke to his adversary in a low voice, almost making the man forget they were about to embark on a fight to the death as he strained to catch the words. 'I am Medicine Feather, brother of the Arapaho and friend of the Sioux. This is the land of the Sioux. It was a mistake to come here.'

The identity of an opponent whose exploits were legendary sent a chill through the guard and caused him to pause a moment, as though reluctant to fight, considering again a yell for assistance – but Wes Gray didn't give him the opportunity. He swayed forward as though about to launch an attack, to which his opponent was forced to respond. Clumsily, the guard swung the axe at Wes's head, but without speed or accuracy. Wes swayed back again, out of reach, but jabbed his arm forward after the axe blade had passed so that the point of his knife almost touched the other's chest.

The guard stepped back, his eyes wide and staring, transfixed almost by the glinting knife in Wes Gray's hand. Desperation drove his next move, and a belief that a greater reach must prove victorious: raising the axe over his shoulder, he swung it in a cruel arc – but that was exactly what Wes had expected. Again he stepped back to avoid the blow, and when its impetus took it beyond recall, he stepped forward and buried the knife into the other man's body. As a squeal of agony came to the guard's lips, Wes covered his mouth with one hand and twisted the knife with the other. He lowered the dead body to the floor, then turned his attention to the prisoners.

119

'Can you walk?' he asked Jem, as he cut away all of the bindings. The answer was affirmative, but even by the time they'd reached the rear door, Wes wasn't sure it was the truth.

SEVEN

Maud Sawbrick rubbed her wrists and ankles where the skin had been chafed by the rough rope with which she'd been tied. Jem leant against the wall, a hand pressed against his brow as though his head needed support to prevent it falling off his shoulders. With a finger to his lips to quell the questions he knew they wanted to ask, Wes carefully reopened the rear door to check for the return of the outside guard. There was no one in sight. He pointed to the stable and urged Maud to make a dash for its far corner. Then, with a supporting arm around Jem's shoulder, the men followed.

It was a short but uncomfortable run for the farm owner. Without Wes Gray's strength he would have fallen twice, and the deep groans that escaped his mouth denoted not only pain but an intense struggle to retain consciousness. The reunion with Vera, although conducted in absolute silence, went some way to revive his spirits.

They paused behind the stable for less than a minute, as Wes was anxious to get the family into the covering trees as quickly as possible. Not only was there a risk of pursuit from the farm when their escape was discovered, but they might also be seen by the men who had been sent to recall Vera's hunters. Ahead was the most perilous part of their flight for freedom – crossing the clearing where they would be exposed to the view of anyone watching from the house. There was no alternative, and Wes could only hope that whatever purpose had taken the men into the barn kept them there long enough to enable his party to reach the woods. Jem, he knew, wasn't capable of completing the crossing unaided, so despite the other's reluctance, he hoisted him across his shoulders and carried him.

Jem's weight was not insignificant, but as long as he could keep it evenly distributed Wes knew he could cover the distance without pausing. The load he was bearing, however, made it impossible to adopt his usual crouched, loping stride, and even though he told the women to stay low, he was forced to run upright. With every stride he expected to hear a shout of alarm or the report of firearms, but they reached the trees without incident and could rest there for a few moments – and the Sawbricks were able to give voice to their pleasure at being together again.

Now that the Sawbricks were out of immediate danger, Wes was free to focus his attention on the farm. His creed for survival demanded revenge, punishment for those who threatened his existence and that of his friends. Because of the way the Sawbricks had been held captive and their daughter had been hunted he was convinced that all the family would be killed before the raiders quit their home. Jake Preston was their leader, which, in Wes's opinion, made him responsible for that decision.

Wes also held Preston responsible for the ambush that had threatened his life and left Tall Horse fighting for his own. Although he was at a loss to understand the motive for either event, Wes couldn't shake off the assumption that they were linked. He was engulfed by curiosity, and needed to know not only why his visit to the camp of the Black Hills miners had raised such enmity, but also why a peaceful family on the banks of the Missouri needed to die. In addition, he wanted to know why the man he'd killed in the storehouse had been dressed like a Sioux warrior.

At present, he had no answers to these questions, but the recent activity suggested that their purpose for invading the farm was about to reach its climax. If he hung around he would know all. Then he would kill Jake Preston, or die in the attempt.

His thoughts were interrupted by noises deeper in the wood, announcing the return of the two men who'd been sent in search of their companions. The speed and recklessness with which they were moving disclosed their location long before they came into view. By that time, Wes had told Vera to guide her parents to the place where he'd left his pony and wait for him there. Vera baulked at the suggestion. Although her father's condition was improving, she clearly doubted her ability to aid him in the event of pursuit. Wes assured the family that that was unlikely, pointing out that the raiders' horses were saddled in readiness for a hasty departure.

'They don't mean to hang around much longer,' he said, 'but I want to know their purpose for coming here. No one will find you in that clearing where we left the pony, so wait there for me. I'll join you as soon as possible.'

They parted company, Vera and her parents heading deeper into the woods, while Wes set a course that circumnavigated the railed pasture. It added some distance to his route to the farm but he knew that no lookouts had been posted, and it kept him out of the eye-line of anyone whose attention had been drawn to the returning pair. These two had begun shouting for attention before they'd completed the crossing of the paddock, and men were beginning to gather to learn the reason for the hullabaloo.

Although most of the saddled horses had been tethered along the paddock rails, one or two were standing under the boughs of a huge oak tree that stood near the house. Wes gained its shadow and watched as men emerged from the barn in response to the calls of the two men. Like the man he'd killed in the storehouse, all those who had been in the barn were disguised as tribesmen, with feathers in their hair and paint on their faces. Only Jake Preston, who came from the house to investigate the excitement, wore his usual attire.

'Dead,' one of the returnees declared. 'All of them bleeding out on the riverbank about a mile from here.'

'Are you saying the girl stabbed them?' Jake Preston was incredulous.

'Don't know that it was the girl, but somebody sure did.'

The murmurs arising from those who had gathered were stilled when the second man spoke. 'It's not just Sam and Joe out there,' he said. 'Found Sol Carter's body, too.'

'Sol Carter!' The speaker was Henry Watkin, pushing through the throng to stand face to face with the man. 'What about my brother, did you see George?'

'No, nobody else.'

'Where's George?' asked Henry Watkin.

Somebody in the assembly wanted to know if their companions had been killed by the Sioux.

'Could have been,' the first man replied. 'They were gutted, but their hair hadn't been lifted.'

It took only a moment for Henry Watkin to grasp the only alternative. His face darkened as he turned it in Jake Preston's direction. 'It's that man Wes Gray,' he said, 'Medicine Feather. He killed them. He's here now.'

Jake Preston had known Henry Watkin for several years, and knew his strengths and his weaknesses. One of the latter was a dependence on his older brother, which made him a liability when left on his own. Now, the thought that his brother was dead was creating a turmoil in his mind capable of causing unrest among the rest of the band. Already the name 'Medicine Feather' was being uttered as though he was more dangerous than the entire Sioux nation.

'He's not here,' Jake Preston spoke with authority, 'and even if he was, he's only one man. Despite the stories that are told about him, he's only human. He can't kill everyone!' He looked around the group to see how his words had been received. Encouraged, he spoke again.

'You men have been well paid for the task in hand. We've had the signal from across the river, which means the boat must be less than half-an-hour away. It'll be coming around that bend soon, and when it does I want us ready for action. There's no rail around its deck so you can charge aboard the moment it comes alongside the jetty. I'm told there's a newspaperman on board. If you can identify him, then crack his head but don't kill him. The independent report of the survivor of a Sioux attack will spread across the continent like wildfire, and it will be backed up by every arrow we leave sticking in the steamer and the bodies on it.'

'And the rest of the people on board?' someone asked.

'No survivors,' said Jake Preston. 'There are soldiers, a guard of eight men commanded by a lieutenant. Apart from those, there are the four members of the delegation and their aide, plus a six-man crew. As soon as the job's completed we ride north to the crossing point. You can clean up and change clothes when we get there. We separate in the morning after crossing the Missouri. Any questions?'

'Indians usually set properties aflame after a successful raid,' a voice announced.

'Why not,' approved Jake Preston. 'Burn down the house and outbuildings, but not the steamer. I want that to be found with its cargo of bodies.'

'What about the prisoners?' someone asked, motioning with his head in the direction of the storehouse.

127

Although he still displayed an outward calmness, the turn of events registered by Sol Carter's failure to kill Wes Gray had unsettled Jake Preston. He experienced a greater sense of urgency to be done with this business, to ride clear from this land of the Sioux and the threat of the man called Medicine Feather. Accordingly, he was happy to undertake anything that could be done before the arrival of the *Far West* that helped to hasten their departure after the attack. In the event of failure, he now considered the value of the Sawbricks negligible. He would take his chance, trust in his own abilities to find another avenue of escape.

'Cut them free and bring them outside.' He pointed to the bundles that had been left on the house porch. 'Use those,' he said. 'Put three or four in each, the way the Sioux do it.'

A man unrolled the blankets and chose a bow and a handful of arrows from those revealed. Another man knelt beside him and did likewise, while a third went off to the storehouse for the condemned prisoners.

Almost immediately he came running out of the building holding short lengths of cut rope in his hands.

'They've gone!' he yelled, '—and Harv's dead!' he added, throwing a glance back inside as though there was some possibility of a mistake, that the man with the gaping wound in his stomach might rise to his feet and follow him into the evening's hastening gloom.

It was Henry Watkin, of course, who voiced the name: 'Medicine Feather. He's here!'

The men, without side-arms to reach for, exchanged looks that expressed their disbelief that a rescue had been made under their noses. Despite Jake Preston's claim that he was only human, there had always been something frighteningly mystical about the stories told about Medicine Feather. Even if they did number two dozen, he seemed to have the ability to isolate and slay his prey at will. No one was eager to face him alone.

Jake Preston, who had taken and examined the cut bindings, now threw them aside. 'Well, he's gone now,' he said, his voice still strong, controlling the anger he felt, 'and we only have a few more minutes to prepare for the boat's arrival.' He pointed to the horses hitched to the oak tree that Wes was using for cover. 'Get those horses moved to the rear of the barn,' he ordered. 'We don't want the people on board to suspect that there is anyone here but the woodman and his family.'

The men showed a reluctance to obey, shuffling their feet, watching each other, looking for someone to provide a lead, either to go about the business of preparing the ambush, or rubbing off the warpaint, mounting up and riding for the northern river crossing.

'What are you worried about?' Jake Preston asked, 'He's just one man!'

'One man who has already killed four of ours.' The speaker glanced at Henry Watkin. 'Perhaps five,' he added. 'He's cutting us out like sick cattle for slaughter!'

'Then stick together in groups of three or four for the remainder of the time we're here. Besides, you've been paid,' Jake reminded them, snapping out his words angrily. When he spoke again he'd regained his more usual, persuasive tone. 'Nothing's changed,' he told them. 'Within the hour we'll be miles away, and by morning you'll be across the river looking for someplace to spend the money that's filling your pockets.'

The men couldn't argue with the fact that they'd accepted Jake's money, and there was no way they would surrender it now that it was snug in their pockets – so with a shrug of acceptance, first one man turned away to move the offending horses, then another followed him. That was the signal for the gathering to break up, and everyone found a task that needed attending to before the arrival of the river steamer.

Crouching at the base of the oak tree, Wes Gray heard every word, and the full implication of Jake Preston's plan was instantly apparent. His purpose was to start a war with the Sioux to gain unhindered access to the gold in the Black Hills. Those miners who had already set up a base in the hills had been lured there with false assurances of military protection. They were there as unwitting sacrifices, and their slaughter at the hands of the Sioux was not only expected, but desired – so far they had been saved only by the fact that the Sioux had been in their winter camps.

Even though the miners were the transgressors of the treaty, their deaths at the hands of the Sioux would surely bring about the reprisals required by Jake Preston and the men he represented. But just in case the government failed to respond with military action, they had planned a greater outrage, one that would certainly bring the army into the field against the tribes. The murder of a Washington delegation could not be allowed to pass unpunished, and if the Sioux were held responsible they would be faced with a war they could not win.

Wes knew that somehow he had to prevent the attack on the riverboat, but that wasn't going to be easy. As Jake Preston had told his men, Wes couldn't fight them all. In fact, tangling with the raiders again would not help at all. If he had any advantage it was that they were unaware that he knew their plan. Perhaps he could find a way to alert the people on the boat. If they were deterred from docking at the riverbank it would greatly weaken Jake Preston's plan. For the moment though, he had to get away from the farm – free of the tension of instant discovery he could then apply his mind to developing a scheme to thwart Jake Preston.

The two raiders sent to collect the tethered horses were approaching the tree. For men who, moments earlier, had been startled by the ghastly deaths of their comrades, they now showed little sign of watchfulness or concern for their own safety. They spoke in low voices, grumbling about their scant clothing, the feathers in their hair and the weapons they were expected to use on armed soldiers. Although Wes was less than five yards away, they failed to see him, his blue shirt and dark hair blending splendidly with the ground shadows. After a moment they walked away, still grumbling, unaware that only his need for secrecy had prevented them from becoming Medicine Feather's next victims.

When they were a dozen steps away, Wes began to squirm backwards, continuing until he found the pasture rails, which he followed back to the place in the woods where he'd parted from the Sawbrick family. He caught up with them just as they reached the place where his pony was tethered. It hadn't been an easy journey for Jem. He slumped against a tree, his chin touching his chest.

'You can build a fire,' Wes told Maud, 'they won't come looking for you.' He related what he'd heard at the camp. All three expressed anger when he spoke of the buildings being burned to represent a Sioux raid. Wes tried to lessen the impact by voicing his intention to warn the people on the riverboat. 'If I can get to the paddleboat before it docks it might be possible to upset their plans.' he said. 'That being so, there wouldn't be any purpose to setting your home ablaze.'

'How will you do it?' Jem asked.

Wes paced as he struggled to come up with an idea. Although getting the boat to stop in the river would probably scupper Jake Preston's immediate plan, it didn't automatically follow that he wouldn't be resourceful enough to form another. Even worse, in Wes Gray's opinion, was the thought that a set-back might persuade Jake Preston to abandon the scheme altogether and ride clear of this place. Wes didn't want that: Jake Preston's crimes were personal – an ambush, a raid on the home of his friends, and now a plot against the whole Sioux nation, the people of *Apo Hopa*, his wife. His crimes were too great to go unpunished.

'I need to get a message to the soldiers on the paddleboat,' he said, his words spoken quietly, almost like a thought escaping through his mouth, 'but there is so little time!' Delivering a warning meant intercepting the *Far West* before it reached the wood station, but to do that he first had to get across the White river flowing swiftly below. As its junction with the Missouri was less than a mile

133

upstream, there seemed to be little possibility of finding a suitable crossing place. The cause seemed hopeless.

Until Vera said, 'We have a boat.'

EIGHT

With the safety of his family in mind, Jem Sawbrick's carpentry skills had been put to practical use with the construction of a boat. The purpose of the sturdy, willow-framed craft had been to provide an independent means of transporting his family downriver: in the event of an emergency they could quit their farm and reach the nearest town or settlement without delay. It had never been used for that purpose. Indeed, because of its weight and awkward manoeuvrability for one person, it had rarely been in the water, and had never travelled beyond the bend that would take it out of sight of the farm. However, during the summer months when the Missouri was less ferocious, its river worthiness had been proven by fishing jaunts enjoyed by Jem and Vera, even though fish were as easy to catch from the bank as they were midstream.

The exact location of the *Far West* was unknown

to Wes, but the activity at the farm indicated an advanced state of readiness for the raiders' planned attack. He therefore had no time to lose if he wanted to intercept the boat on the river. It was possible that he was already too late, but he had to try – and he could think of no alternative for forewarning the people on board of the ambush. It was the need to avoid unnecessary delays that overcame Wes's reluctance to accept Vera's offer to show him where the boat was stored. He had no liking for taking her back to the farm, but her arguments proved persuasive. The boat, she told him, had not been uncovered from its winter storage and would not be easy to find without guidance – and in addition, getting it into the water without a lot of noise was a difficult task for one man. Jem's confirmation of his daughter's words settled the matter.

It was very nearly dusk when they made their way back towards the farm. Although it was too big for her, hanging to her knees like a fringed dress, Wes had insisted that Vera should continue to wear his jacket. Its necessity as effective camouflage was reduced by the gathering gloom, but he was anxious that she had all the protection that he, at least, could provide. From the woods, the farmhouse appeared deserted: only one lantern had been lit at the side of the house, but no one passed through the short range of its glow. Wes guessed that the raiders were posted at the riverside, in position to storm the paddleboat when it drew alongside the dock.

Vera led the way when they moved, skirting the rear of the buildings and entering the shrubbery that spread down to the bank downriver of the house. His scheme would have been ruined if the boat had been at the other side of the house, as passing the dock without discovery would have been impossible. As it was, they were able to crawl unseen to the small inlet where the boat had been stored. It was no more than forty yards from the timber planking of the jetty, and although there was little excitement in the tone of the men who were stationed there, their voices still carried along the river to Wes and Vera.

The boat was upside down and hidden under a few skins and a lot of foliage. Wes had to concede that without Vera to guide him, it would have been difficult to find. He was also surprised by its size, and acknowledged that, unlike the canoes that were his usual waterway vehicle, it was too heavy to take out of the water and lift on his shoulders to avoid steering through cataracts and stretches of whitewater. In the fashion of canoes and bull boats the sides consisted of skin-covered ribs, but the floor was solid wood, which accounted for the additional weight.

'Let's get it in the water,' he said softly to Vera.

Again the girl took the lead, showing him the routine she used with her father to get the boat afloat. Although she'd rolled up the sleeves of the buckskin jacket to her elbows, its length and weight were still proving to be an encumbrance. Disregarding her companion's look of disapproval, she took off the jacket and laid it aside on the river-bank. Together, with Wes lifting and Vera manoeuvring, they turned the boat into the right position for entry into the water: the execution was perfect until the last moment, when the boat hit the water with more force than they had intended. The resultant slap and splash brought a moment of concern and caused them to stop all movement, while Wes strained his senses for any sign that the noise had attracted the attention of those on the jetty. They waited, completely still, for almost a full minute, then, assured that their activities had not startled anyone into investigation, Wes collected a paddle and climbed into the boat.

Eager though he was to set off downriver, Wes still experienced a moment of misgiving. He wasn't keen to leave Vera on her own. He had no doubt that she could find her way back to the place where they'd left her parents, but he was troubled by the risk that she might be discovered by the raiders. It was an element of danger he couldn't resolve. Vera, however, disposed of that worry, but only by pre-senting him with another cause for concern: she picked up the other paddle and followed him on to the boat.

'What are you doing?' The rasp-like tone in his low voice told of his alarm.

'I'm coming with you,' she said. 'The boat is too big for just one person. Dad can't manage single-handed. We always do it together.'

'If we're seen, the men on the jetty will open fire. It's too dangerous for you to be here.'

'It's more dangerous for you to try to go down-river alone. We don't know how this boat will behave when it reaches the confluence with the White.' As she was talking she used the paddle to push the boat away from the inlet. Instantly, the flow of the river carried it into the main stream.

Although his disgruntlement was unabated, Wes stopped talking. His reason was two-fold: sounds carried along the river and he had no wish to advertise his presence to Jake Preston, and the pull of the river was strong and he needed to concentrate on steering the craft before they were swept into midstream and into the view of those on the bank. Vera had settled in the bows, and without any direction from Wes had plunged the paddle into the water, dragging on it to counteract the pull of the current which was trying to sweep them away from the river's edge. They needed to keep close to the bank where the darkness of evening was enhanced by the shadows cast by the riverside trees. For a brief moment he thought they'd been seen by the men on the fast receding jetty, as a single voice called what sounded like a lookout's alarm, but it wasn't repeated and no shots were sent in their direction.

Progress was rapid, and the bend of the river was reached in a few minutes – negotiating that took them out of sight of the jetty and away from the threat of the raiders' guns, enabling them to move away from the riverbank and its associated dangers. Twice they had come close to collisions with partially submerged trees, which might have ripped apart the craft's exposed side.

Night seemed to have descended on the river more quickly than on the land, and as Wes peered ahead there was little to see but blackness. Unless some accident had befallen it, the *Far West*, he figured, had to be close now. Something moved ahead, a dim light, a lantern in the wheelhouse or on a promenade deck – or perhaps it was only in Wes's imagination, because when he looked another time it had gone again. If it was the boat he ought to be able to hear the battering of the water with its great rear wheel – but soon another noise began to dominate all other sounds, and they were approaching the source of it with almost reckless speed. Vera looked over her shoulder, and for the first time Wes could see real apprehension in her eyes.

'It's the White River,' she yelled. 'This is where it

falls into the Missouri.'

Customarily when passing this point, Wes steered to the far bank where the effect of the falls caused less disturbance. On this occasion, the need to avoid detection had robbed him of that option, and had forced him into the right-hand bank until he was out of sight of the jetty. Now he had to move into the middle of the river and trust that the boat didn't flounder in the tumult. He shouted an instruction to Vera and they worked together to get the boat into less dangerous waters.

Keeping the boat on a straight course wasn't easy. Overcoming the strength of the Missouri's current was almost challenge enough for the paddlers, requiring a great effort on their part to steer the craft towards the centre of the river. At the same time, however, sudden swirls and eddies generated by the falling cross river surged around them, occasionally twisting the small boat until it was broadside on in the water, and sometimes tossing it, lifting the front end high out of the water before it crashed down again with jarring savagery. There were moments when the river seemed determined to destroy the boat and the voyagers, and it took every ounce of their combined strengths to get the craft beyond the maelstrom and gain control of it.

Vera, her face and hair damp from the river's spray, turned to look at Wes. The exertion had left her gulping for air but nonetheless exultant at their safe passage. Her smile was wide and not without a hint of pride in her effort to keep the boat afloat.

A quick nod of the head was Wes Gray's response. One obstacle had been overcome, but until they'd intercepted and boarded the *Far West* their mission was incomplete. Mentally, however, he did acknowledge that the girl had been right: if he'd tackled the river alone he would have come to grief. She'd met the river's challenge head on, not only with skilful use of the paddle, but by adjusting her position to counteract the boat's lurches. Vera was a slim girl, no heavier than a drink of water, Wes might have said, but judicious use of her slight weight had been enough to keep the boat from flipping over. Each time the front end had reared up she had leant forwards, then pressed down on the bow until it dropped back down to the water. Wes was impressed, not only by her courageous behaviour, but also the coolness with which she'd reacted to the predicament.

Now his thoughts were centred on the steamboat, his eyes searching again for the light he thought he'd seen earlier. Instead, it was a movement in the water that caught his eye. For a moment he thought he'd seen a dark shape, a log perhaps, carried downriver on the spring flood, but thorough though his examination of the surface was, he was unable to espy it again. The oncoming night, shadows on the water and river swells were all capable of confusing the eye, and a shout from Vera distracted him altogether.

'There it is,' she said, pointing ahead to where the shape of the paddleboat had begun to rise above the dark line of the background hills.

They were separated by a hundred yards, but the gap was closing quickly. The sound of the blades of the huge rear wheel striking the water carried to them, the noise increasing in volume as it drew nearer, bearing a message of danger for anyone unfortunate enough to be caught in their rotation. Wes had no wish for such a fate to befall him and Vera, but he was suddenly aware that they were in an awkward situation. They were low in the water, and although army lookouts had probably been posted on board, the chances of being seen by the *Far West* were remote. Wes knew it was imperative to attract the ship's attention, so getting to his feet, he drew his pistol and prepared to fire a couple of shots in the air.

But before he could pull the trigger the small boat was struck amidships with violent force, and not only did Wes lose his balance but also his pistol, which fell into the river. He followed immediately after, the sound of the splash he made mingling with Vera's shout of surprise – and the unexpected growl of a grizzly.

As Wes went under the water he could make out the figure of the bear above him, the action of its

143

legs convincing Wes that it was continuing its attack on the boat. His immediate thought was for Vera's safety, but he was still trying to arrest his descent, which was being increased by the pull of the current. Above him the boat was being rocked ferociously, and a moment later it overturned completely. Some feet away, Vera tumbled into the river, sinking quickly despite the frantic movement of her arms and legs. At that instant, Wes was unable to assist her, needing to establish his own position first. He was pulled forwards by the current, and he lifted his head out of the water to grab a breath of air.

The bear was still in combat with the boat, submitting it to bites and blows that were ripping it apart. A section of the hull broke away and was carried on the flow towards Wes, but too far wide of the place where he was trying to tread water for it to be useful to him. Now that the boat was shattered beyond repair, the bear had lost interest in it. The reason for its attack was a mystery to Wes – perhaps it had simply been angered by the interruption to its cross-river swim – but it had now resumed its journey to the bank with a demonstration of strength against the river's flow that Wes could only envy. For now, though, he had other matters to consider.

Hoping to find Vera, Wes dipped under the surface again, but visibility was so poor that unless they'd been able to touch hands it was unlikely he'd see her. He swam back to the surface where the remnants of the capsized boat were now downstream and being carried further and further away with every passing moment. Any hopes entertained by Wes that it might provide some assistance in the struggle against the mighty river were dashed. Beyond the wreckage he could see the *Far West* steaming towards him and closing rapidly. He had no idea how he could prevent it passing him in the water, but he knew that all the passengers and crew would die if he failed to get on board. The fear of losing both Vera and the *Far West* overwhelmed any concern for the fact that his own life was in danger, but in truth the struggle against the force of the water was eating away at his strength.

Then he saw Vera, her head just above the water, but her arms were pulling with strong strokes that were propelling her in his direction. He had no doubt that she'd seen him, and that she was trying to reach him, and he tried to swim against the current to get near to her. It was impossible for him to make progress in her direction, but at least he wasn't being swept downstream at the same rate as the girl. At the same time he realized that the steamboat was bearing down on them, and that they were in as much danger of being struck by it as they were of being bypassed.

The ship loomed large above him – the side spars

that were used for 'grasshopping' sandbars towered high at the front, and behind were the twin, smoke-spouting funnels. He could see the upper pilot's cabin lit by the lanterns he had seen earlier, and he could even make out the ship's name painted in green letters above its windows. But he couldn't see any people, even though the cargo deck was lower than he'd expected, perhaps no more than two feet above the water. The bitter-sweet knowledge that they could have drawn alongside in Jem's little boat and just stepped aboard highlighted how close to success they'd been.

Then suddenly the ship's bows were cleaving the water and washing him aside, and a wave swept over his head so that even if a shout could have been heard by someone on board, he wasn't able to deliver it. The momentum with which he was being carried downriver seemed more accentuated by the passing ship, but he could find no means of arrest-ing it. For a moment he was prepared to submit to his fate: either to be crushed under the rear paddle wheel, or to struggle in the river until his strength was completely exhausted and he sank to a watery grave. But at that most disheartening moment there appeared a chance, a hope of preservation.

A hawser, a stout rope which had come loose from the nearest tall spar, was trailing in the water, providing an unlikely and unexpected opportunity for survival. Wes grasped it, his hand only just able to close around its thickness, but he clung to it despite the dreadful wrench to his shoulder joint. The river was still intent upon taking him, and one-handed, it was difficult to resist its drag. His hand slipped along the rope's length for several inches, and only when he could get both hands around it did he have any sense of success. But that respite was short-lived, because no sooner had his left hand reached the rope than it was needed for another purpose: Vera, her pale face clear against the dark water, would have gone to her doom if he hadn't grabbed the shoulder of her shirt as she passed.

For several moments they were hauled through the water, Wes pulled by the trailing rope and Vera by him. The strain on Wes's arms was tremendous as the paddleboat pulled them one way while the powerful river tried to take them in the opposite direction. More than once, Wes's hand slipped along the wet rope, filling him with the fear that he would reach its end and they would perish in the river. In addition, his hold on Vera was tenuous: he was gripping only her clothing, and any attempt to draw her nearer to him promised disaster. He could feel it shifting in his hand, as though the river's counter flow might cause a division of the spoils, leaving him with nothing in his hand but her shirt.

The same concern filled Vera's mind, and she was as aware as Wes Gray that their lives were hanging by a thread. Despite reaching out a hand to hold on to the frontiersman's waist, she knew that the sleeve he was holding was in danger of separating from the rest of the shirt. She began kicking against the water, trying to swim against the current to get nearer to Wes to ease the strain on the stitching. Her feet touched the boat's smooth hull, and provided momentary purchase to lift her forward. That small success encouraged her to try again, pushing away with greater determination so that it lifted her to a point where her head was level with his chest. Gasping with the effort, water streamed out of her mouth.

Vera's change of position was not only a surprise for Wes, but also eased the strain on his left arm. 'Grab my neck,' he shouted. She obeyed, eventually encircling his neck with both arms so that he was able to release his grip on her shirt. If he could save her, lift her on to the deck of the *Far West*, she could warn those aboard of the planned ambush. Never before had he doubted the strength of his arms, yet now they were the source of such pain that he wasn't sure they were capable of another effort. His will, however, was still cast in iron, and his resolution to succeed undaunted. Crooking his left forearm into a seat under her haunches, Wes heaved Vera towards the side of the paddle steamer while yelling one word in her ear: 'Climb!'

Vera's struggle to reach the low deck was little more than a desperate, unplanned, inelegant lunge, only achieved by using Wes Gray's body as a stepping stone. Her bid for safety pushed him under the water. He could barely remember rising once more to the surface, and perhaps he only did so because his survival instinct compelled him to maintain his grip on the rope. Above the rush of the river he could hear voices, and even though his arms ached intolerably he was satisfied that Vera and those on board were safe. Then hands gripped his shoulders and he was raised from the river and deposited on the ship's deck.

Wes was surrounded by a dozen blue-uniformed legs as he coughed water on to the planks on which he lay. The voices he'd heard while in the water were becoming clearer as his mind cleared of the tumult of survival. Some were solicitous, caring of his health and safety, while the other questions were of a more military nature, wondering at his purpose for being in the water – as though a near-drowned girl and man posed some kind of threat to the stability of the government. Then he could hear Vera's voice, insisting that they were heading for an ambush.

'Get your senior officer,' Wes told the nearest soldier. 'There isn't a moment to lose. An armed gang is waiting to attack at the wood station.'

A sergeant among the rescuing soldiers was deferred to for a decision, which he seemed reluctant to make. He cast a glance to the upper deck where the few state rooms and salons were situated. His hesitation brought an angry shout from Wes.

'They mean to slaughter everyone!' Wes yelled. 'You've got to defend the ship immediately!'

'The gentlemen are dining,' he said.

'Disturb them!' Wes snapped as he struggled to his feet. '*Now!*'

'Wes? Wes Gray!'

Wes turned to face the man who had called his name, and was pleased to see Luther Kelly pushing through the group that had gathered around. When the plot was hastily explained to Lieutenant Faraday, the senior officer aboard, and Wes Gray's character vouched for by Luther Kelly, preparations to overcome the attackers were swiftly made.

The lack of a built-up side to the paddle steamer's lower deck had been an asset in rescuing Vera and Wes from the river, but now it was a boon to the ambushers, whose attack when the ship berthed would be unhindered. However, forewarned, the defenders had the upper hand. The lower deck was a storage area, not only of lumber to feed the furnace but also goods in transit along the river. Although stacks of lumber were currently few, the army had seized the opportunity to send supplies to the far fort on the boat contracted to transport the Washington commission into the north country. As a consequence, there were several crates and bundles that provided good cover for the waiting soldiers.

The fight began the moment the *Far West* abutted the landing stage. It was swift and a total victory for the army. In the mistaken belief that their attack would be a complete surprise to those on the paddle steamer, Jake Preston's men ran forwards emitting shrieks and whoops that were meant to be the war cries of Sioux warriors. Although one or two of their number were armed with rifles, the majority were only carrying those primitive weapons that had, over the centuries, proved inferior even in more capable hands. They were met with a fearsome first fusillade from the soldiers that left men dead on the staging or floating down the Missouri, never to be seen again. Within two minutes every attacker was dead, their half-naked bodies shattered by the overpowering military fire-power.

Wes had been given a rifle to enable him to take part in the battle. When it was clear that the ambush had failed he was the first one ashore, picking his way through the bodies in search of Jake Preston. He had looked for him during the fight, and had assumed he'd be easy to find as he was the only member of the gang who had not adopted a disguise – but without success. He ran up past the house towards the place where the horses had been tethered, leaving behind the final shots of a conflict that would culminate with a single arm wound for one side and total annihilation of the other.

Jake Preston was in the saddle when Wes ran into

the yard between the house and outbuildings. He was kicking his heels against the flanks of his horse, urging it to gallop with hands, feet and voice. Even so, he heard the challenge from Wes Gray, heard his name called in such a manner that it was clearly an order to stop. He didn't. His right hand slipped inside his jacket and produced a gun, which he fired once, twice, three times at Wes. The shots were wayward, accuracy restricted by the movement of his horse. By the time he'd triggered the third shot the gun was pointing backwards, the horse pounding a northbound route.

Wes had wanted answers, wanted to know who was responsible for the plot, but he could live without knowing, but he couldn't allow Jake Preston to escape. Jake Preston had tried to kill him, and for that he had to be punished. He raised the rifle to his shoulders and sent three bullets after the rider. All three hit their target, and Jake Preston fell dead from his horse.

The stub of a thick cigar burned between Senator Jeremiah Goodwin's lips as he examined the bodies that littered the landing strip against which the *Far West* was berthed. For company he had Lieutenant Faraday, Luther Kelly and Wes Gray. Wes was pointing out the obvious fact that all the dead men were Americans.

'These men are not Sioux warriors,' he said, 'but

their disguise and weapons were meant to put the blame on them for your death.'

'If the plot was to kill everyone, I wonder why they bothered with a disguise,' said Senator Goodwin.

Wes wasn't sure if the air of indifference in the Senator's tone was a demonstration of bravado, or a reflection that either he didn't believe the purpose of the plot, or he thought that the handful of soldiers on board the paddle steamer would have repelled it with or without an advance warning. 'All but one,' Wes said. 'You have a newspaperman in your group. He was meant to survive to provide a first-hand account.'

That item brought a twitch of concern to the Senator's lips. 'Mark Kellogg only joined us at the last minute,' he said. 'Not many people know he's on board. He's hoping we'll reach Fort Union before Custer leaves.'

'Custer?'

'Rumours of gold in the Black Hills are rife. Washington wants to know the truth, and Custer is leading an expedition to do an official survey.'

Wes was stunned by the news. An unannounced foray into Sioux territory by a military force of any size would unsettle the tribes, and the fact that Custer was leading them was capable of putting them on to an immediate war footing.

'The Sioux won't allow it. The Black Hills are in

the heart of their Reservation.'

'There's nothing they can do to stop it. Even the Great Sioux Reservation is part of the United States of America, over which the government has absolute control.'

'Not according to the terms of the Laramie Treaty,' argued Wes.

'It's gold, Mr Gray,' announced the Senator, and the glint in his eye told Wes that the man had more than a passing interest in finding it. 'This great country of ours needs access to its wealth in every form. If there is gold in the Black Hills, we must have it.'

'But if there is gold in the Black Hills then it belongs to the Sioux.'

Senator Goodwin dismissed Wes's argument with a wave of his hand. 'They'll be recompensed,' he asserted, as though the import of the matter was small and its consequences irrelevant, 'but the land is ours and the gold it holds is ours.'

'And is this what you intend to tell them at Five Squaws Meadow?'

'Of course not. My mission is to consolidate the Treaty. Tell them how pleased the Great Father is that the Sioux people are observing its terms, and listen to any grievances they might have.'

'They have a grievance that there are miners already in the Black Hills, and the government is doing nothing to remove them.'

'Well, as I've already said, gold is important.'

'Those men will be killed if they don't get off the Reservation.'

An angry look lit up the Senator's eyes. 'If the Sioux resort to violence they will feel the full force of the army's might.'

'You can't make a treaty and expect only one party to obey its terms!' The Senator turned away, showing a disinclination to continue the conversation. 'Do you know a man called Mark Owenfield?' asked Wes.

Senator Goodwin turned his head to look at Wes. 'I know him.'

'He is responsible for putting those men in danger, convincing them that they are safe from attack when it is just not so.' Wes wondered if Mark Owenfield was also the instigator of the attack on the Washington delegation, but he kept that thought to himself.

Senator Goodwin adopted a haughty tone when he replied: 'Mark Owenfield is a respectable lawyer who represents many influential people and companies in the east.'

'Companies who hope to profit from Black Hills gold?'

'Accusations like that could get you into serious trouble, Mr Gray.'

'I'm trying to help you,' retorted Wes. 'Just because today's attempt to kill you failed, it doesn't mean tomorrow's won't. Someone is determined to get that gold, and they are prepared to start a war that will see an end to the way of life of the tribespeople. And they don't care who else dies to achieve it.'

Senator Goodwin walked away without another word, followed by Lieutenant Faraday. Luther Kelly, who'd been listening to the exchange, sidled up to Wes. 'One thing you should know,' he said. 'Mark Owenfield isn't just a highly respected lawyer, he's also the Senator's son-in-law. It's the people you know who advance your career in Washington. So be careful, Wes. Back there he's powerful enough to do you harm without ever seeing you again.'

On the second day after leaving the wood station Wes returned to Black Buffalo's village to collect his packs. The chief and several of the warriors had gone north for the meeting at Five Squaws Meadow, so there was a quietness about the village that was reminiscent of the days when the warriors were away on the summer hunt – but now it was overlain with a forlorn atmosphere. Painted Elk had remained behind, and it was he who imparted the three items of bad news that afflicted the village. First, Tall Horse had died; his wounds had been too severe to survive the journey back to the village.

Then, Yellow Hawk's medicine ceremony had culminated in a sweat lodge vision which he revealed to the village. Its interpretation boded ill not only for the village, but for the whole of the Sioux nation. The dream had involved buffalo, Lakota and Bluecoats. In the beginning there had been many more buffalo than the Lakota people, against whom the Bluecoats were few. But the buffalo dwindled, their few surrounded by the hunters of the tribe who were likewise surrounded by as many Bluecoats. Eventually, the world was full of *wasicuns*, and it was impossible to see either buffalo or Sioux. The white men covered the world, the Lakota would walk the land no more.

The third item related by Painted Elk concerned the miners in the Black Hills. They were all dead at the hands of Tashunka Witco – Crazy Horse – and his Ogallalah warriors. Now the people of Black Buffalo's village awaited army reprisals. The onset of Yellow Hawk's vision was before them.

Wes kept to himself the news that Custer was on his way to the Black Hills. There was nothing he could do to prevent it, nothing he could do to avert the clash that surely lay ahead. He loaded his packs into a canoe and set off along the Cheyenne river.

Vera was on the bank watching Wes as he pulled the canoe ashore. The moment she'd seen him afar off she'd returned to the house and tied a strip of yellow ribbon in her hair. He didn't mention it when he greeted her, but it was clear he'd noticed it, and that pleased her. She knew it was a cavalry tradition, but she saw no reason why it shouldn't have the same meaning for civilians. She had a gift for him, too, a hat to replace the one he'd lost in the fight with George Watkin. It was white and had belonged to one of the raiders, and she'd affixed a band of her own hand-strung beads around the brim. Jem and Maud welcomed him, too. When he told them that he was stopping only long enough for a cup of coffee their disappointment was evidently not as great as their daughter's.

'You need to get away from here.' The words were addressed to Jem, but were meant for the whole family. 'In any circumstances, the Sioux will fight to protect their territory and their way of life. Sending Custer into the Black Hills is almost a declaration of war. Perhaps the negotiators will prevent all-out hostilities this summer, but it won't be forever. Already the miners that were in the Black Hills have been killed, and if others follow in Custer's wake, they'll suffer the same fate. Get your family out now, Jem.'

Jem tried to shrug off the suggestion that they were in danger, cited instances of friendship with several Sioux, men and women. 'Why would they attack us?'

'The Cheyenne along the Washita could cite friendships with white people before Custer's troops destroyed their village and slaughtered the women and children. If war develops, the scalp of a settler will bring as much honour to a brave as that of a soldier. If you become a target they'll attack without warning.'

Jem was uneasy. 'You'll frighten my family with that sort of talk,' he said.

'That's my intention. It's time to go, Jem.'

'I've got a home here, and if I desert it I might lose the wood concession for all time.'

'If boats are still using this part of the river they can gather their own timber.'

Jem wanted to argue, wanted to tell Wes that the Treaty had put an end to the days of Indian wars. His wife was watching him, knowing him, knowing it was a decision he couldn't make alone. Vera's eyes were fixed on Wes. He'd saved her life and risked his own to do so.

If he was urging them to leave, there had to be a good reason. If he offered to take her with him when he left, then she would go. But he didn't.

'If you take my advice,' he said, 'you'll pack up your things and get on board the *Far West* when she comes back downriver.'

There wasn't anything more he could do, so he pushed his canoe away from the shore and paddled towards the centre of the stream where the flow was strongest. It carried him quickly towards the bend that was just above the junction with the White. Before taking the bend he looked back. Vera continued to watch him, her black hair lifting in the breeze along the valley. He hoped that the next time he saw it, it wasn't a trophy on a Sioux war lance.

KT-389-734

WED FOR HIS
SECRET HEIR

WED FOR HIS SECRET HEIR

CHANTELLE SHAW

MILLS & BOON

First published in Great Britain 2018
by Mills & Boon, an imprint of HarperCollins*Publishers*
1 London Bridge Street, London, SE1 9GF

Large Print edition 2018

© 2018 Chantelle Shaw

ISBN: 978-0-263-07445-1

MIX
Paper from
responsible sources
FSC
www.fsc.org   FSC™ C007454

This book is produced from independently certified
FSC™ paper to ensure responsible forest management.
For more information visit www.harpercollins.co.uk/green.

Printed and bound in Great Britain
by CPI Group (UK) Ltd, Croydon, CR0 4YY

For my gorgeous grandson Casey James

CHAPTER ONE

THE PRE-DINNER DRINKS seemed to be lasting for ever. Giannis Gekas glanced at his watch as his stomach rumbled. He had been in meetings all day and the tired-looking sandwich his PA had brought him at lunchtime had lived up to its appearance.

He sipped his Virgin Mary cocktail and considered eating the celery stalk that garnished the drink. The voices of the other guests in the banqueting hall merged into a jangle of white noise, and he edged behind a pillar to avoid having to make small talk with people he did not know and had no interest in.

It was then that he spotted a woman rearranging the place name cards on one of the circular dining tables. He supposed she might be a member of the events management team responsible for organising the charity fundraising dinner and auction. But she was wearing an evening gown, which suggested that she was a guest, and she cast a furtive glance over her shoulder as she switched the name cards.

When Giannis had taken the private lift from his penthouse suite in the exclusive London hotel, down to the foyer, he had checked the seating plan in the banqueting hall to find out where he would be sitting for the dinner. He wondered why the woman had put herself next to him. It was not the first time such a thing had happened, he acknowledged with weary cynicism. The phenomenal success of his cruise line company had propelled him to the top of the list of Europe's richest businessmen.

He had been blessed with good looks and even before he had accrued his wealth women had pursued him, since he was a teenager taking tourists on sailing trips around the Greek islands on his family's boat. At eighteen, he had relished the attention of the countless nubile blondes who had flocked around him, but at thirty-five he was more selective.

The woman was blonde, admittedly, but she was not his type. He thought briefly of his last mistress Lise—a tall, toned Swedish swimwear model. He had dated her for a few months until she had started dropping hints about marriage. The dreaded 'm' word spelled the end of Giannis's interest, and he had ended the affair and arranged for Lise to be sent a diamond bracelet from an exclusive London jewellers, where he had an account.

Dinner would be served at seven-thirty and guests were beginning to take their places at the various tables. Giannis strolled over to where the woman was holding on tightly to the back of a chair as if she expected to be challenged for the seat. Her hair was the colour of honey and fell in silky waves to halfway down her back. As he drew closer to her, he noted that her eyes were the soft grey of rain clouds. She was attractive rather than beautiful, with defined cheekbones and a wide, pretty mouth that captured his attention. The full lips were frankly sensual, and as he watched her bite her lower lip he felt a frisson of desire to soothe the place with his tongue.

Surprised by his body's response, after he had decided that the woman did not warrant a second look, Giannis roamed his eyes over her. She was average height, with a slim waist and unfashionably curvaceous breasts and hips. Once again he felt a tightening in his groin as he allowed his gaze to linger on the creamy mounds displayed to perfection by the low-cut neckline of her black silk jersey dress.

She wore no jewellery—which was unusual at a high society event. Most of the other female guests were bedecked with gold and diamonds, and her lack of sparkling adornments focused his attention on the lustrous creaminess of her shoulders and décolleté.

He halted beside the table. 'Allow me,' he said smoothly as he drew out her chair and waited for her to sit down, before he lowered his tall frame onto the seat next to her. 'It appears that we will be companions for the evening...' he paused and glanced down at the table '... Miss Ava Sheridan.'

Wary grey eyes flew to his face. 'How do you know my name?'

'It is written on the card in front of you,' he said drily, wondering if she would explain why she had swapped the place cards.

A pink stain swept along her cheekbones but she quickly composed herself and gave him a hesitant smile. 'Oh, yes. Of course.' She caught her lower lip between her even white teeth and a flame flickered into life inside him. 'I'm pleased to meet you, Mr Gekas.'

'Giannis,' he said softly. He leaned back in his chair, turning his upper body so that he could focus his full attention on her, and smiled. With a sense of predictability, he watched her eyes darken, the pupils dilating. Charm came effortlessly to him. He had discovered when he was a youth that he had something: charisma, magnetism—whatever it was called, Giannis had it in bucketfuls. People were drawn to him. Men respected him and wanted his friendship—often only discovering after he had beaten them in a business deal that his laid-back air hid a ruthless determination to succeed. Women were fascinated by him and wanted him to take them to bed. Always.

Ava Sheridan was no different. Giannis offered her his hand and after an infinitesimal hesitation she placed her fingers in his. He lifted her hand to his mouth and she caught her breath when he brushed his lips across her knuckles.

Yes, she was attracted to him. What surprised

him more was the shaft of white-hot desire that swept through him and made him uncomfortably hard. Thankfully, the lower half of his body was hidden beneath the folds of the tablecloth. He was relieved when more guests took their seats at the table and while introductions were made and waiters arrived to pour the wine and serve the first course Giannis regained control of his libido. He even felt amused by his reaction to Ava Sheridan, who was simply not in the same league as the sophisticated models and socialites he usually dated. He hadn't had sex for over a month, since he'd broken up with Lise, and celibacy did not suit him, he acknowledged wryly.

He finished his conversation with the hedge fund manager sitting on the other side of him and turned his head towards Ava, hiding a smile when she quickly jerked her gaze away. He had been aware of the numerous glances she had darted at him while he had been chatting to the other guests around the table.

As he studied the curve of her cheek and the elegant line of her neck, he realised that he had been wrong to dismiss her as merely attractive. She was beautiful, but her beauty was understated and entirely natural. Giannis suspected that she used minimal make-up to enhance her English rose complexion, and her round-as-peaches breasts did not owe their firmness to implants or a cosmetic surgeon's skill. In a room full of primped and pampered women adorned in extravagant jewellery, Ava Sheridan was like a rare and precious pearl found in the deepest depths of the ocean.

She was also as stubbornly resistant as an oyster shell, he thought, frustrated by her refusal to turn her head in his direction even though she must be aware of his scrutiny.

'Can I pour you some more wine?' He took his cue when she placed her half-empty glass down on the table. Now she could not avoid looking at him and, as their eyes met, Giannis felt the sizzle, the intangible spark of sexual attraction shoot between them.

'Just a little, thank you.' Her voice was low and melodious and made him think of cool water. A tiny frown creased her brow as she watched him top up her glass before he replaced the wine bottle in the ice bucket. 'Don't you want any wine?'

'No.' He gave her another easy smile and did not explain that he never drank alcohol.

She darted him a glance from beneath the sweep of her lashes. 'I have heard that you regularly make generous donations to charities… Giannis. And you are especially supportive of organisations which help families affected by alcohol misuse. Is there a particular reason for your interest?'

Giannis tensed and a suspicion slid into his mind as he remembered how she had contrived to sit next to him at dinner. The media were fascinated with him, and it would not be the first time that a member of the press had managed to inveigle their way onto the guest list of a social function in order to meet him. Mostly they wanted the latest gossip about his love life, but a few years ago a reporter had dug up the story from his past that he did not want to be reminded of.

Not that he could ever forget the mistake he'd made when he was nineteen, which had resulted in his father's death. The memories of that night would haunt Giannis for ever, and guilt cast a long shadow over him.

His expression hardened. 'Are you a journalist, Miss Sheridan?'

Her eyebrows rose. Either she was an accomplished actress or her surprise was genuine. 'No. Why do you think I might be?'

'You changed the seating arrangement so that we could sit together. I watched you switch the place cards.'

Colour blazed on her cheeks and if Giannis had been a different man he might have felt some sympathy for her obvious embarrassment. But he was who he was, and he felt nothing.

'I…yes, I admit I did swap the name cards,' she muttered. 'But I still don't understand why you think I am a journalist.'

'I have had experience of reporters, especially those working for the gutter press, using underhand methods to try to gain an interview with me.'

'I promise you I'm not a journalist.'

'Then why did you ensure that we would sit together?'

She bit her lip again and Giannis was irritated with himself for staring at her mouth. 'I… I was hoping to have a chance to talk to you.'

Her pretty face was flushed rose-pink but her intelligent grey eyes were honest—Giannis did not know why he was so convinced of that. The faint desperation in her unguarded expression sparked his curiosity.

'So, talk,' he said curtly.

'Not here.' Ava tore her gaze from Giannis Gekas and took a deep breath, hoping to steady the frantic thud of her pulse. She had recognised him instantly when he had walked over to the dining table where Becky, bless her, had allocated her a place. But her seat had been on the other side of the table—too far away from Giannis to be able to have a private conversation with him.

She had taken a gamble that no one would notice her swapping the name cards around. But she *had* to talk to Giannis about her brother. She'd forked out a fortune for a ticket to the charity dinner and bought an expensive evening dress that she'd probably never have the chance to wear again. The only way she could keep Sam from being sent to a young offender institution was if she could persuade Giannis Gekas to drop the charges against him.

Ava took a sip of her wine. It was important that she kept a clear head and she hadn't intended to drink any alcohol tonight, but she had not expected Giannis to be so *devastatingly* attractive. The photos she'd seen of him on the Internet when she'd researched the man dubbed Greece's most eligible bachelor had not prepared her for the way her heart had crashed into her ribs when he'd smiled. Handsome did not come close to describing his lethal good looks. His face was a work of art—the sculpted cheekbones and chiselled jaw softened by a blatantly sensual mouth that frequently curved into a lazy smile.

Dark, almost black eyes gleamed beneath heavy brows, and he constantly shoved a hand through his thick, dark brown hair that fell forwards onto his brow. But even more enticing than his model-perfect features and tall, muscle-packed body was Giannis's rampant sexuality. He oozed charisma and he promised danger and excitement—the very things that Ava avoided. She gave herself a mental shake. It did not matter that Giannis was a bronzed Greek god. All she cared about was saving her idiot of a kid brother from prison and the very real possibility that Sam would be drawn into a life of crime like their father.

Sam wasn't bad; he had just gone off the rails because he lacked guidance. Ava knew that her mother had struggled to cope when Sam had hit puberty and he'd got in with a rough crowd of teenagers who hung around on the streets near the family home in East London. Even worse, Sam had become fascinated with their father and had even reverted to using the name McKay rather than their mother's maiden name, Sheridan. Ava had been glad to move away from the East End and all its associations with her father, but she felt guilty that she had not been around to keep her brother out of trouble.

She took another sip of wine and her eyes were drawn once more to the man sitting next to her. Sam's future rested in Giannis Gekas's hands. A waiter appeared and removed her goat's cheese salad starter that she had barely touched and replaced it with the Dover sole that she had chosen for the main course. Across the table, one of the other guests was trying to catch Giannis's attention. The chance to have a meaningful conversation with him during dinner seemed hopeless.

'I can't talk to you here.' She caught her bottom lip between her teeth and a quiver ran through her when his eyes focused on her mouth. She wondered why he suddenly seemed tense. 'Would it be possible for me to speak to you in private after dinner?'

His dark eyes trapped her gaze but his expression was unreadable. Afraid that he was about to refuse her request, she acted instinctively and placed her hand over his where it rested on the tablecloth. *'Please.'*

The warmth of his olive-gold skin beneath her fingertips sent heat racing up her arm. She attempted to snatch her hand away but Giannis captured her fingers in his.

'That depends on whether you are an entertaining dinner companion,' he murmured. He smiled at her confused expression and stroked his thumb lightly over the pulse in her wrist that was going crazy. 'Relax, *glykiá mou.* I think there is every possibility that we can have a private discussion later.'

'Thank you.' Relief flooded through her. But she could not relax as concern for her brother changed to a different kind of tension that had everything to do with the glitter in Giannis's eyes. She couldn't look away from his sensual mouth. His jaw was shadowed with black stubble and she wondered if it would feel abrasive against her cheek if he kissed her. If she kissed him back.

She took another sip of wine before she remembered that she hadn't had any lunch. Alcohol had a more potent effect on an empty stomach, she reminded herself. Her appetite had disappeared but she forced herself to eat a couple of forkfuls of Dover sole.

'So tell me, Ava—you have a beautiful name, by the way.' Giannis's husky accent felt like rough velvet stroking across Ava's skin, and the way he said her name in his lazy, sexy drawl, elongating the vowels—*Aaavaaa*—sent a quiver of reaction through her. 'You said that you are not a journalist, so what do you do for a living?'

Explaining about her work as a victim care officer might be awkward when Giannis was himself the victim of a crime which had been committed by her brother, Ava thought ruefully. Sam deeply regretted the extensive damage that he and his so-called 'friends' had caused to Giannis's luxurious yacht. She needed to convince Giannis that her brother had made a mistake and deserved another chance.

She reached for her wine glass, but then changed her mind. Her head felt swimmy—although that might be because she had inhaled the spicy, explicitly sensual scent of Giannis's aftershave.

'Actually I'm between jobs at the moment.' She was pleased that her voice was steady, unlike her see-sawing emotions. 'I recently moved from Scotland back to London to be closer to my mother…and brother.'

Giannis ate some of his beef Wellington before he spoke. 'I have travelled widely, but Scotland is one place that I have never visited. I've heard that it is very beautiful.'

Ava thought of the deprived areas of Glasgow where she had been involved with a victim support charity, first as a volunteer, and after graduating from university she had been offered a job with the victim support team. In the past few years some of the city's grim, grey tower blocks had been knocked down and replaced with new houses, but high levels of unemployment still remained, as did the incidence of drug-taking, violence and crime.

She had felt that her job as a VCO—helping people who were victims or witnesses of crime—made amends in some small way for the terrible crimes her father had committed. But living far away in Scotland meant she had missed the signs that her brother had been drawn into the gang culture in East London. Her father's old haunts.

'Why do you care what I get up to?' Sam had demanded when she had tried to talk to him about his behaviour. 'You moved away and you don't care about me.' Ava felt a familiar stab of guilt that she hadn't been around for Sam or her mother when they had both needed her.

She dragged her thoughts back to the present and realised that Giannis was waiting for her to reply. 'The Highlands have some spectacular scenery,' she told him. 'If you are thinking of making a trip to Scotland I can recommend a few places for you to visit.'

'It would be better if you came with me and gave me a guided tour of the places you think would interest me.'

Ava's heart gave a jolt. *Was he being serious?*

She stared into his dark-as-night eyes and saw amusement and something else that evoked a coiling sensation low in her belly. 'We...we don't know each other.'

'Not yet, but the night is still young and full of endless possibilities,' he murmured in his husky Mediterranean accent that made her toes curl. He gave a faint shrug of his shoulders, drawing her attention to his powerful physique beneath the elegant lines of his dinner jacket. 'I have little leisure time and it makes sense when I visit somewhere new to take a companion who has local knowledge.'

Ava was saved from having to reply when one of the event organisers arrived at the table to hand out catalogues which listed the items that were being offered in the fundraising auction.

Giannis flicked through the pages of the catalogue. 'Is there anything in the listings that you intend to bid for?'

'Unfortunately I can't afford the kind of money that a platinum watch or a luxury African safari holiday are likely to fetch in the auction,' she said drily. 'I imagine that art collectors will be keen to bid for the Mark Derring painting. His work is stunning, and art tends to be a good investment. There are also some interesting wines being auctioned. The Chateau Latour 1962 is bound to create a lot of interest.'

Giannis gave her a thoughtful look. 'So, I have already discovered that you are an expert in art and wine. I confess that I am intrigued by you, Ava.'

She gave a self-conscious laugh. 'I'm not an expert in either subject, but I went to a finishing school in Switzerland where I learned how to talk confidently about art, recognise fine wines and understand the finer points of international etiquette.'

'I did not realise that girls—I presume only girls—still went to finishing schools,' Giannis said. 'What made you decide to go to one?'

'My father thought it would be a good experience for me.' Ava felt a familiar tension in her shoulders as she thought of her father. The truth was that she tried not to think about Terry McKay. That part of her life when she had been Ava McKay was over. She had lost touch with the friends she had made at the Institut Maison Cécile in St Moritz when her father had been sent to prison. But the few months that she had spent at the exclusive finishing school, which had numbered two European princesses among its students, had given her the social skills and exquisite manners which allowed her to feel comfortable at high society events.

It was a pity that the finishing school had not given advice on how to behave when a gorgeous Greek god looked at her as if he was imagining her naked, Ava thought as her eyes locked with Giannis's smouldering gaze. Panic and an inexplicable sense of excitement pumped through her veins. She was here at the charity dinner for her brother's sake, she reminded herself. Giannis had said he would give her an opportunity to speak to him in private on the condition that she entertained him during dinner. She did not know if he had been serious, but she could not risk losing the chance to plead with him to show leniency to Sam.

'It's not fair,' she murmured. She had to lean towards Giannis so that he could hear her above the hum of chatter in the banqueting hall, and the scent of him—spicy cologne mixed with an elusive scent of male pheromones—made her head spin. 'I have told you things about me but you haven't told me anything about yourself.'

'That's not true. I've told you that I have never visited Scotland. Although I have a feeling that I will take a trip there very soon,' he drawled. His voice was indulgent like rich cream and the gleam in his eyes was wickedly suggestive.

A sensuous shiver ran down Ava's spine. Common sense dictated that she should respond to Giannis's outrageous flirting with cool amusement and make a witty remark to put him in his place and let him know she wasn't interested in him. Except that he fascinated her, and she felt like a teenager on a first date rather than an experienced woman of twenty-seven.

She wasn't all that experienced, a little voice in her head reminded her. At university she'd dated a few guys but the relationships had fizzled out fairly quickly. It had been her fault—she'd been wary of allowing anyone too close in case they discovered that she was leading a double life. Two years ago, she had met Craig at a party given by a work colleague. She had been attracted to his open and friendly nature and when they had become lovers she'd believed that they might have a future together. A year into their relationship, she had plucked up the courage and revealed her real identity. But Craig had reacted with horror to the news that she was the daughter of the infamous London gangland boss Terry McKay.

'How could we have a family when there is a risk that our children might inherit your father's criminal genes?' Craig had said, with no trace of warmth in his voice and a look of distaste on his face that had filled Ava with shame.

'Criminality isn't an inherited condition,' she had argued. But she continued to be haunted by Craig's words. Perhaps there *was* a 'criminal gene' that could be passed down through generations and she would not be able to save Sam from a life of crime.

Ava forced her mind away from the past. She refused to believe that her kind, funny younger brother could become a violent criminal like their father. But the statistics of youths reoffending after being sent to prison were high. She needed to keep her nerve and seize the right moment to throw herself on Giannis's mercy.

In normal circumstances Ava would have found the bidding process at the charity auction fascinating. The sums of money that some of the items fetched were staggering—and far beyond anything her finances could stretch to. Giannis offered the highest bid of a six-figure sum for a luxury spa break at an exclusive resort in the Maldives for two people. Ava wondered who he planned to take with him. No doubt he had several mistresses to choose from. But if he wanted more variety, she was sure that any one of the women in the banqueting hall who she had noticed sending him covetous glances would jump at the chance to spend four days—and nights—with a gorgeous, wealthy Greek god. Giannis was reputed to have become a billionaire from his successful luxury cruise line company, The Gekas Experience.

'Congratulations on your winning bid for the spa break. I don't blame you for deciding that a visit to the Maldives would be more enjoyable than a trip to Scotland,' she said, unable to prevent the faint waspishness in her voice as she pictured him cavorting in a tropical paradise with a supermodel.

'I bought the spa break for my mother and sister. My mother has often said that she would like to visit the Maldives, and at least my sister will be pleased.' There was an odd nuance in Giannis's tone. 'Perhaps the trip will make my mother happy, but I doubt it,' he said heavily.

Ava looked at him curiously, wanting to know more about his family. He had seemed tense when he spoke about his mother, but she was heartened to know that he had a sister and perhaps he would understand why she was so anxious to save her brother from a prison sentence.

The auction continued, but she was barely aware of what was going on around her and her senses were finely attuned to the man seated beside her. While she sipped her coffee and pretended to study the auction catalogue she tried not to stare at Giannis's strong, tanned hands as he picked up his coffee cup. But her traitorous imagination visualised his hands sliding over her naked body, cupping her breasts in his palms as he bent his head to take each of her nipples into his mouth.

Sweet heaven! What had got into her? Hot-faced, she tensed when he moved his leg beneath the table and she felt his thigh brush against hers. He turned his head towards her, amusement gleaming in his eyes when he saw the hectic flush on her cheeks.

'It is rather warm in here, isn't it?' he murmured.

She was on fire and desperate to escape to the restroom so that she could hold her wrists under the cold tap to try to bring her temperature down. Perhaps spending a few minutes away from Giannis would allow her to regain her composure. 'Please excuse me,' she muttered as she shoved her chair back and stood up abruptly.

'Ow!' For a few seconds she could not understand why scalding liquid was soaking into the front of her dress. The reason became clear when she saw a waiter hovering close by. He was holding a cafetière, and she guessed that he had leaned over her shoulder in order to refill her coffee cup at the same time that she had jumped up and knocked into him.

'I am so sorry, madam.'

'It's all right—it was my fault,' Ava choked, wanting to die of embarrassment. She hated being the centre of attention but everyone at the table, everyone in the banqueting room, it seemed, was looking at her. The head waiter hurried over and added his profuse apologies to those of the waiter who had spilled the coffee.

Giannis had risen from his seat. 'Were you burned by the hot coffee?' His deep voice was calm in the midst of the chaos.

'I think I'm all right. My dress took the brunt of it.' The coffee was cooling as it soaked through the material, but her dress was drenched and her attempts to blot the liquid with her napkin were ineffective. At least it was a black dress and the coffee stain might wash out, Ava thought. But she couldn't spend the rest of the evening in her wet dress and she would have to go home without having had an opportunity to speak to Giannis about her brother.

The hotel manager had been called and he arrived at the table to add his apologies and reprimand the hapless waiter. 'Really, it's my fault,' Ava tried to explain. She just wanted to get out of the banqueting hall, away from the curious stares of the other diners.

'Come with me.' Giannis slipped his hand under her elbow, and she was relieved when he escorted her out of the room. She knew she would have to call for a taxi to take her home, but while she was searching in her bag for her phone she barely noticed that they had stepped into a lift until the doors slid smoothly shut.

'We will go to my hotel suite so that you can use the bathroom to freshen up, and meanwhile I'll arrange for your dress to be laundered,' Giannis answered her unspoken question.

Ava was about to say that there was no need for him to go to all that trouble. But it occurred to her that while she waited for her dress to be cleaned she would have the perfect opportunity to ask him to drop the charges against her brother. Was it sensible to go to a hotel room with a man she had never met before? questioned her common sense. This might be her only chance to save Sam, she reminded herself.

The doors opened and she discovered that the lift had brought them directly to Giannis's suite. Ignoring the lurch of her heart, she followed him across the vast sitting room. 'The bathroom is through there,' he said, pointing towards a door. 'There is a spare robe that you can use and I'll call room service and have someone collect your dress. Would you like some more wine, or coffee?'

'I think I've had enough coffee for one night.' She gave him a rueful smile and her stomach muscles tightened when his eyes focused intently on her mouth.

She had definitely had enough wine, Ava thought as she shot into the opulent marble-tiled bathroom and locked the door, before releasing her breath on a shaky sigh. It must be her out-of-control imagination that made her think she had seen a predatory hunger in Giannis's gaze. She wondered if he looked at every woman that way, and made them feel as though they were the most beautiful, the most desirable woman he had ever met. Probably. Giannis had a reputation as a playboy and he possessed an effortless charm that was irresistible.

But not to her. She was immune to Giannis's magnetism, she assured herself. As she stripped off her coffee-soaked dress and reached for the folded towelling robe on a shelf, she caught sight of her reflection in the mirror above the vanity unit. Her face was flushed and her eyes looked huge beneath her fringe. Usually she wore her hair up in a chignon but tonight she had left it loose and it reached halfway down her back. The layers that the hairdresser had cut into it made her hair look thick and lustrous, gleaming like spun gold beneath the bright bathroom light.

Ava stared at herself in the mirror, startled by her transformation from ordinary and unexciting to a sensual Siren. She had bought a seamless black bra to wear beneath her dress and her nipples were visible through the semi-transparent cups. The matching black thong that she had worn for practical reasons—so that she would not have a visible panty-line—was the most daring piece of lingerie she had ever owned.

She ran her hands over her smooth thighs above the lacy bands of her hold-up stockings and felt a delicious ache low in her pelvis. She felt sexy and seductive for the first time since Craig had dumped her as she pictured Giannis's reaction if he saw her in her revealing underwear.

She shook her head. It must be the effects of the wine that had lowered her inhibitions and filled her mind with erotic images. Cursing her wayward thoughts, she slipped her arms into the robe and tied the belt firmly around her waist. Of course he was not going to see her underwear. She had come to his hotel suite for one purpose only—to ask him to give her brother another chance. Taking a deep breath, Ava opened the bathroom door and prepared to throw herself on Giannis Gekas's mercy.

CHAPTER TWO

HE WAS SPRAWLED on a sofa, his long legs stretched out in front of him and his arms lying along the back of the cushions. He had removed his jacket and tie and unfastened the top few shirt buttons, to reveal a vee of olive-gold skin and a sprinkling of black chest hairs. Giannis looked indolent and yet Ava sensed that beneath his civilised veneer he was a buccaneer who lived life by his rules and ruthlessly took what he wanted. Plenty of women would want to try to tame him but she was sure that none would succeed. Giannis Gekas answered to no one, and her nerve almost deserted her.

He stood up as she entered the sitting room and walked over to take her dress from her. 'I rinsed out most of the coffee and wrung out as much water as I could,' she explained as she handed him the soggy bundle of material.

'I have been assured that your dress will be

laundered and returned to you as quickly as possible,' he told her as he strode across the room and opened the door of the suite to give the dress to a member of the hotel's staff who was waiting in the corridor.

Giannis closed the door and came back to Ava. 'I ordered you some English tea and some petits fours,' he said, indicating the silver tea service on the low table in front of the sofa. 'Please, sit down.'

'Thank you.' She tore her eyes from him, her attention caught by a large canvas leaning against the wall. 'That's the Mark Derring painting from the auction.'

'I followed your advice and bid for it. You were sitting next to me,' he reminded her in a sardonic voice that made her think he was remembering how she had swapped the place name cards. 'Didn't you realise that I had offered the highest bid for the painting?'

Heat spread across her face. She could hardly admit that she had been so busy trying to hide her fierce awareness of him that she hadn't taken much notice of the auction. Giannis gave one of his lazy smiles, as if he knew how fast her heart was beating, and Ava forgot to breathe as she was trapped by the gleam in his eyes. She did not remember when he had moved closer to her, but she was conscious of how much taller than her he was when she had to tilt her head to look at his face.

He was utterly gorgeous, but it was not just his impossibly handsome features that made her feel weak and oddly vulnerable. Self-assurance shimmered from him and, combined with his simmering sensuality, it was a potent mix that made her head spin.

'Congratulations on winning the painting in the auction,' she murmured, desperate to say something and shatter the spell that his fathomless dark eyes and his far too sexy smile had cast on her. She was stupidly flattered that he had taken her advice about the artwork. Her self-confidence had been knocked by Craig's attitude when she'd admitted that she was the daughter of one of the UK's most notorious criminals. Thinking of her father reminded her of her brother, and she sank down onto the sofa while she mentally prepared what she was going to say to Giannis. It did not help her thought process when he sat down next to her.

'Help yourself to a petit four,' he said, offering her the plate of irresistible sweet delicacies.

'I shouldn't,' Ava murmured ruefully as she reached for a chocolate truffle. She bit into it and gave a blissful sigh when it melted, creamy and delicious, on her tongue. 'Chocolate is my weakness, unfortunately.'

He shrugged. 'Are you one of those women who starve themselves because the fashion industry dictates that the feminine figure should be stick-thin?'

'I think it's patently obvious that I don't starve myself,' she said drily. The belt of the towelling robe had worked loose and she flushed when she glanced down and saw that the front was gaping open, revealing the upper slopes of her breasts above her bra. She quickly pulled the lapels of the robe together.

'I am glad to hear it. Women should have curves.' Giannis looked deeply into her eyes and the heat in his gaze caused her heart to skip a beat. 'Before the regrettable incident with the coffee you looked stunning in your dress, and you have an exquisite figure, Ava,' he said softly. 'I am flattered that you wanted to sit next to me at dinner.'

Clearly, Giannis believed she had swapped the name cards because she was interested in him, but her motive had been completely different. Ava swallowed. 'I need to…' She did not finish her sentence and her breath caught in her throat when he lifted his hand and lightly brushed his thumb pad across the corner of her mouth.

'You had chocolate on your lips,' he murmured, showing her the smear of chocolate on his thumb that he had removed from her mouth. Her eyes widened when he put his thumb into his own mouth.

How could such an innocuous gesture seem so erotic? She was mesmerised as she watched his tongue flick out to lick his thumb clean. Unconsciously her own tongue darted out to moisten her lips and the feral growl that Giannis gave caused her stomach muscles to clench.

Remember why you are here, Ava ordered herself. But it was impossible to think about her brother when Giannis shifted along the sofa so that he was much too close. Her heart was thumping so hard in her chest that she was surprised it wasn't audible. It felt unreal to be in a luxurious hotel room with a devastatingly gorgeous man who was looking at her as if she was his ultimate fantasy. Somewhere in a distant recess of her brain she knew she should deliver her rehearsed speech, but her sense of unreality deepened when Giannis lifted his hand and stroked her cheek before he captured her chin between his fingers.

'What are you doing?' she gasped. It was imperative that she should seize her chance to talk to him about Sam.

'I would like to kiss you, beautiful Ava.' His voice was soft like velvet caressing her senses. 'And I think that perhaps you would like me to kiss you? Am I right? Do you want me to do this…?' He brushed his mouth over hers, tantalising her with a promise of sweeter delight to follow.

On one level Ava was appalled that she was allowing a stranger to kiss her, but she did not pull away when Giannis slid his hand beneath her hair to cup her nape and drew her towards him.

Sexual chemistry had fizzed between them

from the moment they had set eyes on one another, she acknowledged. Neither of them had eaten much at dinner because they had been sending each other loaded glances. She could not fight her body's instinctive response to Giannis and with a helpless sigh she parted her lips. A tremor ran through her when he kissed her again and reality disappeared.

It was as though she had been flung to the far reaches of the universe where nothing existed but Giannis's lips moving over hers, tasting her, enticing her. His warm breath filled her mouth and she felt the intoxicating heat of his body through his white shirt when she placed her hands flat on his chest.

In a minute she would end this madness and push him away, she assured herself. She had been curious to know what it would be like to be kissed by an expert. And Giannis was certainly an expert. Ava did not have much experience of men but she recognised his mastery in the bone-shaking sensuality of his caresses.

He lifted his mouth from hers and trailed his lips over her cheek and up to her ear, exploring its delicate shape with his tongue before he gently nipped her earlobe with his teeth. A quiver ran through her and she arched her neck as he kissed his way down her throat and nuzzled the dip where her collarbone joined. Her skin felt scorched by the heat of his mouth. She wanted more—she wanted to feel his lips everywhere, tasting her and tantalising her with sensual promise.

At last he lifted his head. He was breathing hard. Ava stared at him with wide, unfocused eyes. She had never felt so aroused before, except in her dreams. Perhaps this was a dream, and if so she did not want to wake up.

'Your skin is marked where that idiot waiter spilled boiling-hot coffee down you,' Giannis murmured. She followed his gaze and saw that the front of her robe had fallen open again. There was a patch of pink skin on the upper slope of one breast.

'It's nothing.' She tried to close the robe but he brushed her hand away and deftly untied the belt before he stood up and drew her to her feet. It was as if she were trapped in a strange dreamlike state where she could not speak, and she did not protest when he pushed the robe off her shoulders and it fell to the floor.

Giannis rocked back on his heels and subjected her to a slow, intense scrutiny, starting with her stiletto-heeled shoes and moving up her stockings-clad legs and the expanse of creamy skin above her lacy stocking tops. Ava could not move, could hardly breathe as his gaze lingered on her black silk thong before he finally raised his eyes to her breasts with their pointed nipples jutting provocatively beneath the semi-transparent bra cups.

'Eísai ómorfi,' he said hoarsely.

Even if she hadn't understood the Greek words—which translated to English meant *you are beautiful*—there was no mistaking the heat in his gaze, the hunger that made his eyes glitter like polished jet. Ava knew she wasn't really beautiful. Passably attractive was a more realistic description. But Giannis had sounded as if he genuinely thought she was beautiful. The desire blazing in his eyes restored some of her pride that had been decimated by Craig's rejection.

Soon she would end this madness, she assured herself again. But for a few moments she wanted to relish the sense of feminine power that swept through her when Giannis reached for her and she saw that his hand was shaking. Europe's most sought-after playboy was *shaking* with desire for her. It was a heady feeling. A wildness came over her, a longing to just once throw off the restraints she had imposed on herself since she was seventeen and had discovered the truth about Terry McKay.

When she was younger she had never told anyone that her father was a criminal, but the strain of keeping her shameful secret had meant that she was always on her guard. Even with Craig, she had never been able to completely relax and enjoy sex. She'd assumed she had a low sex drive, but now the fire in her blood and the thunderous drumbeat of desire in her veins revealed a passionate, sensual woman who ached for fulfilment.

Giannis pulled her into his arms and crushed her against his broad chest, making her aware of how strong he was, how muscular and *male* compared to her soft female body. But she was strong too, she realised, feeling him shudder when she arched into him so that the hard points of her nipples pressed against his chest. He claimed her mouth, his lips urgent, demanding her response, and with a low moan she melted into his heat and fire. She kissed him back with a fervency that drew a harsh groan from his throat when at last he lifted his head and stared into her eyes.

'I want you,' he said in a rough voice that made her tremble deep inside. 'You drive me insane, lovely Ava. I want to see you naked in my bed. I want to touch your body and discover all your secrets, and then I want to...' He lowered his head and whispered in her ear in explicit detail all that he wanted to do to her.

Ava's stomach dipped. Somewhere back in the real world the voice of her common sense urged her to stop, *now*, before she did something she might regret later. But another voice insisted that if she let this moment, this man slip away she would regret it for ever. She did not understand what had happened to sensible Ava Sheridan, but shockingly she did not care. Only one thing was in her mind, in her blood. *Desire, desire—* it pulsed through her veins and made her forget everything but the exquisite sensations Giannis was creating when he cupped one of her breasts in his hand and stroked her nipple through the gossamer-fine bra cup.

She gave a low moan as he slipped his hand inside her bra and played with her nipple, rolling the hard peak between his fingers, causing exquisite sensation to shoot down to that other pleasure point between her legs. '*Oh.*' She would die if he did not touch her *there* where she ached to feel his hands.

His soft laughter made her blush scarlet when she realised that she had spoken the words out loud. 'Come with me.' Giannis caught hold of her hand and something—disappointment? Frustration?—tautened his features when she hesitated. 'What is it?'

She wanted to tell him that she did not have one-night stands and she had never, ever had sex with a stranger. She wasn't impetuous or daring. She was old before her time, Ava thought bleakly. Just for once she wanted to be the sexually confident woman that Giannis clearly believed she was.

He smiled, his eyes lit with a sensual warmth that made her insides melt. 'What's wrong?' he said softly, lifting his hand to brush her hair back from her face. The oddly tender gesture dispelled her doubts and the hunger in his gaze caused a sensuous heat to pool between her thighs.

'Nothing is wrong,' she assured him in a breathy voice she did not recognise as her own. She slid her hands over his shirt and undid the rest of the buttons before she pushed the material aside and skimmed her palms over his bare chest. His skin felt like silk overlaid with wiry black hairs that arrowed down to the waistband of his trousers. She heard him draw a quick breath when she stroked her fingertips along his zip.

'You're sure?'

She didn't want to step out of the fantasy and question what she was doing. The new, bold Ava tilted her head to one side and sent him a lingering look from beneath the sweep of her lashes. 'What are you waiting for?' she murmured.

He laughed—a low, husky sound that caused the tiny hairs on her skin to stand on end. Every cell of her body was acutely aware of him and the promise in his glittering dark eyes sent a shiver of excitement through her.

Without saying another word, he led her by the hand into the bedroom. Ava was vaguely aware of the sophisticated décor and the lamps dimmed so that they emitted a soft golden glow. In the centre of the room was an enormous bed. Someone—presumably the chambermaid—had earlier turned back the bedspread and Ava's heart skipped a beat when she saw black silk sheets.

The four-poster bed had been designed for seduction, for passion, and it occurred to her that Giannis would surely not have intended to spend the night alone. Perhaps he regularly picked up women for sex. The slightly unsettling thought quickly faded from her mind and anticipation prickled across her skin when he shrugged off his shirt and deftly removed his shoes and socks before he unzipped his trousers and stepped out of them.

He was magnificent—lean-hipped and with a powerfully muscular chest and impressive six-pack. In the lamplight his skin gleamed like polished bronze, his chest and thighs overlaid with black hairs. Her gaze dropped lower to his tight black boxer shorts which could not conceal his arousal, and the growl he gave as she stared at him evoked a primitive need to feel him inside her.

'Take off your bra,' he ordered.

Her stomach flipped. She would have preferred him to undress her, and on some level her brain recognised that he was giving her the opportunity to change her mind. He wasn't going to force her to do anything she did not want to do. She roamed her eyes over his gorgeous body and desire rolled through her. Slowly she reached behind her back and unclipped her bra, letting the cups fall away from her breasts.

Giannis swallowed audibly. 'Beautiful.' His voice was oddly harsh, as if he was struggling to keep himself under control. He shook his head when she put her hands on the lacy tops of her hold-up stockings and prepared to roll them down her legs. 'Leave them on,' he growled. 'And your shoes.' He closed the gap between them in one stride and pulled her into his arms so that her bare breasts pressed against his naked chest. Ava felt a shudder run through him. *'Se thélo,'* he muttered.

She knew the Greek words meant *I want you* and she was left in no doubt when he circled his hips against hers and she felt the solid ridge of his arousal straining beneath his boxers. Driven beyond reason by a hunger she had never felt before, had never believed she was capable of feeling, she slipped her hand into the waistband of his boxers and curled her hand around him.

'Witch.' He pulled off his boxer shorts and kicked them away. Ava felt a momentary doubt when she saw how hugely aroused he was. But then he scooped her up and laid her down on the bed, and the feel of his hard, male, totally naked body pressing down on her blew away the last of her inhibitions. She trapped his face between her hands and tugged his mouth down to hers, arching against him when he claimed her lips in a devastating kiss.

It was wild and hot, passion swiftly spiralling out of control and shooting her beyond the stratosphere to a place she had never been before, where there was only the sensation of his warm skin pressed against hers and his seeking hands exploring her body and finding her pleasure spots with unerring precision.

'*Oh.*' She gave a thin cry when Giannis bent his head to her breast and flicked his tongue back and forth across its distended peak.

'Do you like that?' His voice was indulgent as if he knew how much she liked what he was doing to her, but Ava was too spellbound by him to worry about his arrogance. She sighed with pleasure when he drew her nipple into his mouth and sucked hard so that she almost climaxed right then. He transferred his attention to her other breast and she dug her fingers into his buttocks, feeling the awesome length of his erection pushing between her legs. There was no thought in her head to deny him, when to do so would deny her the orgasm that she could already sense building deep in her pelvis.

Somehow he untangled their limbs and shifted across the mattress. Frantically she grabbed hold of him and he laughed softly. Ignoring her hands tugging at him, he reached for his wallet on the bedside table and took out a condom. 'You *are* eager, aren't you?' he murmured. 'Here—' he put the condom into her hand '—you put it on for me.'

Ava fumbled with the foil packet, not wanting to admit that she had never opened a condom before. Craig had always prepared himself for sex, and when they had made love it had been over quickly, leaving her dissatisfied and convinced that the problem lay with her.

Finally she managed to tear the foil with her fingernail and then unrolled the condom down his length.

'*Theos*, you're going to kill me.' His chest heaved when she finally completed her task. He pushed aside her flimsy black silk thong and stroked his fingers over her silken flesh, parting her so that he could slide one finger inside her.

It felt amazing but it wasn't enough—not nearly enough. Ava could hear her panting breaths as she lifted her hips towards his hand, needing more, needing him... 'Please...'

'I know,' he growled. She heard a ripping sound as he tore her thong, and then he simply took her with a hard, deep thrust that expelled the breath from her lungs in a shocked gasp.

He stilled and stared down at her, his shoulder muscles bunching as he supported himself on his hands. The lamplight cast shadows over his face, emphasising the angles and planes of his chiselled features. A beautiful stranger who had claimed her body. 'Did I hurt you?' The concern in his voice touched her heart.

'No...' She clutched his shoulders as she felt him start to withdraw. The shock of his penetration was receding and her internal muscles stretched so that she could take him deeper inside her, filling her, fulfilling her most secret fantasies when he began to move.

He must have sensed that he needed to slow the pace and at first he was almost gentle as he circled his hips against hers and kissed her breasts and throat, making his way up to her mouth to push his tongue between her lips while he drove deep inside her.

She arched her hips to meet each stroke, unaware of the frantic cries she made as he established a powerful rhythm. He thrust deeper, harder, taking her higher until she clawed her nails down his back, desperate to reach a place that she had never managed to reach before, except when she pleasured herself.

He laughed softly. 'Relax, and it'll happen.'

'It won't. I can't...' Ava gave a sob of frustration. There must be something wrong with her that made it impossible for her to reach an orgasm during sex.

She felt Giannis slip his hand between their joined bodies and then he did something magical with his fingers, while he continued his rhythmic thrusts, faster, faster...

It felt so good. The way he expertly moved his hand, as if he knew exactly how to give her the utmost pleasure. It felt unbelievably good and the pressure inside her was building, building to a crescendo. Suddenly she was there, suspended for timeless seconds on the edge of ecstasy before the wave crashed over her and swept her up in a maelstrom of intense pleasure that went on and on, pulsing, pounding through her, tearing a low cry from her throat.

Even when the ripples of her orgasm started to fade, he continued to move inside her with an urgency that took her breath away. He gripped her hips and reared over her, his head thrown back so that the cords on his neck stood out. Incredibly, Ava climaxed for a second time, swift and sharp, as Giannis gave a final thrust and emitted a savage groan as he pressed his face into her neck while great shudders racked his body.

In the afterglow, a sense of peace enfolded her and she lay quite still, not wanting him to move away, not ready to face the reality of what had just happened. Gradually the thunderous beat of his heart slowed. She loved the feel of his big, strong body lying lax on top of her and of his arms around her, holding her close. Her limbs felt heavy and the lingering ripples of her orgasm triggered delicious tingles deep in her pelvis.

So *that* was what poets wrote sonnets about, she thought, smiling to herself. There wasn't something wrong with her, as Craig had suggested. Sex with Giannis had been mind-blowing and had proved that her body was capable of experiencing the most intense passion. From Giannis's reaction he had enjoyed having sex with her. She wasn't frigid. She was a responsive, sexually confident woman.

He lifted his head at last and looked down at her, his dark eyes unfathomable, making Ava realise once again that even though they had just shared the most intimate act that two people could experience, she did not know him. Oh, she'd gleaned a few facts about him on the Internet. Mainly about his business success or which model or actress he'd dated, although there was actually very little information about him. She knew nothing about the real Giannis Gekas— his family, his interests, even mundane things such as what kind of food he liked. There was an endless list of unknowns—all the tiny snippets of information that people at the beginning of a conventional relationship would find out about each other.

All she knew was that they had been drawn together by a combustible sexual chemistry, and when she became aware of him hardening once more while he was still buried deep inside her, nothing else mattered.

'You are irresistible, *omorfiá mou*,' he murmured. 'I want you again.'

Excitement coiled through her and she wrapped her legs around his back to draw him deeper inside her. He groaned. 'You would tempt a saint. But first I need to change the condom. Don't go away.' He dropped a brief but utterly sensual kiss on her mouth—a promise of further delights to follow—before he lifted himself off her and strode into the bathroom.

Ava watched him, her gaze clinging to his broad shoulders before sliding lower to the taut curves of his buttocks, and molten heat pooled between her thighs. Everything about tonight felt unreal, as if she was in the middle of an erotic dream that she did not want to end.

CHAPTER THREE

GIANNIS STEPPED OUT of the shower cubicle and blotted the moisture from his skin before he knotted a towel around his hips and walked into the bedroom. He glanced at the bed and saw that Ava was still fast asleep. Her honey-blonde hair spilled across the black silk pillows and her hand was tucked under her cheek. She looked young and unexpectedly innocent but looks were deceptive and there had been no hint of the ingénue about her last night.

The memory of her standing in front of him in stiletto heels, sheer black stockings and a minuscule pair of knickers had a predictable effect on his body, and he was tempted to whip off his towel and wake her for morning sex. But there wasn't time, and he felt no more than a fleeting regret as he turned away from the bed, striding over to the wardrobe to select a shirt to wear with his suit. While he dressed, he thought about his schedule for the day.

He had meetings in Paris in the afternoon and a social function to attend in the evening. But first he planned to drive to his house in Hertfordshire that he had recently purchased, to inspect the renovations that had been completed and pay the workmen a bonus. It would be useful to have a permanent base in the UK, but another reason he had bought Milton Grange was because the grounds included a particularly fine garden. Giannis hoped that his mother might like to visit the house in the summer, and perhaps tending to the roses would lift her spirits, which had been low lately. Although there was nothing new about that, he thought heavily.

He had spent most of his adult life trying to make his mother happy. His conscience insisted that caring for her was a small penance and could never atone for his terrible lapse of judgement that had resulted in the death of his father. He despised himself even more because he found his mother difficult. Even his sister had suggested that their *mitera*'s relentless misery was intended to make him feel guilty.

Giannis sighed as his thoughts switched from his mother to another thorn in his side. Ever since Stefanos Markou had announced that he intended to sell Markou Shipping and retire from business, Giannis had tried to persuade the old man to sell his ships to him. The Markou fleet of six small cargo ships would be an ideal addition to The Gekas Experience.

TGE already operated ten vessels offering luxurious cruises around the Mediterranean and the Caribbean. River cruising was becoming increasingly popular and Giannis wanted to expand the company and make TGE the world leader in this emerging tourist market. The Markou fleet of ships would need major refurbishments to turn them into high-end luxury river cruisers, but it was cheaper to upgrade existing ships than to commission a new fleet of vessels.

To Giannis's intense frustration, Stefanos had rejected his very generous financial offer. That was to say—Stefanos had not actually turned him down but he kept adding new conditions before he would sell. Giannis had already agreed to employ the entire Markou Shipping workforce and retrain the staff so that they could work on his cruise ships. Far more problematic was Stefanos's insistence that he wanted to sell his company to a married man.

'Markou Shipping's ethos is family first,' Stefanos had told Giannis. 'Many of the current staff are second or even third generation employees and they share the company's values of loyalty and propriety. How do you think they would feel if I sold the company to you—a notorious playboy who regards women only as pleasurable diversions? But if you were to choose a wife and settle down it would show that you believe in the high ideals which my great-grandfather, who started Markou Shipping one hundred years ago, held dear.'

Giannis had no desire to marry, but a rival potential buyer had shown interest in purchasing the Markou fleet of vessels. Norwegian businessman Anders Tromska was married and the father of two children. Stefanos approved of Tromska for being a dedicated family man who had never been involved in any kind of scandal or photographed by the paparazzi with a different blonde on his arm every week.

Giannis was prepared to increase his financial

offer for the fleet of ships. But for once he had discovered that money could not solve a problem. It seemed that the only way he might persuade Stefanos to sell to him was if he magically conjured himself a wife.

He slipped his arms into his jacket and pushed the Markou problem to the back of his mind for now, turning his thoughts instead to a happier situation. His beloved *Nerissa*—a classic motor yacht which had been his father's first boat— had been repaired and restored after it had been vandalised.

Giannis had kept the boat moored at St Katharine Dock and he stayed on it whenever he visited London. He had been furious when he'd heard that a gang of youths had boarded the boat one night and held a party. A fire had somehow started in the main cabin and quickly ripped through the boat. It turned out that a cleaner who worked for the valeting company employed to maintain the boat had stolen the keys and taken his thuggish friends aboard *Nerissa*. The gang had escaped before the police arrived, apart from the cleaner, who had been arrested and charged with criminal damage.

The manager of the boat valeting company had been deeply apologetic. 'The youth who took the keys to your boat has a police record for various petty crimes. His social worker persuaded me to give him a job. To be honest he seemed like a nice lad, and his sister who accompanied him to his interview was anxious for me to give him a chance. But they say that bad blood will out in the end,' the manager had said sagely.

In Giannis's opinion, the cleaner who he held responsible for wrecking his boat deserved to be locked up in jail and the keys thrown away. *Nerissa* was special to him and he had wonderful memories of idyllic days spent on her with his father. Now that the boat had been repaired he had arranged for her to be taken back to Greece, to his home on the island of Spetses.

The sound of movement from the bed compelled Giannis to turn his head and look across the room. Ava rolled onto her back and the sheet slipped down to reveal one perfect round breast, creamy pale against the black silk sheet and adorned with a dusky pink nipple that Giannis had delighted in tormenting with his mouth the previous night.

One night with the golden-haired temptress was not enough to sate his desire for her, he acknowledged. His arousal was uncomfortably hard beneath his close-fitting trousers. He would take her phone number and call her on his next trip to London, he decided. Maybe he would instruct his PA to clear his diary for a few days so that he could fly up to Scotland with Ava. His imagination ran riot as he pictured them staying at a castle and having hot sex in front of a blazing log fire. He had heard that it often rained in the Highlands, and they would have to pass the time somehow.

But that was for the future. Right now he had a busy day ahead of him. He glanced at his watch and strode over to the bed to wake Sleeping Beauty. He had asked for his car to be brought to the front of the hotel ready for him to drive to Hertfordshire and he was keen to be on his way. But his conscience—which was frankly underused—insisted on this occasion that he could not simply disappear and leave Ava asleep.

'Good morning.' He leaned over the bed and watched her long eyelashes flutter and settle back on her cheeks. 'It's time to get up, angel-face.' Impatience edged into his voice, and he put his hand on her shoulder to give her a gentle shake.

Long hazel-coloured lashes swept upwards. Her grey eyes were dazed with sleep before she blinked and focused on his face.

'Oh. My. God.' Her appalled expression was almost comical. 'I thought you were a dream.'

Giannis grinned. 'I aim to please. You were pretty amazing last night too.' His gaze lingered on her bare breast and she made a choked sound as she dragged the sheet up to her chin. 'But it is now morning,' he told her. 'Nine o'clock, to be precise. And incredibly tempting though you are, I have a busy schedule and you need to get dressed.'

'Oh, my God,' Ava said again. She sat up and pushed her tangled blonde hair out of her eyes. The faint quiver of her lower lip made her seem oddly vulnerable. Giannis was surprised by the inexplicable urge that came over him to hold her in his arms and comfort her. But why did he think she needed to be comforted when he was certain she had enjoyed the passionate night they had spent together as much as he had? Just as pertinently, what qualified him to offer comfort to anyone? He destroyed things, and Ava, with her curiously innocent air, would do well to stay away from him, he reminded himself.

He was used to being instantly obeyed and he frowned when, instead of jumping out of bed, Ava slumped back against the pillows and covered her face with her hands. Giannis struggled to hide his irritation. 'You were not so shy last night,' he drawled.

'Last night was a mistake.' Her voice was muffled behind her hands. 'I must have had too much to drink.'

His jaw hardened. 'You drank a small glass of wine during dinner. Don't try to make out that you were unaware of what you were doing when you undressed in front of me, or suggest that I took advantage of you. When I asked if you were sure you wanted to have sex, you more or less begged me to take you.'

She jerked upright and dropped her hands away from her face, shaking her head so that her hair swirled around her shoulders like a curtain of gold silk. 'I did not *beg*.' There was outrage in her voice but she continued in a low tone, 'I know what I did. I was responsible for my behaviour and I'm not blaming you. But I shouldn't have slept with you. What I mean is that I should have spoken to you…asked you… Oh, this is so awkward.' Her eyes widened even more. 'Did you say that it's nine o'clock? Oh, my *God*.'

She scrambled off the bed and tugged the sheet around her, but not before Giannis had glimpsed her naked body. At some point during the night he had removed her stockings using his teeth to tug them down her legs. He watched Ava struggle to put her bra on while she clutched the sheet to her like a security blanket. 'Don't you think it's a little late for modesty?' he said sardonically.

She picked up her torn thong from the floor and looked as though she was about to burst into tears. 'I have to go,' she said wildly. 'Sam will be going mad wondering where I am. I was supposed to have an important conversation with you last night.'

'About what?'

She bit her lip. 'It's a delicate matter.'

Giannis counted to ten beneath his breath. 'I'm in a hurry, so whatever it is you want to say—for God's sake get on with it.'

This couldn't be happening, Ava thought frantically. In a minute she would wake up from a nightmare. But in the cold light of morning she could not fool herself that having wild sex with Giannis last night had been a dream. She felt a sensation like wet cement congealing in the pit of her stomach with the knowledge that, as a result of her irresponsible behaviour, she had lost her chance to plead with Giannis to drop the charges against her brother. She felt sick with shame and guilt.

The sound of a familiar ringtone cut through the tense atmosphere and she scrabbled in her handbag to retrieve her phone. Her heart lurched when she saw that it was her brother calling.

'Sam, I've been…unavoidably delayed.' She dared not look at Giannis. 'You will have to ring for a taxi to take you to the courthouse, and I'll meet you there. You'll have to hurry—' she felt her anxiety rise '—your case is due to be heard by the magistrate in half an hour, and you mustn't be late.'

'The magistrate is ill,' Sam said when Ava paused for breath. 'I've just heard that the court cases today have been postponed.'

Ava heard relief in her brother's voice and she felt a rush of emotion. Sam hadn't said much in the weeks leading up to his court hearing, but she knew he was scared at the prospect of being sent to prison. 'Thank goodness.' She breathed out a heavy sigh. 'I don't mean it's good that the magistrate is ill, of course, but it gives us a bit more time.'

'Time to do what?' her brother said flatly. 'My case has only been delayed for a few days and it's still likely that I'll be sent to a YOI.'

Ava knew that young offender institutions tended to be grim places and she understood why Sam was scared. He might be eighteen but he would always be her kid brother. 'Not necessarily.' She tried to sound optimistic. 'I can't talk now. I'll see you at home later.'

She replaced her phone in her bag, and her eyes widened as she watched Giannis open his briefcase and throw some documents on top of a pile of bank notes. He closed the briefcase but Ava had a sudden flashback to when she had been a little girl, and had seen her father counting piles of bank notes on the kitchen table.

'Payday,' he'd told her when she had asked him about the money.

'You must be a good businessman to earn so much money, Daddy,' Ava had said trustingly. She had idolised her father.

Terry had winked at her. 'Oh, I'm an expert, honey-bunch. I'm going to use this money to buy a house in Cyprus. What do you think of that?'

'Where's Cyprus?'

'It's near to Greece. The villa I'm buying is next to the beach, and it has a big swimming pool so you will be able to teach your baby brother to swim when he's older.'

'Why aren't we going to live in England any more?'

Her father had given her an odd smile. 'It's too hot for me to live here.' It had been the middle of winter at the time and Ava had felt confused by her father's reply. But years later she had learned that Terry McKay had moved his family abroad after he'd received a tip-off that he was about to be arrested on suspicion of carrying out several armed raids on jewellery shops in London.

She dragged her mind from the past as she caught sight of her reflection in the full-length mirror. She looked like a tart with her just-got-out-of-bed hair and panda eyes where her mascara had smudged. Her lips were fuller and redder than usual, and remembering how Giannis had covered her mouth with his and kissed her senseless made her feel hot all over. She could not have a serious conversation with him about her brother while she was naked and draped in a silk sheet.

As if he had read her thoughts, Giannis walked over to the wardrobe and took out her evening gown. 'Your dress has been cleaned, but I guessed you would not want to be seen leaving the hotel this morning wearing a ball gown so I ordered you something more appropriate to wear.' He handed her a bag with the name of a well-known design house emblazoned on it. 'I'll leave you to get dressed. Please hurry,' he said curtly before he strode out of the bedroom.

Ava scooted into the en suite bathroom and looked longingly at the bath, the size of a small swimming pool. She had discovered new muscles and she ached everywhere. But Giannis was no longer the charming lover of last night and he had not hidden his impatience this morning, she thought ruefully as she bundled her hair into a shower cap before taking a quick shower.

The bag he had given her contained a pair of beautifully tailored black trousers and a cream cashmere sweater. There was also an exquisite set of silk and lace underwear. Remembering her ripped thong brought a scarlet flush to her cheeks. She did not recognise the shameless temptress she had turned into last night. Giannis had revealed a side to her that she hadn't known existed.

Grimacing at the sight of her kiss-stung lips in the mirror, she brushed her hair and caught it up in a loose knot on top of her head. At least she looked respectable, although she shuddered to think how much the designer clothes must have cost. Everything fitted her perfectly, and when she slipped on the black stiletto heels she'd worn the previous evening she was pleasantly surprised by how slim and elegant she looked. Stuffing her evening gown into the bag that had held her new clothes, she walked into the sitting room.

Giannis was speaking on his phone but he finished the call when he saw her and strolled across the room. His intent appraisal caused her heart to miss a beat. 'I see that the clothes fit you.'

'How did you know my size?'

'I have had plenty of experience of the female figure,' he drawled.

Inexplicably Ava felt the acid burn of jealousy in her stomach at the idea of him making love with other women. Love had nothing to do with it, she reminded herself. Giannis was a notorious womaniser and she was simply another blonde who had shared his bed for one night. No doubt he would have forgotten her name by tomorrow.

'Obviously I'll pay for the clothes,' she said crisply. 'Can you give me your bank details so that I can transfer what I owe you, or would you prefer a cheque?'

'Forget it. I don't want any money.'

'No way will I allow you to buy me expensive designer clothes. I'll find out what they cost and send a cheque for the amount to your London office.'

His eyes narrowed. 'How do you know that I have an office in London?'

'I found out from the Internet that you own a cruise line company called The Gekas Experience. TGE UK's offices are in Bond Street.' Ava hesitated. 'I wrote to you a few weeks ago about a serious matter, but you did not reply.'

'Sheridan,' he said slowly. 'I wondered why your name on the place card at dinner last night seemed familiar.' He frowned. 'I'm afraid you will have to jog my memory.'

She took a deep breath. 'My brother, Sam McKay, used to work for a boat valeting company called Spick and Span.' Giannis's expression hardened, and she continued quickly. 'Sam had got involved with a gang of rough youths who made out that they were his friends. They coerced him into taking them aboard one of the boats that he valeted in St Katharine Dock. I don't know if the gang meant to vandalise the boat, but a fire broke out. My brother was horrified, and he stayed on board to try to put the flames out while the rest of the gang got away. He was the only one to be arrested and charged with criminal damage. But he never meant for your boat to be damaged.' Ava's voice wavered as Giannis's dark brows drew together in a slashing frown. 'It was just a silly prank that got out of hand.'

'A prank? The *Nerissa* was nearly destroyed. Do you know how many thousands of pounds of damage your brother and his friends caused?' Giannis said harshly. 'It wasn't just the financial cost of having the boat repaired. The sentimental value of everything that was lost is incalculable. My father designed every detail of *Nerissa*'s interior and he was so proud of that boat.'

'I'm sorry.' Ava was shocked by the raw emotion in Giannis's voice. She had only considered the financial implications of the fire, and it hadn't occurred to her that the boat might be special to him. It made the situation even worse. 'Sam really regrets that he allowed the gang on board. He thought that they just wanted to have a look at the boat, and he was horrified by what happened.' She bit her lip. 'My brother is scared of the gang members, which is why he refused to give their names to the police. He's young and impressionable, but honestly he's not a bad person.'

Giannis's brows rose. 'The manager of the boat valeting company told me that your brother already had a criminal record by the age of sixteen. Sam McKay clearly has a complete disregard for the law.'

He picked up his briefcase and walked over to the penthouse suite's private lift. 'I remember the letter you sent asking me to drop the charges against your brother. I did not reply because frankly I was too angry. Sam broke the law and he must face the consequences,' he said coldly.

'Wait!' Ava hurried across the room as the lift doors opened and she followed Giannis inside. She jabbed her finger on the button to keep the door open. 'Please hear me out.'

'I'm in a hurry,' he growled.

'When I read in a newspaper that you would be attending the charity fundraising dinner I decided to try to meet you. My friend works for the event's management company which organised the evening, and Becky arranged for me to sit at the same table as you. I hoped to persuade you to find it in your heart to give my brother another chance.'

'I don't have a heart.' Giannis reached out and pulled her hand away from the button and the lift doors instantly closed. 'Your methods of persuasion were impressive, I'll grant you. But it was a wasted performance, angel-face.'

Ava gave him a puzzled look. 'What do you mean?'

'Oh, come on. You obviously had sex with me because you thought I would let your brother off the hook.'

'I did *not*. I didn't plan to go to bed with you—it just…happened,' she muttered, shame coiling through her like a venomous serpent. To say that she had handled things badly would be an understatement. Last night she had behaved like the slut that Giannis clearly believed she was, but she refused to give up trying to help Sam.

The lift doors opened on the ground floor and she shot out behind Giannis when he stepped into the foyer. 'My reason for having sex with you had nothing to do with my brother,' she told him, her stiletto heels tapping out a staccato beat on the marble floor as she tried to keep pace with his long stride. Her voice seemed to echo around the vast space and she blushed when she became aware of the curious glances directed at her by other hotel guests. The terribly sophisticated receptionist standing behind the front desk arched her brows.

'Why don't you announce on national TV that

we slept together?' Giannis threw her a fulminating look, his dark eyes gleaming like obsidian.

'I'm sorry.' Ava lowered her voice. 'I don't want you to have the wrong impression of me. I don't usually sleep with men I've only just met and I don't understand why I behaved the way I did last night. I suppose it was chemistry. There was an instant attraction that neither of us could resist.'

He growled something uncomplimentary beneath his breath. 'Next you'll be telling me that we were both shot through the heart by Cupid's arrow.' Giannis halted beside a pillar. 'Last night was fun, angel-face, and maybe I'll look you up the next time I'm in town. But I'm not going to drop the charges against your hooligan brother. Even if I wanted to, I don't think it would be possible. As I understand English law, it is the Crown Prosecution who decide if the case should go to court.'

'You could instruct your lawyer to withdraw your complaint of criminal damage inflicted on your boat, and if you refuse to provide evidence to the court the case against Sam will be dropped.'

She grabbed Giannis's arm as he turned to

walk away and felt his rock-hard bicep ripple beneath his jacket. 'It's true that Sam has a police record. Like I said, he was drawn into the gang culture through fear. It's not easy being a teenager in the East End,' she said huskily. 'Sam will almost certainly be given a custodial sentence and I'm scared of what will happen to him in a young offender institution. My brother is not a hardened criminal; he's just a silly kid who made a mistake.'

'Several mistakes,' Giannis said sardonically. 'Perhaps spending a few uncomfortable weeks in prison will teach him to respect the law in future.'

Giannis had not been lying when he'd stated that he did not have a heart, Ava thought bleakly. His phone rang, and she dropped her hand from his arm and moved a few steps away from him, although she was still able to overhear his conversation. A few minutes later he finished the call, and his expression was thunderous as he strode across the lobby without glancing in her direction.

She gave chase and caught up with him, positioning herself so that she was standing between him and the door of the hotel. 'I appreciate you must be annoyed that, from the sound of it, you might have lost a business deal to buy a fleet of ships. But I can't... I *won't* stand by and watch my brother be sent to prison.'

His dark brows lowered even further. 'How the hell do you know about my business deal?'

'I can speak Greek and I couldn't help but hear some of your conversation just now, concerning someone called Markou who has rejected your offer to buy his shipping company.' Ava bit her lip, and something flashed in Giannis's dark eyes that reminded her of the stark sexual hunger in his gaze when he had taken her to bed last night. 'I'm sure your business deal is important to you, but my brother is important to me,' she said huskily. 'Is there any way I can persuade you to give Sam another chance?'

He did not reply as he stepped past her and nodded to the doorman, who sprang forwards to open the door.

Ava followed Giannis out of the hotel and shivered as a gust of wind swirled around her and tugged at her chignon. Although it was early in September, autumn had already arrived with a vengeance. A thunderstorm was forecast but at the moment drizzle was falling and she could feel it soaking through her cashmere jumper. The miserable weather suited her mood of hopelessness as through a blur of tears she saw a sleek black car parked in front of the hotel.

She watched Giannis unlock the car and throw his briefcase onto the back seat. The knowledge that she had failed to save her brother from a likely prison sentence felt like a knife in Ava's heart.

'Have you never done anything in your past that you regret?' she called after him. He hesitated and swung round to face her, his dark brows snapping together.

Desperate to stop him getting into his car and driving away, Ava raced down the hotel steps but she stumbled in her high heels and gave a cry as she felt herself falling. There was nothing she could do to save herself. But then, miraculously, she felt two strong arms wrap around her as Giannis caught her and held her against his chest. In the same instant, on the periphery of her vision she saw a bright flash and wondered if it had been a lightning strike as the storm blew up.

The thought slipped away as the evocative scent of Giannis's aftershave swamped her senses. Still in a state of shock after her near fall, she rested her cheek on his shirt front and heard the erratic thud of his heart beneath her ear. She wished she could remain in his arms for ever. The crazy notion slid into her mind and refused to budge.

There was another flash of bright light. 'Who is your mystery blonde, Mr Gekas?' a voice called out.

Ava heard Giannis swear beneath his breath. 'What's happening?' she asked dazedly, lifting her head from his chest and blinking in the blinding glare of camera flashes.

When a taxi had dropped her at the hotel entrance the previous evening she had noticed the crowd of paparazzi who had gathered to take photos of the celebrity guests arriving at the party. Evidently some of them had waited all night to snap guests leaving the hotel the next morning, and they had struck gold when they had spotted Europe's most notorious playboy and a female companion.

'Hey, Mr Gekas, over here.' A photographer

aimed a long-lens camera at them. 'Can you tell us the name of your girlfriend?'

'I certainly can,' Giannis said calmly. To Ava's surprise, he did not move away from her as she had expected. Instead he kept his arm clamped firmly around her waist as he turned her to face the paparazzi. 'Gentlemen,' he drawled, 'I would like to introduce you to Miss Ava Sheridan—my fiancée.'

She couldn't have heard him correctly. Ava jerked her eyes to his face. *'What...?'* she began, but the rest of her words were obliterated as his dark head swooped down and he crushed her lips beneath his.

The kiss was a statement of pure possession. Giannis ground his mouth against hers, forcing her lips apart and demanding her response, re-igniting the flame inside her so that she was powerless to resist him.

Ava felt dizzy from a lack of oxygen when he finally lifted his head a fraction. *'What the hell?'* she choked, struggling to drag air into her lungs when he pressed her face into his shoulder.

'I need you to be my fake fiancée,' he growled, his lips hovering centimetres above hers. 'Play along with me and I'll drop all the charges against your brother.'

Her eyes widened. 'That's *blackmail.*'

His fingers bit into her upper arms as he hauled her hard up against his whipcord body. To the watching photographers they must have looked like lovers who could not keep their hands off each other. 'It's called business, baby. And you and I have just formed a partnership.'

CHAPTER FOUR

'YOU'VE GOT A damned nerve.'

Giannis flicked a glance at Ava, sitting stiffly beside him. It was the first time she had uttered a word since he had bundled her into his car and driven away from the hotel. But her simmering silence had spoken volumes.

Tendrils of honey-blonde hair had worked loose from her chignon to curl around her cheeks. She smelled of soap and lemony shampoo and he had no idea why he found her wholesome, natural beauty so incredibly sexy. He cursed beneath his breath. She was an unwelcome distraction but she might be the solution to his problem with Stefanos Markou.

He focused his attention on the traffic crawling around Marble Arch. 'It was damage limitation,' he drawled. 'Thanks to social media, pictures of us leaving the hotel will have gone viral within minutes. I couldn't risk my reputation. Anyone who saw the photographs of us together would have assumed that you are my latest mistress.'

Ava made a strangled sound. 'You couldn't risk *your* reputation? What about mine? Everyone will believe that I am engaged to the world's worst womaniser. I can't believe you told the photographers that I am your fiancée.' She ran a hand through her hair, evidently forgetting that she had secured it on top of her head. Her chignon started to unravel and she cursed as she pulled out the remaining pins and combed her fingers through her hair.

'You're right,' she muttered, scrolling through her phone. 'The news of our so-called engagement is all over social media. Thankfully my mother is at a yoga retreat in India where there is no Internet connection. She was seriously stressed about my brother and I persuaded her to go abroad and leave me to deal with the court case. But Sam is bound to see this nonsense and I can't imagine what he's going to say.'

'Presumably he will be grateful to you for helping him to avoid going to prison,' Giannis said drily. He sensed Ava turn her head to stare at him, and a brief glance in her direction revealed that her eyes were the icy grey of an Arctic sky.

'You can't really expect me to go through with the ridiculous charade of pretending to be your fiancée,' she snapped.

'Oh, but I can, *glykiá mou.*'

For some reason her furious snort made him want to smile. Usually he avoided highly emotional women but Ava's wildly passionate nature fascinated him. She was beautiful when she was angry and even more gorgeous when she was aroused, he brooded. Memories of her straddling him, her golden hair tumbling around her shoulders and her bare breasts, round and firm like ripe peaches, caused Giannis to shift uncomfortably in his seat.

He cleared his throat. 'I thought you wanted to keep your brother out of jail?'

'I do. But two minutes before we walked out of the hotel you had refused to help Sam. I don't understand why you have changed your mind, or why you need me to be your fake fiancée.'

'Like I said, the reason is business. More specifically, the only chance I have of doing a deal with Stefanos Markou is if I can prove to him that

I am a reformed character. He has refused to sell Markou Shipping to me because he disapproves of my lifestyle and he thinks I am a playboy.'

'You *are* a playboy,' Ava interrupted.

'Not any more.' Giannis grinned at her. 'Not since I fell in love with you at first sight and decided to marry you and produce a tribe of children. Markou is an old-fashioned romantic and you, angel-face, are going to persuade him to sell his ships to me.'

Her expression became even more wintry. 'There's not a chance in hell that I'd marry you and even less chance I'd agree to have your children.'

Giannis's fingers tightened involuntarily on the steering wheel as a shaft of pain caught him unawares. He had thought he'd dealt with what had happened five years ago, but sometimes he felt an ache in his heart for the child he might have had. Caroline had told him she'd suffered a miscarriage, but in his darkest hours he wondered if she had decided not to allow her pregnancy to continue because she hadn't wanted to be associated with him after he'd admitted that he had spent a year in prison.

He forced his mind away from the past. 'Forgive me for sounding cynical, but I am a very wealthy man and most women I've ever met would happily marry for hard cash. However, I have no intention of marrying you. I simply want you to pretend that we are engaged and planning our wedding. I'm gambling that Stefanos would prefer to sell Markou Shipping to me rather than to a rival company because he knows I will have the ships refurbished in Greece and employ the local workforce. All we have to do is convince him that I have turned into a paragon of virtue thanks to the love of a good woman.'

'How are *we* going to do that?' Ava's tone dripped ice.

'I will make a formal announcement of our engagement and ensure that our relationship receives as much media coverage as possible. Stefanos has invited all the bidders who are interested in buying his company to meet him on his private Greek island in one month's time. With you by my side, an engagement ring on your finger, I am confident that he will sell Markou Shipping to me. The deal is as good as done,' he said with satisfaction.

She frowned. 'Are you saying that—supposing I was mad enough to agree to the pretence—I would have to be your fake fiancée for a whole month and go to Greece with you?'

'One month is less than the prison sentence your brother would be likely to receive,' Giannis reminded her. 'It will be necessary for you to live at my home in Greece because Stefanos is not stupid and he will only believe our relationship is genuine if we are seen together regularly. From now on, every time we are out in public we must act as if we are madly in love.'

'It would require better acting skills than I possess,' Ava muttered.

'On the contrary, I thought you were very convincing when you kissed me outside the hotel.'

She made a choked sound as if she had swallowed a wasp. 'I was in a state of shock after hearing you tell the photographers that I was your fiancée.' After a tense pause, she said, 'What will happen if Stefanos sells his company to you and then we end our fake engagement and you go back to your bachelor lifestyle that he disapproves of? Won't he be angry when he realises he was duped?'

Giannis shrugged. 'There will be nothing he can do once the sale is finalised.'

'Isn't that rather unfair?'

'Life is not always fair.' Irritation made his voice curt. He really did not need a lecture on morals from Ava. 'It was not fair that your brother wrecked my boat, but I am offering you a way to help Sam stay out of prison. Face it, angel-face, we both need each other.'

'I suppose so,' she muttered. 'But I can't give up a month of my life. What am I supposed to do about my job, for instance?'

'You told me you are between jobs since you moved from Scotland to London. What do you do, anyway? I noticed you avoided talking about your career.'

She grimaced. 'I am a victim care officer, and I try to help people who have been the victims of crime. I worked for a victim support charity in Glasgow and I have been offered a similar role with an organisation in London.'

'When will you start the new job?'

Ava seemed reluctant to answer him. 'The post starts in November.'

'So there is nothing to stop you posing as my fiancée now.'

'You are *so* arrogant. Do you always expect people to jump at your command? How do you know that I don't have a boyfriend?'

'If you do, I suggest you dump him because he clearly doesn't satisfy you in bed.' Giannis's lips twitched when Ava muttered something uncomplimentary. She was prickly and defensive and he had no idea why she fascinated him. Well, he had some idea, he acknowledged derisively as he pictured her sprawled on black silk sheets wearing only a pair of sheer stockings. He glanced at her and she quickly turned her head away, but not before he'd seen a flash of awareness in her eyes.

Last night they had been dynamite in bed and sex with her had been the best he'd had in a long, long time. Was that why he had come up with the fake engagement plan? Giannis dismissed the idea. He'd been forced to take drastic action when the paparazzi had snapped him and Ava leaving the hotel, having clearly spent the night together. He could not risk that his playboy reputation might lose him the deal with Stefanos Markou.

His inconvenient desire for Ava would no doubt fade once he had secured Markou's fleet of ships. The only thing he cared about was fulfilling the promise he had made over his father's coffin, to provide for his mother and sister. Money and the trappings of wealth were all that he could give them to try to make up for what he had stolen from them. Yet sometimes his single-minded pursuit of success felt soulless, and sometimes he wondered what would happen if he ever opened the Pandora's Box of his emotions. It was safer to keep the lid closed.

'Did you choose to work with crime victims because your brother got into trouble with the police?' Giannis succumbed to his curiosity about Ava. She had made an unusual career choice for someone who had learned etiquette and social graces at a Swiss finishing school. At dinner last night he had noted how comfortable she was with the other wealthy guests, and he was confident she would act the role of his fiancée with grace and charm that would delight Stefanos Markou.

She shook her head. 'Sam was still in primary school when I went to university to study criminology.'

'Why criminology?'

For some reason she stiffened, but her voice was non-committal. 'I found it an interesting subject. But moving away to study and work in Scotland meant I wasn't around to spot the signs that Sam was having problems, or that my mother didn't know how to cope with him when he fell in with a rough crowd.' She sighed. 'I blame myself.'

'Why do you blame yourself for your brother's behaviour? Each of us has to take responsibility for our actions.'

Every day of the past fifteen years, Giannis had regretted that he'd drunk a glass of wine when he and his father had dined together at a *taverna*. Later, on the journey back to the family home, he had driven too fast along the coastal road from Athens and misjudged a sharp bend. Nothing could excuse his fatal error of judgement. If there was any justice in the world then he would have died that night instead of his father.

Ava insisted that her brother regretted taking a gang of thugs aboard *Nerissa* and damaging the boat. She clearly loved her brother, and Giannis felt a begrudging admiration for her determination to help Sam. He remembered how scared *he* had felt at nineteen when he had stood in a courtroom and heard the judge sentence him to a year in prison.

He had deserved his punishment and prison had been nothing compared to the lifetime of self-recrimination and contempt he had sentenced himself to. The car accident had been a terrible mistake, yet not one of his relatives had supported him. His sister had been too young to understand, but his mother would never stop blaming him, Giannis thought heavily.

He looked at Ava and she blushed and quickly turned her head to the front as if she was embarrassed that he had caught her staring at him.

'What about your father?' he asked her as he slipped the car into gear and pulled away from the traffic lights. At least the traffic was flowing better as they headed towards Camden. 'Did he try to give guidance to your brother?'

'Dad…left when Sam was eight years old.'

'Did you and your brother have any contact with him after that?'

'No.'

'It is my belief that children, especially boys,

benefit from having a good relationship with their father. Although I realise my views might be regarded as old-fashioned by feminists,' Giannis said drily.

'I suppose it would depend on how good the father was,' Ava muttered.

She glanced at Giannis's hard profile and wondered what he would say if she told him that it had been difficult for her and Sam to have a relationship with their father after he had been sentenced to fifteen years in prison. Her mother had refused to allow Sam to visit Terry McKay at the maximum-security jail which housed some of the UK's most dangerous criminals. Ava had visited her father once, but she had found the experience traumatic. It had been bad enough having to suffer the indignity of being searched by a warden to make sure she was not smuggling drugs or weapons into the jail.

Seeing her father in prison had been like looking at a stranger. She had found it impossible to accept that the man she had trusted and adored had, unbeknown to his family, been a violent criminal and ruthless gangland boss. The name

Terry McKay was still feared by some people in the East End of London. Perhaps if Sam had seen the grim reality of life behind bars he might not hero-worship his father as a modern-day Robin Hood character, Ava thought heavily. She was prepared to do everything in her power to prevent her brother from turning to a life of crime, and keeping him out of a young offender institution was vital. Giannis had offered her a way to give Sam another chance, but could she really be his fake fiancée?

She had assumed after they had spent the night together that she would never see him again. Memories of her wildly passionate response to his lovemaking made her want to squirm with embarrassment, but she remembered too how he had groaned when he had climaxed inside her. Did he intend that they would be lovers for the duration of their fake engagement? The little shiver of anticipation that ran through her made her despair of herself. If she had an ounce of common sense she would refuse to have anything more to do with him.

But there was Sam to consider.

Desperate to stop her thoughts from going

round in circles, she searched for something to say to Giannis. 'Do you have a good relationship with your father?' If she could build up a picture of him—his family and friends, his values, she might have a better understanding of him.

He was silent for so long that she thought he was not going to answer. 'I did,' he said at last in a curt voice. 'My father is dead.'

'I'm sorry.' Evidently she had touched a raw nerve, and his forbidding expression warned her to back off. She sighed. 'This isn't going to work. We are two strangers who know nothing about each other. We'll never convince anyone that we are madly in love and planning to get married.'

To her surprise, Giannis nodded. 'We will have to spend some time getting to know each other. I can't afford any slip-ups when we meet Stefanos. Let's start with some basics. Why do you and your brother have different surnames? Have you ever been married?'

'No.' Her voice was sharper than she had intended, and she flushed when he threw her a speculative look before he turned his eyes back to the road. For some reason she found herself explaining. 'There was someone who I was sure...'

She bit her lip. 'But I was wrong. He didn't love me the way I'd hoped.'

'Did you love him?'

'I thought I did.' She did not want to talk about Craig. 'After my parents divorced I took my mother's maiden name.'

Ava breathed a sigh of relief when he did not pursue the subject of her brother's surname. Giannis was Greek and it was possible that he did not associate the name McKay with an East End gangster. If he knew of the crimes her father had committed she was sure he wouldn't want her to pose as his fake fiancée and he was likely to refuse to drop the charges against Sam.

Giannis slowed the car to allow a bus to pull out. 'Where did you learn Greek? I did not think the language is routinely taught in English schools.'

'My family lived in Cyprus when I was a child, although I went to boarding school in France and then spent ten months at a finishing school in Switzerland.'

'Why did your parents choose not to live in England?'

'Um…my mother hated the English weather.'

It was partly the truth, but years later Ava had learned that the real reason her father had taken his family to live abroad had been the lack of an extradition agreement between the UK and Cyprus, which had meant that Terry could not be arrested and sent back to England.

Her thoughts were distracted when a cyclist suddenly swerved in front of the car. Only Giannis's lightning reaction as he slammed on the brakes saved the cyclist from being knocked off his bike.

'That was a close call.' She looked over at Giannis and was shocked to see that he was grey beneath his tan. His skin was drawn so tight across his face that his sharp cheekbones were prominent. Beads of sweat glistened on his brow and she noticed that his hand shook when he raked his fingers through his hair.

Ahead there was an empty space by the side of the road and Ava waited until he had parked the car and switched off the engine before she murmured, 'You didn't hit the cyclist. He was riding like an idiot and it was fortunate for him that you are a good driver.'

Giannis gave an odd laugh that almost sounded

as though he was in pain. 'You don't know anything about me, angel-face.'

'That's the point I've been making,' she said
quietly. 'We are not going to be able to carry off
a fake engagement.'

'For your brother's sake you had better hope
that we do.' The stark warning in Giannis's voice
increased Ava's tension, and when he got out of
the car and walked round to open her door she
froze when she recognised an area of London
that was painfully familiar to her.

'Why have we come here? I thought you were
taking me home.' It occurred to her that he had
not asked where she lived, and she had been so
stunned after he'd told the photographers she was
his fiancée that she had let him drive her away
from the hotel without asking where they were
going.

'Hatton Garden is the best place to buy jewellery.'

'That doesn't explain why you have brought
me here.' She was aware that Hatton Garden was
known worldwide as London's jewellery quarter
and the centre of the UK's diamond trade. It was

also the place where her father had masterminded and carried out his most audacious robbery.

Ava remembered when she was a little girl, before the family had moved to Cyprus, her father had often taken her for walks to Covent Garden and St Paul's Cathedral. They had always ended up in Hatton Garden and strolled past the many jewellery shops with their windows full of sparkling precious gems. She had loved those trips with her father, unaware that Terry McKay had been assessing which shops would be the easiest to break into.

'For our engagement to be believable you will need to wear an engagement ring. Preferably a diamond the size of a rock that you can flash in front of the photographers,' Giannis drawled. He glanced at his watch. 'Try not to take too long choosing one.' He took his phone out of his jacket pocket. 'I need to tell my pilot to have the jet ready for us to leave earlier than I'd originally planned.'

Ava stared at him. 'You own a *jet*?'

'It's the quickest way to get around. We should be in Paris by lunchtime. I'm going to be busy this afternoon but I'll arrange for a personal shopper to help you choose some suitable clothes. This evening we will be attending a high-profile function at the Louvre that is bound to attract a lot of media interest. By tomorrow morning half the world will believe that we are in love.'

'Wait…' She stiffened when he slid his hand beneath her elbow and tried to lead her towards a jewellery store. Her heart plummeted when she saw the name above the shop front.

Ten years ago her father had carried out an armed robbery at the prestigious Engerfield's jewellers and stolen jewellery with a value of several million pounds. But Terry McKay's luck had finally run out and he had been caught trying to flee back to Cyprus on his boat. In court, CCTV footage had shown him threatening a young female shop assistant with a shotgun.

Ava had been devastated to discover that her father was a ruthless gangster. Even worse, several national newspapers had published a photo of her and her mother with the suggestion that they must have been aware of Terry's criminal activities. If Julie McKay *had* harboured suspicions about her husband, she had not told her daughter.

But Ava knew that her mother had worshipped Terry and been blind to his faults.

She stared at the jewellery shop. 'I can't go in there.'

Giannis frowned. 'Why not? Engerfield's is arguably the best jewellers in London.'

'What I mean is that I can't wear an engagement ring or go to Paris with you until I've seen my brother and explained that our relationship is fake.'

'You cannot tell anyone the truth in case someone leaks information to the press. I mean it,' Giannis said harshly as Ava opened her mouth to argue. 'No one must have any idea that our engagement is not real.'

'But what am I going to say to Sam?'

He shrugged. 'You'll have to invent a story that we met a few weeks ago, and after a whirlwind romance I asked you to marry me. That will explain why I dropped the charges against Sam because I did not want to prosecute my future brother-in-law.'

'I don't want to lie to my brother,' she choked. 'I hate deception.'

'Do you really want to have to admit to him

that you slept with me the night we met? *That* is the truth, Ava, and I will have no qualms about telling Sam how we got into this situation.'

'*You* told the paparazzi that I am your fiancée. The situation is all your fault.' She winced when Giannis tightened his grip on her arm and escorted her through the door of the jewellers.

'Smile,' he instructed her in a low tone when a silver-haired man walked over to meet them.

Somehow Ava managed to force her lips to curve upwards, but inside she was quaking as she recognised Nigel Engerfield. Ten years ago he had been commended for his bravery after he had tried to protect his staff from the gang of armed thieves led by her father. At the time of her father's trial Ava remembered seeing the shop manager's photograph in the newspapers. Would he remember *her* from the photo of Terry McKay's family that had appeared in the press a decade ago? She was sure she did not imagine that the manager gave her a close look, but to her relief he turned his gaze from her and smiled at Giannis.

'Mr Gekas, what a pleasure to see you again. How can I help you?'

'We would like to choose an engagement ring. Wouldn't we, darling?' Giannis slid his arm around Ava's waist and his dark eyes glittered as he met her startled glance. 'This is my fiancée...'

'Miss Sheridan,' Ava said quickly, holding out her hand to Nigel Engerfield. She was scared he might remember that Terry McKay had a daughter called Ava.

'Please accept my congratulations, Mr Gekas and... Miss Sheridan.' The manager's gaze lingered on Ava. 'If you would like to follow me, I will take you to one of our private sitting rooms so that you can be comfortable while you take your time to peruse our collection of engagement rings. Is there a particular style or gemstone that you are interested in?'

'What woman doesn't love diamonds?' Giannis drawled.

Nigel Engerfield nodded and left the room, returning a few minutes later carrying several trays of rings, and accompanied by an assistant bearing a bottle of champagne and two glasses. The champagne cork popped and the assistant handed Ava a flute of the sparkling drink. She took a cautious sip, aware that she had not eaten breakfast. Maybe Giannis had the same thought because he set his glass down on the table without drinking from it.

'Please sit down and take as much time as you like choosing your perfect ring,' the manager invited Ava, placing the trays of rings on the table in front of her.

She looked down at the glittering, sparkling rings and felt sick as she remembered how, when she was a little girl, she had loved trying on her mother's jewellery. After her father had been arrested, the police had confiscated all the jewels that Terry had stolen—including her mother's wedding ring. Everything from Ava's privileged childhood—the luxury villa in Cyprus, the exotic holidays and expensive private education—had been paid for with the proceeds of her father's criminal activities. There was nothing she could do to erase her sense of guilt, but working as a VCO was at least some sort of reparation for what her father had done.

'Do you see anything you like, darling?' Giannis's voice jolted her from the past. She looked over to where he was standing by the window.

Sunlight streamed through the glass, and his dark hair gleamed like raw silk when he ran a careless hand through it. His face was all angles and planes, as beautiful as a sculpted work of art. But he was not made from cold marble. Last night his skin had felt warm beneath her fingertips when she had explored his magnificent body.

Ava could recall every detail of his honed musculature that was now hidden beneath his superbly tailored suit. Oh, yes, she saw something she liked, she silently answered his question. His eyes captured hers, and her heart missed a beat when she glimpsed a predatory gleam in his gaze.

Hastily she looked down at the glittering rings displayed against black velvet cushions. Even though the shop manager had suggested she should take her time to choose a ring, she knew that Giannis wanted her to hurry up.

Inexplicably a wave of sadness swept over her. Choosing an engagement ring was supposed to be a special occasion for couples who were in love. The young assistant who had poured the champagne had looked enviously at Giannis and clearly believed that their romance was genuine. But Ava knew she was an imposter. The web of deceit they were spinning would grow and spread as they sought to convince Stefanos Markou that Giannis had given up his womanising ways because he had fallen in love with her. But of course he never would love her. He needed her so that he could win a business deal and she needed him to save her brother from prison.

What they were doing was wrong, Ava thought miserably. How could she even trust that Giannis would keep his side of their arrangement? He was playing the role of attentive lover faultlessly, but it was just an act—although that did not stop a stupid, idiotic part of her from wishing that his tender smile was real.

'Sweetheart?' Giannis walked over to the sofa and sat down beside her. 'If you don't like any of the rings, I am sure Mr Engerfield has others that you can look at.'

She swallowed. 'I can't do this…'

The rest of her words were smothered by Giannis's mouth as he swiftly lowered his head and kissed her. 'I think you are a little overwhelmed by the occasion,' he murmured, smiling softly at her stunned expression. He looked over at the shop manager. 'Would you mind leaving us alone?'

As soon as Nigel Engerfield and his assistant had stepped out of the room, Giannis did not try to hide his impatience. 'What is the matter?' he growled to Ava. 'All you have to do is choose a diamond ring, but anyone would think you are about to undergo root canal treatment.'

'I never wear jewellery and I hate diamonds,' she muttered.

He swore. 'I thought we had an agreement, but if you've changed your mind I will find another way to persuade Stefanos Markou to sell his ships to me—and your brother will go to prison.'

Ava bit her lip. 'How do I know that you will drop the charges against my brother?'

'You have my word.'

'Your word means nothing.' She ignored the flash of anger in his eyes. 'Phone your lawyer now and instruct that you no longer want to press charges against Sam.'

Giannis glared at her. 'How do I know you won't immediately go to the press and deny that you are my fiancée?'

'You'll have to trust me.' Ava glared back at

him and refused to be cowed by his black stare. In the tense silence that stretched between them she could hear the loud thud of her heart in her ears. Giannis was a man used to being in control, but if he thought she was a pushover he had a nasty surprise coming to him.

Finally he took out his phone and made a call. 'It's done,' he told her moments later. 'You heard me inform my lawyer that I have decided not to press a charge of criminal damage against Sam McKay. Now it is your turn to keep to your side of the bargain.'

Ava felt light-headed with relief that Sam would not face prosecution and prison. 'I won't let you down,' she assured Giannis huskily. She glanced at the trays and selected an ostentatious diamond solitaire ring. 'Does this have enough bling to impress the paparazzi?'

He frowned at her choice and studied the other rings. 'This one is better,' he said as he picked out a ring and slid it onto her finger.

She stared down at her hand, and her throat felt oddly constricted. 'Really?' she tried to ignore the emotions swirling inside her as she said sarcastically, 'Don't you think a pink heart is romantic overload?'

'It's a pink sapphire. You said you dislike diamonds, although there are a few small diamonds surrounding the heart. But the ring is pretty and elegant and it suits your small hand.'

The ring was a perfect fit on her finger and, despite Ava's insistence that she did not like jewellery, she instantly fell in love with the pink sapphire's simplicity and delicate beauty. Once again she felt a tug on her heart. Didn't every woman secretly yearn for love and marriage, for the man of her dreams to place a beautiful ring on her finger and tell her that he loved her?

Giannis was hardly her fairy tale prince, she reminded herself. If they had not been spotted by the paparazzi leaving the hotel together, she would have been just another of his one-night stands. She stood up abruptly and moved away from him. 'I don't care which ring I have. It's simply to fool people into thinking that we are engaged and I'll only have to wear it for a month.'

He followed her over to the door but, before she could open it, he caught hold of her shoulder and spun her round to face him. His brows lowered when he saw her mutinous expression. 'For the next month I will expect you to behave like you are my adoring fiancée, not a stroppy adolescent, which is your current attitude,' he said tersely.

'Let go of me.' Her eyes darkened with temper when he backed her up against the door. He was too close, and her senses leapt as she breathed in his exotic aftershave. 'What are you doing?'

'Giving you some acting lessons,' he growled and, before she had time to react, he covered her mouth with his and kissed the fight out of her.

He kissed her until she was breathless, until she melted against him and slid her arms up the front of his shirt. The scrape of his rough jaw against her skin sent a shudder of longing through Ava. It shamed her to admit it, but Giannis only had to touch her and he decimated her power of logical thought. She pressed herself closer to his big, hard body, a low moan rising in her throat when he flicked his tongue inside her mouth.

And then it was over as, with humiliating ease, he broke the kiss and lifted his hands to unwind her arms from around his neck. Only the slight unsteadiness of his breath indicated that he was not as unaffected by the kiss as he wanted her to think.

His voice was coolly amused as he drawled, 'You are an A-star student, *glykiá mou*. You almost had *me* convinced that you are in love with me.'

'Hell,' Ava told him succinctly, 'will freeze over first.'

CHAPTER FIVE

PARIS IN EARLY autumn was made for lovers. The September sky was a crisp, bright blue and the leaves on the trees were beginning to change colour and drifted to the ground like red and gold confetti.

Staring out of the window of a chauffeur-driven limousine on his way back to his hotel from a business meeting, Giannis watched couples holding hands or strolling arm in arm next to the Seine. What it was to be in love, he thought cynically. Five years ago he had fallen hard for Caroline when he'd met her during a business trip to her home state of California. *Theos*, he had believed that she loved him. But the truth was she had loved his money and had hoped he would pay for her father's political campaign to become the next US President.

Caroline's pregnancy had been a mistake but, as long as they were married, a baby, especially if it was a boy, might help her father's campaign, she'd told Giannis. Images of widower Brice Herbert cuddling his grandchild would appeal to the electorate.

However, having a son-in-law who had served a prison sentence would have been a disaster for Brice Herbert's political ambition. Caroline had reacted with horror when Giannis had revealed the dark secret of his past. He'd sensed that she had been relieved when she'd lost the baby. Motherhood had not been on her agenda when there was a chance she could be America's First Lady. It was probably a blessing in disguise, she'd said, and it meant that there was no reason for them to marry. But he could never believe that the loss of his child was a blessing. It had felt as if his heart had been ripped out, and confirmed his belief that he did not deserve to be happy.

The limousine swept past the Arc de Triomphe while Giannis adeptly blocked out thoughts of his past and focused on the present. Specifically on the woman who was going to help him prove to Stefanos Markou that he had given up his playboy lifestyle. He should have predicted that Ava would argue when he had given her his credit card and sent her shopping, he brooded.

'I packed some things when you drove me home to collect my passport. There is nothing wrong with my clothes,' she'd told him in a stiff voice that made him want to shake her.

'I am a wealthy man and when we are out together in public, people will expect my fiancée to be dressed in haute couture,' he had explained patiently. 'Fleur Laurent is a personal shopper and she will take you to the designer boutiques on the Champs-Élysées.'

Most women in Giannis's experience would have been delighted at the chance to spend his money, but not Ava. She was irritating, incomprehensible and—he searched for another suitable adjective that best summed up his feelings for her. *Ungrateful.* She did not seem to appreciate that he was doing her a huge favour by dropping the criminal damage charge against her brother.

Giannis frowned as he remembered meeting Sam McKay briefly when he'd driven Ava home before they had flown to Paris. He had been surprised when she'd directed him to pull up outside a shabby terraced house. It was odd that her family had moved from Cyprus to a run-down area of East London. Perhaps there had been a change in her parents' financial circumstances, he'd mused.

He had insisted on accompanying Ava into the house to maintain the pretence of their romance. He wasn't going to risk her brother selling a story to the press that their engagement was fake. But, instead of a swaggering teenager, he'd discovered that Sam was a lanky, nervous-looking youth who had stammered his thanks to Giannis for dropping the criminal charges against him. Sam had admitted that he'd been stupid and regretted the mistakes he had made.

Giannis understood what it was like to regret past actions and, to his surprise, he'd found himself feeling glad that he had given Ava's brother a chance to turn his life around. While Ava had gone upstairs to look for her passport, Sam had shyly congratulated him on becoming engaged to his sister and had voiced his opinion that Ava deserved to be happy after her previous boyfriend had broken her heart.

The limousine drew up outside the hotel and Giannis glanced at his watch. His meeting had overrun but there was just enough time for him to shower and change before the evening's function at the Louvre started. He hoped Ava would be ready on time. *Theos*, he hoped she hadn't run out on him.

He was aware of a sinking sensation in his stomach as the possibility occurred to him. He acknowledged that he had struggled to concentrate during his business meeting because he had been anticipating spending the evening with Ava. If he hadn't known himself better he might have been concerned by his fascination with her. But experience had taught him that desire was a transitory emotion.

'I wouldn't have thought that you would be interested in a fashion show,' she had remarked when he'd told her about the evening's event.

'The show is for new designers to demonstrate their talent. I sponsor a young Greek designer called Kris Antoniadis. You may not have heard of him, but I predict that in a few years he will be highly regarded in the fashion world. At least I certainly hope so because I am Kris's main financial sponsor and I have invested a lot of money in him.'

'Is money the only thing you are interested in?' she'd asked him in a snippy tone which gave the impression she thought that making money was immoral.

He had looked her up and down and allowed his eyes linger on the firm swell of her breasts beneath her cashmere sweater. 'It's not the *only* thing that interests me,' he'd murmured, and she'd blushed.

There was no sign of her in their hotel suite, but Giannis heard the sound of a hairdryer from the en suite bathroom. Stripping off his jacket and tie as he went, he strode into the separate shower room and then headed to the dressing room to change into a tuxedo.

He returned to the sitting room just as Ava emerged from the bedroom, and Giannis felt a sudden tightness in his chest. His brain acknowledged that the personal shopper had fulfilled the brief he'd given her to find an evening gown that was both elegant and sexy. But as he stared at Ava he was conscious of the way another area of his anatomy reacted as his blood rushed to his groin.

'You look stunning,' he told her, and to his own

ears his voice sounded huskier than usual as his customary sangfroid deserted him.

'Thank you. So do you.' Soft colour stained her cheeks. Giannis was surprised by how easily she blushed. It gave her an air of vulnerability that he chose to ignore.

'The personal shopper said I should wear a statement dress tonight—whatever a statement dress is. But I don't think you will approve when I tell you how many noughts were on the price tag,' she said ruefully.

'Whatever it cost it was worth it.' Giannis could not tear his eyes off her. The dress was made of midnight-blue velvet, strapless and fitting tightly to her hips before the skirt flared out in a mermaid style down to the floor. Around her neck she wore a matching blue velvet choker with a diamanté decoration. Her hair was caught up at the sides with silver clasps and rippled down her back in silky waves.

He had a mental image of her lying on the bed wearing only the velvet choker, her creamy skin and luscious curves displayed for his delectation. Desire ran hot and urgent through his veins and he was tempted to turn his vision into reality.

Perhaps Ava could read his mind. 'I don't know why you booked a hotel suite with only one bedroom. The deal was for me to be your *fake* fiancée.' She walked past him and picked up the phone. 'I'm going to call reception and ask for a room of my own.'

Giannis crossed the room in two strides and snatched the receiver out of her hand. 'If you do that, how long do you think it will take for a member of the hotel's staff to reveal on social media that we don't share a bed? We are supposed to be madly in love,' he reminded her.

'Did you assume I would be your convenient mistress for the next month? You've got a damned nerve,' she snapped.

He considered proving to her that it had been a reasonable assumption to make. Sexual chemistry simmered between them and all it would take was one kiss, one touch, to cause a nuclear explosion. He watched her tongue dart out to moisten her lower lip and the beast inside him roared.

Somehow Giannis brought his raging hormones under control. What was important was that their 'romance' gained as much public exposure as possible so that Stefanos Markou believed he was a reformed character preparing to devote himself to marriage and family—the ideals that Stefanos believed in.

Throughout the day Giannis had asked himself why he was going to the lengths of pretending to be engaged, simply to tip a business opportunity in his favour. But the truth was that he needed Markou Shipping's fleet of ships to enable him to expand his cruise line company into the river-cruising market. The ships could be refitted during the winter and be ready to take passengers early next summer, which would put TGE ahead of its main competitors.

'We can sort out sleeping arrangements later,' he told Ava. 'The car is waiting to take us to the Louvre. Are you ready for our first performance, *agápi mou*?'

'I am not your love.'

'You are when we are out in public.' He took hold of her arm and frowned when she flinched away from him. 'You'll have to do better than that if we are going to convince anyone that our relationship is genuine.' Impatience flared in him at her mutinous expression. 'We made a deal and I have carried out my side of it,' he reminded her.

'You told me that I would have to trust you, and I did. But perhaps I was a fool to believe your word?'

'I am completely trustworthy,' she said in a fierce voice. 'I will pretend to be your fiancée. But why would anyone believe that you—a handsome billionaire playboy who has dated some of the world's most beautiful women—have fallen in love with an ordinary, nothing special woman like me?' She worried her bottom lip with her teeth. 'What are we going to say if anyone asks how we met?'

He shrugged. 'We'll tell them the truth. We met at a dinner party and there was an immediate attraction between us. And, by the way, there is nothing ordinary about the way you look in that dress,' he growled, his eyes fixed on her pert derrière encased in tight blue velvet when she turned around to check her appearance in the mirror.

'Sexual attraction is not the same thing as falling in love,' she muttered.

She was nervous, Giannis realised with a jolt of surprise. If he had been asked to describe Ava he would have said that she was determined and strong—he guessed she'd have to be in her job working with crime victims. But the faint tremor of her mouth revealed an unexpected vulnerability that he could not simply dismiss. For their fake engagement to be successful, he realised that he would have to win her confidence and earn her trust.

He lifted his hand to brush a stray tendril of hair off her face. 'But mutual attraction is how all relationships begin, isn't it?' he said softly. 'You meet someone and *wham*. At first there is a purely physical response, an alchemy which sparks desire. From those roots love might begin to grow and flourish.' His jaw hardened as he thought of Caroline. 'But it is just as likely to wither and die.'

'Are you speaking from experience?' Ava's gentle tone pulled Giannis's mind from the past and he stiffened when he saw something that looked worryingly like compassion in her grey eyes. If she knew the truth about him he was sure that her sympathy would fade as quickly as Caroline had fallen out of love with him.

For a fraction of a second he felt a crazy impulse to admit to Ava that sometimes when he saw a child of about four years old he felt an ache in his heart for the child he might have had. If Caroline hadn't... *No.* He would not think of what she might have done. There was no point in torturing himself with the idea that Caroline had ended her inconvenient pregnancy after he had told her he'd been to prison. The possibility that his crass irresponsibility when he was nineteen had ultimately resulted in the loss of two lives was unbearable.

Ignoring Ava's question, he walked across the room and opened the door. 'We need to go,' he told her curtly, and to his relief she preceded him out of the suite without saying another word.

Ava applauded the models as they sashayed down the runway in the magnificent Sculpture Hall of the Musée du Louvre. The venue of the fashion show was breathtaking, and the clothes worn by the impossibly slender models ranged from exquisite to frankly extraordinary. The collection by the Greek designer Kris Antoniadis brought delighted murmurs from the audience, and the fashion journalist sitting in the front row next to Ava endorsed Giannis's prediction that Kris, as he was simply known, was the next big thing in the fashion world.

'Of course Kris could not have got this far in his career without a wealthy sponsor,' Diane Duberry, fashion editor of a women's magazine, explained to Ava. 'Giannis Gekas is regarded as a great philanthropist for his support of the Greek people during the country's recent problems. He set up a charity which awards bursaries to young entrepreneurs trying to establish businesses in Greece. But I don't know why I am telling you about Giannis when you must know everything about him.'

Diane looked at Giannis's hand resting possessively on Ava's knee, and then at the pink sapphire ring on Ava's finger, and speculation gleamed in her eyes. 'You succeeded where legions of other women have failed and tamed the tiger. Where did the two of you meet?'

'Um…we were seated next to each other at a dinner party.' Ava felt herself flush guiltily even though technically it was the truth.

'Lucky you.' Diane winked at her. 'Who needs a dessert from the sweet trolley when a gorgeous Greek hunk is on the menu?'

Ava was saved from having to think of a reply when the compère of the fashion show came onto the stage and announced that the Young Designer award had been won by the Greek designer, Kris Antoniadis. Kris then appeared on the runway accompanied by models wearing dresses from his bridal collection.

Giannis stood up and drew Ava to her feet. 'Showtime,' he murmured in her ear. 'Just smile and follow my lead.'

Without giving her a chance to protest, he slid his arm around her waist and whisked her up the steps and onto the runway, just as Kris was explaining to the audience how grateful he was to Giannis Gekas for supporting his career. There was more applause and brilliant flashes of light from camera flashes when Giannis stepped forwards, tugging Ava with him.

'I cannot think of a better place to announce my engagement to my beautiful fiancée than in Paris, the world's most romantic city,' he told the audience. With a flourish he lifted Ava's hand up to his mouth and pressed his lips to the pink sapphire heart on her finger.

He was a brilliant actor, she thought caustically.

Her skin burned where his lips had brushed and she wanted to snatch her hand back and denounce their engagement as a lie. The idea of deceiving people went against her personal moral code of honesty and integrity. But she must abide by her promise to be Giannis's fake fiancée because he had honoured his word and halted criminal proceedings against her brother.

And so she obediently showed her engagement ring to the press photographers and looked adoringly into Giannis's eyes for the cameras.

At the after-show party she remained by his side, smiling up at him as if she was besotted with him. For his part he kept his arm around her while they strolled around the room, stopping frequently so that he could introduce her to people he knew.

Waiters threaded through the crowded room carrying trays of canapés and drinks. Ava sipped champagne and felt the bubbles explode on her tongue. Her senses seemed sharper, and she was intensely aware of Giannis's hand resting on her waist and the brush of his thigh against hers. He was holding a flute of champagne but she noted that he never drank from it.

'Do you ever drink alcohol?' she asked him curiously. 'You didn't have any wine at the fundraising dinner, and I noticed that you are not drinking tonight.'

'How very perceptive of you, *glykiá mou.*' He spoke lightly, but Ava felt him stiffen. 'I avoid drinking alcohol because I like to keep a clear head.'

Something told her there was more to him being teetotal than he had admitted. But, before she could pursue the subject, he took her glass out of her fingers and gave it and his own glass to a passing waiter. Catching hold of her hand, he led her onto the dance floor and swept her into his arms.

Her head swam, not from the effects of the few sips of champagne she'd had, but from the intoxicating heat of Giannis's body pressed up against hers and the divine fragrance of his aftershave mixed with his own unique male scent. He was a good dancer and moved with a natural rhythm as he steered them around the dance floor, hip to hip, her breasts crushed against the hard wall of his chest. He slid one hand down to the base of her spine and spread his fingers over her bottom.

Her breath caught in her throat when she felt the solid ridge of his arousal through their clothes.

Ava closed her eyes and reminded herself that Giannis's attentiveness was an act to promote the deception that they were engaged. But there was nothing pretend about the sexual chemistry that sizzled between them. She had never been more aware of a man, or of her own femininity, in her life. Her traitorous mind pictured the big bed in the hotel suite they were sharing. Of course she had no intention of also sharing the bed with him, she assured herself. She had agreed to be his fake fiancée in public only.

But, to keep up the pretence, when the disco music changed to a romantic ballad and Giannis pulled her closer, she slid her hands up to his shoulders. And when he bent his head and brushed his mouth over hers, she parted her lips and kissed him with a fervour that drew a low groan from him.

'We have to get out of here,' he said hoarsely.

Her legs felt unsteady when he abruptly dropped his arms away from her. 'Come,' he growled, clamping his arm around her waist and practically lifting her off her feet as he hurried them out of the museum. The car was waiting for them and, once he had bundled her onto the back seat and closed the privacy screen between them and the driver, he lifted her onto his lap, thrust one hand into her hair and dragged her mouth beneath his.

His kiss was hot and urgent, a ravishment of her senses, as passion exploded between them. Ava sensed a wildness in Giannis that made her shake with need. She remembered Diane Duberry, the fashion journalist at the show, had congratulated her for having tamed the tiger. But the truth was that Giannis would never allow any woman to control him.

Her head was spinning when he finally tore his mouth from hers to allow them to drag oxygen into their lungs. His chest heaved, and when she placed her hand over his heart she felt its thudding, erratic beat. The car sped smoothly through the dark Paris streets and Ava succumbed to the master sorcerer's magic. Giannis trailed his lips down her throat and over one naked shoulder. She did not realise he had unzipped her dress until he tugged the bodice down and cradled her breasts in his big hands.

Her sensible head reminded her that it was shockingly decadent to be half naked in the back of a car and her wanton behaviour was not what she expected of herself. But her thoughts scattered when Giannis bent his head and his warm breath teased one nipple before he closed his mouth around the rosy peak and sucked, hard. Ava could not repress a moan of pleasure, and when he transferred his attention to her other nipple she ran her fingers through his silky dark hair and prayed that he would never stop what he was doing to her.

'I have no intention of stopping, *glykiá mou,*' he said in an amused voice. Colour flared on her face as she realised that she had spoken her plea aloud. But when he returned his mouth to her breasts she tipped her head back and gasped as lightning bolts of sensation shot down to her molten core between her thighs.

Giannis yanked up her long flared skirt and skimmed his hand over one stocking-clad leg, but the dress was designed to fit tightly over her hips and he could not go any further. He swore. 'I hope the other clothes you bought are more accessible.'

Ava shared his frustration but while she was wondering if she could possibly wriggle out of her dress the car came to a halt and Giannis shifted her off his knees. 'We've arrived at the hotel,' he said coolly, straightening his tie and running a hand through his hair. 'You had better tidy yourself up.'

His words catapulted her back to reality and she frantically pulled the top of her dress into place. 'Will you zip me up?'

He refastened her dress seconds before the driver opened the rear door. Giannis stepped onto the pavement and offered Ava his hand. She blinked in the glare of camera flashes going off around them. Photographers were gathered outside the entrance to the hotel and she felt mortified as she imagined how dishevelled she must look as she emerged from the car.

'Here, have this.' Giannis slipped off his jacket and draped it around her shoulders. Glancing down, Ava saw that she had failed to pull the top of her dress up high enough, and her breasts were in danger of spilling out. Hot-faced, she huddled into his jacket as he escorted her into the hotel.

They entered the lift and Ava's reflection in the

mirrored walls confirmed the worst. 'I look like a harlot,' she choked, running her finger over her swollen mouth. 'The photographers must have guessed we were making out on the back seat of the car. If the pictures they took just now appear in tomorrow's newspapers, everyone will think that we can't keep our hands off each other.'

Giannis was leaning against the lift wall, one ankle crossed over the other and his hands shoved into his trouser pockets. His bow tie was dangling loose and Ava flushed as she remembered how she had frenziedly torn off his tie and undone several of his shirt buttons. He looked calm and unruffled, the exact opposite of how she felt.

'The point of tonight was to advertise the news of our engagement to the press.' He dropped his gaze to where her breasts were partially exposed above the top of her dress. 'Thanks to your wardrobe malfunction we certainly got maximum exposure,' he drawled.

He sounded amused, and Ava felt sick as she realised what a fool she was. 'I suppose you knew that the paparazzi would be at our hotel,' she said stiffly. 'Is that why you made love to me in the car?'

'Actually I didn't know. But I should have guessed that they would find out which hotel we are staying at.' His eyes narrowed on her flushed face. 'I'm sorry if the photographers upset you.'

'I'm sorry that I ever agreed to be your fake fiancée.' The lift stopped at the top floor and she preceded Giannis along the corridor, despising herself for her fierce awareness of him even now, after he had humiliated her.

'But you are not sorry that your brother has avoided a prison sentence,' he said drily as he opened the door of their suite and ushered her inside. He caught hold of her arm and spun her round to face him. 'I kissed you because you have driven me insane all evening and I couldn't help myself. I have never wanted any woman as badly as I want you.'

With an effort Ava resisted the lure of his husky, accented voice that almost fooled her into believing he meant it. 'You can stop acting now that there is no audience to deceive. We're alone, in case you hadn't noticed.'

His dark eyes gleamed. 'I am very aware of that fact, *glykiá mou.*'

CHAPTER SIX

SOMETHING IN GIANNIS'S voice sent a shiver of apprehension—if she was honest it was *anticipation*—across Ava's skin. She did not fear him. It was her inability to resist his charisma that made her fearful, she admitted. She broke free from him and marched into the suite's only bedroom, intending to lock herself in. But he was right behind her and his soft laughter followed her as she fled into the en suite bathroom.

Splashing cold water onto her face cooled her heated skin, and she removed the silver clips that were hanging from her tangled hair. But she could not disguise her reddened mouth or the hectic glitter in her eyes. She felt undone, out of control, and it scared the hell out of her. If she was going to survive the next month pretending to be Giannis's fiancée, she would have to make it clear that she would not allow him to manipulate her.

Taking a deep breath, she returned to the bedroom but the sight of him in bed, leaning against the pillows, made her want to retreat back to the bathroom. His arms were folded behind his head and his chest was bare. Her heart lurched at the thought that he might be naked beneath the sheet that was draped dangerously low over his hips. She was fascinated by the fuzz of black hairs that arrowed over his flat stomach and disappeared beneath the sheet. Her eyes were drawn to the obvious bulge of his arousal beneath the fine cotton.

'Feel free to stare,' he drawled.

Blushing hotly, she jerked her eyes back to his face and his expression of arrogant amusement infuriated her. 'When you said we would discuss the sleeping arrangements, I assumed that *you* would spend the night on the sofa,' she snapped.

'The replica eighteenth-century chaise longue looks beautiful but it is extremely uncomfortable.' He picked up the big bolster cushions that he'd piled up behind his shoulders and laid them down the centre of the bed. 'It's a big bed and I won't encroach on your half—unless you invite me to.' He grinned at her outraged expression.

'I must say that I am encouraged by your choice of nightwear.'

It was only then that she noticed the confection of black silk and lace arranged on the pillow next to Giannis. She remembered the personal shopper had picked out several items of sexy lingerie, but Ava hadn't explained that her engagement to Giannis was fake and she would not need them. She guessed that the hotel chambermaid who had unpacked her clothes must have laid out the nightgown. Although gown was an exaggeration, she thought darkly as she snatched the tiny garment off the pillow and stalked into the dressing room.

The clothes she had brought with her from London were still in her suitcase. She found her grey flannel pyjamas and changed into them before she hung the velvet evening dress in the wardrobe. That was the last time she would dare to wear a strapless dress, she vowed, wincing as she remembered how her breasts had almost been exposed to the photographers until Giannis had covered her with his jacket.

She had been grateful for his protective gesture. And he'd insisted that he had not expected the paparazzi to be outside the hotel. Ava bit her lip. Perhaps she was a fool but she believed him. After all, he had kept his side of their deal and halted the criminal case against her brother.

She grimaced as she looked at herself in the mirror. Her passion-killer pyjamas had been designed for comfort and when Giannis saw them she was sure he would have no trouble keeping to his side of the bed. Which was what she wanted—wasn't it?

She pictured him the previous night at the hotel in London, his sleek, honed body poised above her before he'd slowly lowered himself onto her as he'd entered her with one hard thrust. Why not enjoy what he was offering for the next month? whispered a voice of temptation. Sex without strings and no possibility of her getting hurt because—unlike in a normal relationship—she had no expectations that a brief affair with Giannis might lead to something more meaningful. Their engagement was a deception but he had been totally honest with her. Maybe it was time to be honest with herself and admit that she wanted him.

Before she could chicken out, she pulled off her pyjamas and slipped on the black negligee. It was practically see-through, dotted with a few strategically placed lace flowers, and it was the sexiest item of clothing she had ever worn. She walked into the bedroom and the feral sound Giannis made as he stared at her tugged deep in her pelvis.

'I hope you realise that the likelihood of me remaining on my side of the bolsters is zero. You look incredible, *omorfiá mou.*'

There was no doubt that his appreciation was genuine. His arousal was unmissable, jutting beneath the sheet, but more surprising was the flush of dark colour on his cheekbones. Ava's self-confidence rose with every step she took across the room towards him. The light from the bedside lamp sparked off the pink sapphire on her finger as she looked down at the engagement ring, watching its iridescent gleam.

'You can keep the ring after our engagement ends,' Giannis told her.

'No!' She shook her head. 'I am giving you a month of my life but you haven't bought me. I will wear your ring and pretend to be your fiancée in public. But when we are alone—' she pulled off the ring and put it down on the bedside table '—whatever I do, however I behave, is my choice.'

His eyes narrowed as she untied the ribbon at the front of her negligée so that the two sides fell open, exposing her firm breasts and betrayingly hard nipples. 'And what do you choose to do?' he said thickly.

'This.' She whipped the sheet away to reveal his naked, aroused body and climbed on top of him so that she was straddling his hips. 'And this,' she murmured as she leaned forwards and covered his mouth with hers.

For a heart-stopping second he did not respond and she wondered if she had misunderstood, that he didn't want her. But then his arms came around her like iron bands and held her so tightly that she could not escape. He opened his mouth to the fierce demands of her kiss and kissed her back with a barely leashed hunger that made her heart race.

'So you want to take charge, do you?' he murmured as she traced her lips over the prickly black stubble on his jaw. His indulgent tone set an alarm bell off in her head. Clearly, Giannis believed that he was the one in control, and he was simply allowing her to take the dominant role while it suited him.

'You had better believe it,' she told him sweetly. Still astride him, she sat upright and ran her hands over his chest. Her smile was pure innocence as she bent her head and closed her mouth around one male nipple, scraping her teeth over the hard nub.

'Theos...' His body jerked beneath her and he swore when she moved her mouth across to his other nipple and bit him, hard. 'You little vixen.' He tried to grab her hair but she shook it back over her shoulders and moved down his body, pressing hot kisses over his stomach and following the line of dark hairs down lower. Very lightly, she ran her fingertips up and down his shaft and he tensed.

'Not this time, angel,' he muttered. 'I want you too badly.'

She flicked her tongue along the swollen length of him and gave a husky laugh of feminine triumph when he groaned. 'I'm in charge and don't you forget it,' Ava told him. 'I'm not your puppet, so don't think you can control me.'

'You are so fierce.' He laughed but there was something in his voice that sounded like respect. And when he moved suddenly and rolled her beneath him he stared into her eyes for what seemed like eternity, as if he wanted to read her mind. 'You fascinate me. No other woman has done that before,' he admitted.

He slipped his hand between her legs and discovered that she was as turned-on as he was. Keeping his eyes locked with hers, he eased his fingers inside her until she moaned. 'Who is in charge now, angel?' he teased softly. But Ava no longer cared if she won or lost the power struggle. She reached down between their bodies and curled her hand around him, making him groan. Maybe they were both winners, she thought. 'You are ready for me, Ava *mou*.' He swiftly donned a condom before he moved over her and entered her with a slow, deep thrust that delighted her body and touched her soul. With a flash of insight that shook her, she acknowledged that she would always be ready for him. She guessed that Giannis had made a slip of his tongue when he'd called her *my* Ava.

They flew to Greece the next day, and in the evening attended a party held at reputedly Athens' most chic rooftop bar where the cosmopolitan clientele included several international celebrities. The paparazzi swarmed in the street outside the venue and there was a flurry of flashlights as Giannis Gekas and his English fiancée posed for the cameras.

From the rooftop bar the views of the sunset over the city were amazing. But Giannis only had eyes for Ava. She looked stunning in a scarlet cocktail dress that showed off her gorgeous curves, and he was impatient for the party to finish so that he could take her back to his penthouse apartment and reacquaint himself with her delectable body. Their sexual chemistry was hotter than anything he'd experienced with his previous mistresses.

He smiled to himself as he imagined Ava's reaction if he was ever foolish enough to refer to her as his mistress. No doubt she would reply with a scathing comment designed to put him in his place. He enjoyed her fiery nature, and never more so than when they had sex and she became a wildcat with sharp claws. He bore the marks from where she had raked her fingernails down his back when they'd reached a climax together last night. Afterwards, she had reminded him of a contented kitten, warm and soft as she snuggled up to him and flicked her tongue over her lips like a satisfied cat after drinking a bowl of cream.

Giannis had intended to ease his arm from beneath her and move her across to the other side of the bed. But he'd felt reluctant to disturb her and he must have fallen asleep because when he'd next opened his eyes his head had been pillowed on Ava's breasts, and he'd been so aroused that he ached. He had kissed her awake and ignored her protests that had quickly become moans of pleasure when he'd nudged her legs apart with his shoulders and pressed his mouth against her feminine core to feast on her sweetness.

With an effort Giannis dragged his mind from his erotic memories when he realised that he had not been listening to the conversation going on

around him. The group of guests he was standing with were looking at him, clearly waiting for
him to say something. He glanced at Ava for help.

'I was just explaining that we haven't set a date
for our wedding yet,' she said drily. 'We are not
in a rush.'

'On the contrary, *agápi mou*, I am impatient
to make you my wife as soon as possible.' He
slipped his arm around her waist and smiled
with his customary effortless charm at the other
guests. 'I hope you will forgive me for selfishly
wanting to have my beautiful bride-to-be to myself,' he murmured before he led Ava away.

'Why did you say that we will get married
soon?' she demanded while he escorted her out
of the crowded bar. Once they were outside and
walking to where he had parked the car, she
pulled away from him. 'There was no need to
overdo the devoted fiancé act. All that staring
into my eyes as if I was the only woman in the
world was unnecessary.'

He grinned at her uptight expression. 'I need
to convince Stefanos Markou that our engagement is genuine and I am serious about settling
down. The woman in the blue dress who we were

talking to is a journalist with a popular gossip magazine. No doubt the next edition will include several pages devoted to discussing our imminent wedding.'

Ava bit her lip. 'More deception,' she muttered. 'One lie always leads to another. I realise it's just a game to you, but when our fake engagement ends I will face public humiliation as the woman who nearly married Giannis Gekas.'

'It will cost my company in the region of one hundred million pounds to buy Markou's fleet of ships. An investment of that size is hardly a game,' Giannis told her curtly. 'Once I've secured the deal with Stefanos I will give a press statement explaining that you broke off our engagement because you fell out of love with me.'

It wouldn't be the first time it had happened, he brooded. His jaw clenched as he thought of Caroline. At least he'd discovered before he'd made an utter fool of himself that Caroline had been more in love with his money than with him.

Giannis sensed that Ava sent him a few curious glances during the journey back to his apartment block. He parked in the underground car park and when they rode the lift up to the top floor he could not take his eyes off her. She was a temptress in her scarlet dress and vertiginous heels and he had been in a state of semi-arousal all evening as he'd imagined her slender legs wrapped around his back.

His desire for her showed no sign of lessening—yet. But he had no doubt that it would fade and he'd grow bored of her. His mistresses never held his interest for long. Perhaps if he sought some sort of counselling, a psychologist would suggest that his guilt over his father's death was the reason he avoided close relationships. But Giannis had no intention of allowing anyone access to his soul.

After ushering Ava into the penthouse, he crossed the huge open-plan living room and opened the doors leading to his private roof garden. 'Would you like a drink?' he asked her.

'Just fruit juice, please.'

He headed for the kitchen, and returned to find her out on the terrace, standing by the pool. The water appeared black beneath the night sky and reflected the silver stars. 'Is that how you keep in such great physical shape?' she murmured, indicating the pool.

His heart lurched at her compliment. *Theos*,

she made him feel like a teenager with all the uncertainty and confusion brought on by surging hormones, he acknowledged with savage self-derision. 'I complete fifty lengths every morning. But I prefer to swim in the sea when I am at my house on Spetses.'

Ava sipped her fruit juice and glanced at the bottle of beer in his hand. 'You don't need to keep a clear head tonight?' She obviously remembered the reason he had given her for why he hadn't drunk champagne at the fashion show in Paris.

'It's non-alcoholic beer,' he admitted.

'Why are you afraid of not being in control?'

Rattled by her perception, his eyes narrowed. 'I'll ask you the same question.'

'Touché.' She smiled ruefully. 'I don't like surprises.'

'Not even nice ones?'

'I've never had a nice surprise.' She looked at the city skyline. 'The Acropolis looks wonderful lit up at night. Have you always lived in Athens?'

Giannis could not understand why he felt frustrated by her determination to turn the conversation away from herself. In his experience women were only too happy to talk about themselves, but

Ava, he was beginning to realise, was not like any other woman.

He shrugged. 'I grew up just along the coast at Faliron and I am proud to call myself an Athenian.'

'Perhaps I could do some sightseeing while you are at work? I know you have arranged for us to attend various social functions in the evenings so that we are seen together, but you have a business to run during the day.'

'I'll show you around the city. One of the perks of owning my own company is that I can delegate.' As Giannis spoke he wondered what the hell had got into him. He'd never delegated in his life and his work schedule was by his own admittance brutal. Driven by his need to succeed, he regularly worked fourteen-hour days and he couldn't remember the last time he'd spent more than a couple of hours away from his computer or phone.

The more time he spent with Ava, the quicker his inexplicable fascination with her would lead to familiarity and, by definition, boredom, he assured himself. He put down his drink and walked towards her, noting with satisfaction how her eyes widened and her tongue flicked over her lips, issuing an unconscious invitation that he had every intention of accepting.

'There is an even better view of the Acropolis from the bedroom,' he said softly.

She hesitated for a few seconds and when she put her hand in his and let him lead her through the apartment to the master suite he was aware of the hard thud of his heart beneath his ribs. He stood behind her and turned her to face the floor-to-ceiling windows which overlooked Greece's most iconic citadel, situated atop a vast outcrop of rock. 'There.'

'It's so beautiful,' she said in an awed voice. 'What an incredible view. You can just lie in bed and stare at a piece of ancient history.'

'Mmm...' He nuzzled her neck and slid his arms around her to test the weight of her breasts in his hands. 'I can think of rather more energetic things I'd like to do in bed, *agápi mou*.'

She pulled the pink sapphire ring from her finger and dropped it onto the bedside table. 'I'm not your love now that we are alone,' she reminded him.

'But you are my lover.' He unzipped her dress

and when it fell to the floor she stepped out of it before she turned and wound her arms around his neck.

'Yes,' she whispered against his mouth. 'For one month I will be your lover.'

As he scooped her up and laid her down on the bed, Giannis knew he should be relieved that Ava understood the rules. But perversely he felt irritated. Perhaps it was because her words had sounded like a challenge that provoked him to murmur, 'You might want our affair to last longer than a month.'

'I won't.' She watched him undress and reached behind her shoulders to unclip her bra, letting it fall away from her breasts. 'But you might fall in love with me.'

'Impossible,' he promised her. 'I already told you I don't have a heart.' He pushed her back against the mattress and covered her body with his, watching her eyes widen when he pushed between her thighs.

'However, I do have this, *glykiá mou*,' he murmured before he possessed her with one fierce thrust followed by another and another, taking them higher until they arrived at the pinnacle and tumbled over the edge together.

Afterwards, he shifted across the bed and tucked his hands behind his head, determined to emphasise to Ava that sex was all he was prepared to offer. Too many people mistook lust for love, Giannis brooded. He'd made that mistake himself once, when he had fallen for Caroline. But he had learned his lesson and moved on.

After busy, bustling Athens, Ava discovered that life on the beautiful island of Spetses moved at a much slower pace. Thankfully.

She frowned as the thought slipped into her mind. She should be glad that she was halfway through her fake engagement to Giannis. So why did she wish that time would slow down?

She hadn't expected to *like* him, she thought ruefully. They had stayed at his apartment in the city for two weeks, ostensibly so that they could be seen together at high society events. The shock news that Greece's most eligible bachelor had chosen a bride had sparked fevered media interest, leading Ava to remark drily that Stefanos Markou could not have missed reports about their romance, unless he had been visiting remote indigenous tribes in the Amazon rainforest.

But for the most part they'd managed to evade the paparazzi when Giannis had kept his word and showed her Athens. Not just the tourist attractions, although of course they did visit the Acropolis and the nearby Acropolis Museum, as well as the Byzantine Museum.

They climbed the steep winding path to the top of Lycabettus Hill and sat at the top to watch the sunset over the city. He took her to the pretty neighbourhood of Plaka and they strolled hand in hand along the narrow streets lined with pastel-coloured houses where cerise-pink bougainvillea tumbled from window boxes. And he took her to dinner at little *tavernas* tucked away in side streets off the tourist track, where they ate authentic Greek food and Giannis entertained her with stories of the places he had visited around the world and the people he had met. He was an interesting and amusing companion and Ava found herself falling ever deeper under his spell.

Spetses was a twenty-minute helicopter flight from Athens, although most people did not have a helipad in their garden like Giannis, and visitors to the island made use of the red and white water taxis. The island was picturesque, with white-washed houses and cobbled streets around the harbour. Cars were banned in the town centre and the sight of horse-drawn carriages rattling along gave the impression that Spetses belonged to a bygone era. That feeling was reflected in Villa Delphine, Giannis's stunning neo-classical mansion, with its exquisite arches and gracious colonnades. The exterior walls were painted pale yellow, and green shutters at the windows gave the house an elegant yet homely charm.

Ava was relieved that Villa Delphine looked nothing like the extravagant but tasteless house in Cyprus where she had lived for part of her childhood, until her father had been arrested and she had discovered the truth about him. Every happy memory from the first seventeen years of her life now seemed grubby, contaminated by her father's criminality. But at least Sam had been given another chance, and she was hopeful that he would keep out of trouble from now on.

She returned her phone to her bag and watched Giannis walk up the beach towards her. He had been swimming in the sea and water droplets glistened on his olive-gold skin and black chest hairs. His swim-shorts sat low on his hips and Ava's mouth ran dry as she studied his impressive six-pack. Heat flared inside her when he hunkered down in front of her and dropped a tantalisingly brief kiss on her mouth.

'Did you get hold of your brother?'

'I've just finished speaking to him. He is helping out on my aunt and uncle's farm in Cumbria and he says it hasn't stopped raining since he arrived. I didn't tell him that it's twenty-five degrees in Greece. I'm just relieved he's away from the East End and its association with—' She broke off abruptly.

'Association with what?'

'Oh…historically the area of London around Whitechapel was well-known for being a rough place,' she prevaricated. Desperate to avoid the questions that she sensed Giannis wanted to ask, she placed her hands on either side of his face and pulled his mouth down to hers. He allowed her to control the kiss and, as always, passion swiftly flared. But when Ava tried to tug him down beside her, he lifted his lips from hers with an ease that caused her heart to give a twinge.

'Unfortunately there is not time for you to distract me with sex,' he said in a dry tone that made her blush guiltily. 'My mother is joining us for lunch.'

She packed her sun cream and the novel she had been reading into her bag and stood up. 'I thought your mother was in New York?' Giannis had told her that his mother, Filia, and his younger sister, Irini, shared the house next door to Villa Delphine. Irini was an art historian, currently working at a museum in Florence.

'Mitera has flown back from the US early to meet you,' he said as he followed her along the path which led from the private beach up to the house.

Ava halted and swung round to look at him. 'You *have* explained to your mother that I am not really your fiancée—haven't you? We can't lie to her,' she muttered when he remained silent. 'It's not fair. She might be excited that you are going to get married and perhaps give her grandchildren.'

'My mother is an inveterate gossip,' he said curtly. 'If I told her the truth about us, she would be on the phone within minutes to tell a friend, who would tell another friend, and the story that you are my fake fiancée would be leaked to the press within hours.'

He lifted his hand and traced his finger over her lips. 'Don't pout, *glykiá mou,* or it will look as though we have had a lover's tiff,' he teased. His earlier curtness had been replaced by his potent charm and he pulled her into his arms and kissed her until she melted against him. But had his kiss been to distract her? Ava asked herself as she ran upstairs to shower and change out of her bikini before his mother arrived.

When she walked into the salon some half an hour later, wearing an elegant pale blue shift dress from a Paris design house, she heard voices from the terrace speaking in Greek. The woman dressed entirely in black was evidently Giannis's mother. Ava took a deep breath and was about to step outside and introduce herself, but she hesitated as Filia Gekas's voice drifted through the open French doors.

'Have you been honest with this woman who you have decided to marry, Giannis? Have you told Ava *everything* about you?'

CHAPTER SEVEN

SECRETS AND LIES. They lurked in every corner of
the dining room, taunting Ava while she forced
herself to eat her lunch and attempted to make
conversation with Giannis's mother. It was an
uphill task, for Filia was a discontented woman
whose only pleasure in life, it seemed, was criti-
cising her son.

Ava had no idea what the other woman had
meant, or what Giannis was supposed to have told
her. Perhaps it was something that would only
be relevant if he truly intended to marry her—
which, of course, he did not. She was trapped in
a deception that would only end once he had secured his business deal with Stefanos Markou.

She glanced at him across the table and found
he was watching her broodingly as if he was trying to fathom her out. Ava guiltily acknowledged
that she had her own secrets. But why should she
tell Giannis that her father was serving a prison

sentence for armed robbery? In a few weeks' time there might be a brief media frenzy when it was announced that the engagement between Greece's golden boy and his English fiancée was over, but the paparazzi would quickly forget about her, as, no doubt, would Giannis.

She pulled her mind back to the conversation between Giannis and his mother. 'I don't know why you paid a fortune for a holiday to the Maldives,' Filia said sharply. 'You know I dislike long-haul flights.'

'It is hardly any longer than the flight time to New York,' Giannis pointed out mildly. 'I bid for the trip at a charity auction because I hoped you would enjoy a spa break in an exotic location.'

His mother sniffed and turned to Ava. 'I was surprised when Giannis told me that the two of you are engaged to be married. He has never mentioned you before.'

Ava felt heat spread over her cheeks. 'It was a whirlwind courtship,' she murmured.

Filia gave her a speculative look. 'My son is a very wealthy man. Can I ask why you agreed to marry him?'

'Mitera!' Giannis frowned at his mother but she was unabashed.

'It is a reasonable question to ask.' She turned her sharp black eyes back to Ava. 'Well?'

Ava said the only thing she could say. 'I...love him.' Her voice sounded strangely husky and she did not dare look across the table at Giannis. One lie always led to another lie, she thought bleakly. But she must have sounded convincing because his mother gave her a searching look and then nodded.

'Good,' Filia said. 'Love and trust are vital to a successful marriage.'

Ava gave a quiet sigh of relief when Giannis came to her rescue and asked his mother about her trip to New York. Evidently it had been a disaster, for which she blamed him. The five-star hotel where he had arranged for her to stay had, according to Filia, been atrocious. 'Rude staff, and the bed had a lumpy mattress.'

'I am sorry you were disappointed,' he told his mother with commendable patience. Ava glanced at him, telling herself that if he looked amused by her lie about being in love with him she would empty the water jug over his head, and never mind what conclusion his mother might draw.

He met her gaze across the table and the gleam in his dark eyes made her tremble as a shocking realisation dawned on her. It couldn't be true, she assured herself frantically. But the erratic thud of her heart betrayed her. Had she managed to sound convincing to his mother because she was actually falling in love with Giannis?

The helicopter swooped low over the sea and Ava felt her stomach drop. She did not realise that her swift intake of breath had been audible, but Giannis looked up from his laptop. He was seated opposite her in the helicopter's luxurious cabin and leaned forwards to take her hand in his warm grasp.

'Don't worry,' he said reassuringly. 'Vasilis is a good pilot. We will be landing in a few minutes. Stefanos's private island, Gaia, is below us now.'

She nodded and turned her head to look out of the window at the pine tree covered island, edged by golden beaches and set in an azure sea. It was easier to let Giannis think she was nervous of flying in the helicopter. She certainly could not tell him of her terrifying suspicion, which might explain the nauseous feeling she'd experienced for the past few days.

She'd put her queasiness down to some prawns she'd eaten at a restaurant a few evenings before. But while she had packed her suitcase this morning she'd found the packet of tampons she had brought to Spetses with her in the expectation that she would need them.

Her period was only a couple of days late, Ava tried to reassure herself. But a doom-laden voice in her head reminded her that she was never late. Her mind argued that Giannis had used a condom every time they'd had sex. Even when he'd followed her into the shower cubicle and stood behind her so that she had felt his arousal press against her bottom, he had been prepared. She could not be pregnant. Probably her churning stomach and uncomfortably sensitive breasts were signs that her period was about to start.

She sighed. Her mood swings were another indication that she was worrying unnecessarily. When the helicopter had taken off from Spetses she had been thankful that her oversized sunglasses hid her tears. Ava knew she was unlikely to ever return to the island. Giannis had said that they would go to his apartment in Athens after meeting Stefanos Markou and he would arrange for his private jet to fly her back to London.

Apart from the awkward lunch with Giannis's mother, the past two weeks that they had spent at Villa Delphine had been like a wonderful dream where each perfect day rolled into the next, and every night Giannis had made love to her and their wildfire passion blazed out of control. But since Ava had woken early that morning, feeling horribly sick, and crept silently into the bathroom so as not to wake him, her insides had been knotted with dread.

The helicopter landed and Giannis climbed out and offered Ava his hand to assist her down the steps. 'You are still pale,' he said, frowning as he studied her.

'I'm nervous,' she admitted. 'Your hope of buying Markou Shipping is the reason we have spent the last month pretending to be engaged, but what if Stefanos guesses that I am your fake fiancée?'

'Why should he? People tend to believe what they see. That is why conmen are sometimes able to persuade elderly ladies to hand over their life savings.'

Her father had been the cleverest conman of all, Ava thought bitterly. He had fooled his own wife and children with his affable charm. Suddenly she could not wait for the deception she was playing with Giannis to be over. But then her relationship with him would finish—unless her suspicion, and a pregnancy test when she had a chance to buy one, proved positive. The knot of dread in her stomach tightened.

As they walked across the lawn towards a sprawling villa, Giannis slid his arm around her waist and urged her forwards to meet the grey-haired man waiting for them on the terrace. Stefanos Markou shook Giannis's hand before he turned to Ava.

'I admit I was surprised when Giannis announced his decision to marry. But now that I have met you, Ava, I understand why he is in a hurry to make you his wife.' Stefanos smiled. 'My wife read in a magazine that you are planning a Christmas wedding.'

'Christmas is more than two months away and I don't think I can wait that long,' Giannis murmured. Ava's heart gave a familiar flip when he looked down at her with a tender expression in his eyes that her common sense told her was not real. He was a brilliant actor, she reminded herself, but her mouth curved of its own accord into an unconsciously wistful smile.

Stefanos laughed. 'The other bidders who want to buy Markou Shipping are already here. So, let us get down to business, Giannis, while Ava talks of wedding dresses with my wife and daughters.'

He led them into the villa and introduced Ava to his wife, Maria, and his three daughters, who between them had seven children of their own— all girls. Stefanos sighed. 'It seems that I am not destined to have a grandson to pass Markou Shipping on to. Unfortunately my only nephew is a hopeless businessman and so I made the decision to sell the company and retire.'

The small island of Gaia was a picturesque paradise. Stefanos's wife and daughters were friendly and welcoming, but Ava felt a fraud for having to pretend to be excited about her supposed forthcoming wedding. The little grandchildren were a delight, but when she held the youngest baby of just six weeks old she found herself imagining what it would be like to cradle her own baby in her arms. She tried to quell her sense of panic, and inexplicably she felt an ache in her heart as she pictured a baby with Giannis's dark hair and eyes.

Eventually she made the excuse of a headache and slipped away to walk on the beach. When she turned back towards the villa, she saw Giannis striding along the sand to meet her.

'Well?' she asked him anxiously.

A wide grin spread across his face and he looked heartbreakingly handsome. He put his hands on either side of her waist and swung her round in the air. 'It's done,' he told her in a triumphant voice. 'I persuaded Stefanos to sell his company to me. I had to increase my financial offer, but the main reason he agreed was because he is convinced that when you and I marry I will settle down to family life and embrace the values that Stefanos believes are important. Work can start immediately to refit and upgrade the Markou fleet of ships to turn them into luxury cruisers.'

'And I can go home,' Ava said quietly.

Giannis set her back on her feet, but he kept

his arms around her and a faint frown creased between his brows. 'It will take a few days for the paperwork to be finalised and signed. Stefanos is giving a party tonight for all the Markou Shipping employees and he will announce that I am buying the company. It will be an opportunity for me to reassure the workforce that they will continue to be employed by TGE. Stefanos has invited us to spend the night on Gaia and the helicopter will pick us up and take us to Athens in the morning.'

The breeze blew Ava's long hair across her face and Giannis caught the golden strands in his hand and tucked them behind her ear. His dark eyes gleamed with something indefinable that nevertheless made her heart beat too fast. 'I cannot see a reason why you should rush back to England, can you, *glykiá mou*?' he murmured.

She *should* remind him that they had made a deal, and now that she had kept her side of it there was no reason for her to stay in Greece with him. Was he saying that he did not want her to leave? What would he say if she *was* pregnant? Would he still want her and their child? Her thoughts swirled around inside her head. She caught her lower lip between her teeth, and the feral growl he made evoked a wild heat inside her so that when he claimed her mouth and kissed her as if he could never have enough of her she gave up fighting herself and simply melted in his fire.

That evening, the guests were ferried from the mainland to Gaia by boat. As the sun set, the usually peaceful island was packed with several hundred partygoers enjoying Stefanos's generous hospitality. A bar and barbecue had been set up on the beach and a famous DJ had flown in from New York to take charge of the music.

Ava had convinced herself that her niggling stomach ache was a sign that her period was about to start, and with Giannis in an upbeat mood she decided to have fun at the party and live for the moment. He was flatteringly attentive and hardly left her side all evening. She told herself that he was continuing to act the role of adoring fiancé until his business deal with Stefanos had been signed. But the way he held her close while they danced and threaded his fingers through her hair was utterly beguiling.

'Don't go away,' he murmured midway through

the evening. He claimed her mouth in a lingering kiss, as if he was reluctant to leave her, before he went to join Stefanos on the stage at one end of the ballroom. There was loud applause from Markou Shipping's employees when Giannis explained that everyone would keep their jobs and be offered training opportunities at TGE.

'Gullible idiots.' A voice close to Ava sounded cynical. She looked over at the man who had spoken and he caught her curious glance. 'You don't believe that Gekas will keep his word, do you? He has promised to retain Markou's workforce simply to persuade the old fool to sell the company to him. But Gekas isn't interested in saving Greek jobs. All he wants is the ships and in a few months he will sack the workers.'

The man laughed at Ava's startled expression. 'Giannis Gekas fools everyone with his charming manner, including you, it seems. You obviously haven't heard the rumours that Mr Nice Guy has a nasty side.'

It must have been the cool breeze drifting in through the window that made the hairs on the back of Ava's neck stand on end. 'What do you mean?'

'Rumours have circulated for some time that Gekas has links with an organised crime syndicate and that he uses TGE to hide his money-laundering activities.'

'If there was any substance to those rumours, surely the authorities would have investigated Giannis?' Ava said sharply. 'And Stefanos would not have sold Markou Shipping to someone he suspected of being a criminal.'

'It's like I said. Old Markou is a fool who has been taken in by Gekas's apparent saintliness. Setting up a charity to help young Greeks establish new businesses was a clever move.' The man shrugged. 'As for the police, it's likely that some of them are being bribed, or they are too scared of what will happen to them and their families if they start to investigate Gekas's business methods. The Greek mafia are not a bunch of Boy Scouts; they are ruthless mobsters.'

Ava's mouth was dry and she could feel her heart hammering beneath her ribs. 'Do you have any proof to back up your allegations, Mr...?' She paused, hoping the man would introduce himself.

'Of course nothing can be proved. Gekas is too clever for that. And I'm not telling you my name because I don't want to end up at the bottom of the sea with a bullet through my brain.'

Nothing the man had said could be true, Ava tried to reassure herself. But what did she *actually* know about Giannis? whispered a voice in her head. She stared at the man. 'You have no right to make such awful, unsubstantiated accusations against Giannis. Why should I believe you?'

'How do you think that Gekas became a billionaire by his mid-thirties? The luxury cruise market was badly hit by the economic meltdown in Greece and other parts of Europe, yet TGE makes huge profits.'

The man laughed unpleasantly. 'Racketeering is a more likely source of Gekas's fortune. Some years ago a journalist tried to investigate him but your fiancé has powerful friends in high places and I assume the journalist was bribed to keep his nose out of Gekas's private life.'

With another sneering laugh the man walked away and disappeared from Ava's view in the crowded ballroom. The dancing had started again and she saw Giannis walk down the steps at the side of the stage. None of what she had heard

about him could be true. *Could it?* He had cap-
tivated her with his legendary charm but was
she, along with all the other people at the party,
including Stefanos Markou, a gullible fool who
had been taken in by Giannis's charisma?

She had seen it happen before. Everyone who
had met her father had fallen for his cockney
good humour, but at his trial Terry McKay had
been exposed as a ruthless gangland boss who
had used bribery and intimidation to evade the
law. She had no proof that the accusations made
by a stranger against Giannis were true, Ava reminded herself.

A memory pushed into her mind, of the morning in the hotel in London after they had spent
the night together. He had opened his briefcase
and she'd been shocked to see that it contained
piles of bank notes. At the time she had thought
it odd that he carried so much cash around but
she'd been focused on trying to persuade Giannis
to drop the charges against her brother. However,
the incident had reminded her of how her father
had kept large quantities of bank notes hidden in
odd places in the house in Cyprus.

Then there was what she had overheard Giannis's mother say. *'Have you told Ava everything about you?'* What had Filia meant? What secret about himself had Giannis kept from her? And why did his mother disapprove of her only son?

The throbbing music was pounding in Ava's ears and she felt hot and then cold, and horribly sick. The flashing disco ball hanging from the ceiling was spinning round and round, making her dizzy, and she was afraid she was going to faint.

'Ava.' Suddenly Giannis was standing in front of her, his chiselled features softening as he studied her. 'What's the matter, *glykiá mou*?'

His voice was husky with concern, and Ava despised herself for wishing that she could ignore the rumours she had heard about him. But why would the party guest have made up lies about Giannis?

'Migraine,' she muttered. 'I get them occasionally and the bright disco lights are making it worse. If you don't mind I'd like to go to bed and hopefully sleep it off.'

'I'll take you back to our room and stay with you,' he said instantly.

'No, you should remain at the party and cele-
brate winning your business deal.'

Giannis swore softly. 'The deal isn't important.'

'How can you say that, when it was the reason
we have pretended to be engaged?'

His smile made Ava's heart skip a beat, despite
everything she had heard about him. 'Our relationship may have started out as a pretence but
I think we both realise that the spark between
us shows no sign of fading,' he murmured. He
frowned when she swayed on her feet. 'But we
won't discuss it now. You need to take some painkillers.'

She needed to be alone with her chaotic
thoughts, and she was relieved when she saw Stefanos beckon to Giannis from across the room.
'I think you are needed. I'll be fine,' she assured
him, and hurried out of the ballroom before he
could argue.

Later that night, when Giannis quietly entered the bedroom and slid into bed beside her,
Ava squeezed her eyes shut and pretended to be
asleep. And the next morning when she rushed
to the bathroom to be sick he was sympathetic,
believing that a migraine was the cause of her

nausea. His tender concern during the helicopter flight back to Athens added to her confusion. It seemed impossible that he could be involved with the criminal underworld.

Her father had given the appearance of being a loving family man and she had adored him, Ava remembered bleakly. She had been devastated when details of Terry McKay's violent crimes were revealed during his trial. For seventeen years her father had hidden his secret life from her. In the one month that she and Giannis had pretended to be engaged she'd learned virtually nothing about him, except that he was a good actor.

A car was waiting to drive them from Athens airport to the city centre. On the way, she persuaded Giannis to drop her off at a pharmacy, making the excuse that she needed to buy some stronger painkillers for her headache.

'I wish I didn't need to go to the office but I have an important meeting.' He pressed his lips to her forehead. 'Take the migraine tablets and go to bed,' he bade her gently.

One lie always led to more lies, Ava thought miserably when she bought a pregnancy test and hurried back to the penthouse apartment. Her hands shook as she followed the instructions on the test. She still clung to the hope that her late period and bouts of sickness were symptoms of a stomach upset.

The minutes went by agonisingly slowly while she paced around the bathroom. Finally it was time to check the result. Taking a deep breath, she looked at the test and grabbed the edge of the vanity unit as her legs turned to jelly. Her disbelief as she stared at the positive result swiftly turned to terror.

She was expecting Giannis's baby. But who—and more importantly *what*—was Giannis Gekas? Was he the charismatic lover who she had begun to fall in love with? Or was he a criminal who hid his illegal activities behind the façade of a successful businessman and philanthropist?

Feeling numb from the two huge shocks she had received in the space of twenty-four hours, Ava placed a trembling hand on her stomach. It seemed incredible that a new life was developing inside her and she felt an overwhelming sense of protectiveness for her baby. She would have been worried about telling Giannis of her pregnancy *before* she had heard the rumours about him. This was the man, after all, who had insisted that he did not have a heart.

Now the prospect filled her with dread. Supposing he was a man like her father—a criminal and a liar? A cold hand squeezed her heart. What if her ex, Craig, was right and there *was* a criminal gene that her baby might inherit from *both* parents? Ava was the absolute opposite of her father, and she had spent her adult life subconsciously trying to atone for his crimes in her job supporting victims of crime. She would bring her child up to be honest and law-abiding, but would Giannis share her ideals?

She sank down onto the edge of the bath and covered her face with her hands. Even if she could bring herself to ask him outright if he was a criminal, he was bound to deny it. She did not know if she could trust him—and for that reason she dared not tell him that she was having his baby.

Giannis let himself into the apartment and walked noiselessly down the passageway towards the bedroom. He had a ton of work to do following his successful bid to buy Markou Shipping, but he'd been unable to concentrate during his meeting with TGE's board because he had been worried about Ava. She had looked pale and fragile when he'd left her at the pharmacy and he felt guilty that he had not taken care of her. His conscience pricked that he should have brought her home and stayed with her while he sent his housekeeper out to buy medication for Ava's migraine.

He did not understand what had happened to him over the past month. His plan that Ava should pose as his fake fiancée had seemed simple enough. But they had become lovers and, more surprisingly, friends. He had even taken her to Spetses, although he'd never invited any of his previous mistresses to Villa Delphine, which he regarded as his private sanctuary. He'd told himself that the trip to the island was to promote the pretence that they were engaged but, instead of staying for a weekend as he'd intended, they had spent two weeks there. He had even found himself resenting the few hours each day that he'd had to get on with some work because he'd wanted to spend time with Ava, at the pool or the beach or—his preferred option—in bed.

She was beautiful, intelligent, sometimes fierce, often funny and always sexy. It was little things, Giannis mused. Like the way she ate a fresh peach for breakfast every morning with evident enjoyment, licking the juice from her lips with her tongue. Or how she migrated over to his side of the bed in the middle of the night so that when he woke in the morning she was curled up against his chest, warm and soft and infinitely desirable.

Theos, he was behaving like a hormone-fuelled teenager, Giannis thought impatiently as he felt the aching hardness of his arousal. He opened the bedroom door quietly, not wanting to disturb Ava if she was asleep. But the bed was empty. He recognised the suitcase standing on the floor as the one she had brought with her from London. A passport was lying on top of it. The wardrobe doors were open and he could see hanging inside were the dresses that the personal shopper in Paris had helped Ava choose.

Something was not right and he felt a sinking sensation in his stomach as Ava walked out of the bathroom and froze when she saw him. She carefully avoided his gaze and Giannis's eyes narrowed. He leaned nonchalantly against the door frame and kept his tone deliberately bland. 'Are you going somewhere, *glykiá mou*?'

'There is no need for you to refer to me as your sweetheart now that you have secured your deal with Stefanos.' She finally glanced at him and he wondered why she was nervous. 'I managed to book a seat on a flight to London leaving this afternoon.'

Icy fingers curled around his heart. 'You need to get back to the UK in a hurry? How is your headache, by the way?' he said drily.

A pink stain swept along her cheekbones. 'It's much better, thank you.' She caught her bottom lip between her teeth and Giannis fought the urge to walk over to her and cover her mouth with his. 'I thought that now you have persuaded Stefanos to sell his company to you, there is no point in me staying in Greece. I really want to go back and focus on my career.'

Anger flickered inside him and he wanted to tell her that there was every bloody point. They were good together—in bed and out of it. Not that he had any intention of admitting how much he enjoyed her company. This inconvenient attraction he felt for her—he refused to call it an obsession—*would* fade. He just could not say exactly when.

'I thought we decided at Stefanos's party that there was no reason for you to return to the UK immediately.'

'*You* decided. You didn't ask me what I wanted.' She glared at him. 'It sounds familiar, doesn't it?'

What the hell had happened to have brought about a dramatic change in Ava's attitude? Giannis searched his mind for clues that might explain why she was speaking to him in a cool voice that echoed the wintry expression in her grey eyes. Before they had gone to meet Stefanos she had responded to him with an eagerness that made his heart pound. But he noticed how she stiffened when he walked towards her.

She had acted oddly, almost secretively, when she'd shot out of the car and hurried into the pharmacy earlier, he remembered. Maybe her edginess was because it was a certain time in her monthly cycle. Relieved that he had found a likely explanation, he relaxed and murmured, 'I have a suggestion. You are not due to begin your new job in London for nearly another month. Why not stay in Greece until then? And when you return to England we could still meet up. I visit London fairly regularly for business, and I could rent an apartment for us.'

'Are you asking me to be your mistress?'

Giannis hid his irritation. Had she been hoping for more? For him to suggest that they make their fake engagement real, perhaps? Women were all the same, always wanting more than he was prepared to give. With a jolt of surprise he realised that he was not completely opposed to the idea of having a conventional relationship with Ava.

He shrugged. 'Mistress, lover—what does it matter?' He stretched out his hand to stroke her hair and his jaw hardened when she shrank from him. They could play games all day, he thought grimly. He had a sudden sense that he was standing on the edge of a precipice and his gut clenched with something like fear as he prepared to leap into the unknown. 'What matters is that I don't want this...us...to end—yet. I need to know what you want, Ava.'

He thought she hesitated, but maybe he imagined it. She picked up her suitcase and said in a fierce voice that stung Giannis as hard if she had slapped him, 'I want to go home.'

CHAPTER EIGHT

A BLAST OF bitingly cold January air followed Giannis through the door when he strode into TGE UK's plush office building in Bond Street. He disliked winter and London seemed particularly gloomy now that the party season was over. Even the festive lights along Oxford Street had lost some of their sparkle.

He had spent a miserable Christmas with his mother, swamped by guilt, as he was every year, because he knew he was the cause of her unhappiness. For New Year he had stayed at an exclusive ski resort in Aspen. But as the clock had struck midnight he'd made an excuse to the sultry brunette who had hung on his arm all evening and returned to his hotel room alone.

Maybe he was coming down with the flu virus that was going around, he brooded. He was rarely ill, but it might explain his loss of appetite, inability to sleep and a worrying indifference to work, friends and sex. Especially sex.

When Ava had handed him the pink sapphire heart ring before she'd walked out of his apartment in Athens without a backward glance, Giannis had assumed that he would have no trouble forgetting her. He'd thought he had been successful when he'd danced at the New Year's Eve party with the brunette whose name eluded him. But when Dana?—Donna?—had offered to perform a private striptease for him he had thought of Ava's long honey-blonde hair spilling over her breasts, her cool grey eyes and her fiery passion and he had finally admitted to himself that he missed her.

There were a few unopened letters on his desk and he frowned as he flicked through them. His secretary at the UK office had been rushed into hospital with appendicitis shortly before Christmas. The temp who had replaced Phyllis should have opened his private mail and forwarded anything of importance to him. It was obvious that some of the envelopes contained Christmas cards, but as it was now the second week in January he was tempted to throw them in the bin. Exhaling heavily, he opened a card, glanced at the picture of an improbably red-breasted robin and turned it over to read the note inside.

The handwriting was difficult to decipher and he was surprised to see the name 'Sam McKay' scrawled at the bottom of the card. Giannis remembered that Ava had said her brother had struggled at school because he was dyslexic.

Dear Mr Gekas
I wanted to say thanks for letting me off about the damage done to your boat. It was desent of you. Sorry about you and Ava not getting married. Its a shame it didnt work out and about the baby.
Happy christmas
Sam McKay

Baby! Giannis reread the note twice more and tried to make sense of it. Whose baby? He looked at the date stamp on the card's envelope and swore when he saw that Sam had posted it on the fifteenth of December—more than three weeks ago.

He could hear his heartbeat thudding in his ears as a shocking idea formed in his brain. Could Ava be pregnant with *his* baby? If so, then why hadn't she told him? The blood in his veins turned to ice. What the hell had Sam meant in his badly written note when he'd said that it was a shame about the baby? Had Ava suffered a miscarriage? Or had she…?

Giannis swallowed the bile that rose up in his throat. The memory of when Caroline had told him that she was no longer pregnant still haunted him. He had felt as if his heart had been ripped out, but Caroline had regarded her pregnancy as an inconvenience.

He stared at Sam's unsatisfactory note and sucked in a sharp breath when he thought back to the day three months ago at the apartment in Athens when Ava had acted so strangely. Had she known that she was pregnant but had decided that a baby would not fit in with her career?

Theos, he was terrified that history was repeating itself. First Caroline, and now Ava. Something cold and hard settled in the pit of his stomach. He had lost one child, but if Ava was expecting his baby he would move heaven and earth to have a second chance at fatherhood.

Giannis picked up the phone on the desk and

noticed that his hand was shaking as he put a call through to his secretary's office. The temp answered immediately. 'Cancel all my meetings,' he told her brusquely. 'I'll be out for the rest of the day.'

There was a 'sold' sign outside the terraced house in East London where, four months ago, Giannis had taken Ava to collect her passport before they had flown to Paris. If she had already moved away he would find her, he vowed grimly as he walked up the front path and hammered his fist on the door. If she was pregnant and hoped to keep his child from him, she would discover that there was nowhere on earth she could hide.

The front door opened and Ava's eyes widened when she saw him. She quickly tried to close the door but Giannis put his foot out to prevent her.

'What do you want?' she demanded, but beneath her sharp tone he sensed her fear. Of him? He ignored the peculiar pang his heart gave and used his shoulder to push the door wider open so that he could step into the narrow hallway.

'I want the truth.' He handed her the Christmas card he'd received from her brother. Looking puzzled, she read the note inside the card and flushed.

'I haven't explained to Sam that I pretended to be your fiancée so you would drop the charges against him,' she said stiffly. 'I suppose he thinks I'm upset that our engagement is over—which I'm not, of course.'

'Only one part of your brother's note interests me,' Giannis told her coldly. 'Is the baby that Sam refers to *my* baby?' He watched the colour drain from Ava's face and felt dangerously out of control.

'I don't have to tell you anything. And you have no right to force your way into my house.' She backed up along the hallway as he walked towards her.

'Were you pregnant when you left Athens?'

Instead of replying, she spun round and ran into the sitting room. Giannis was right behind her and he found that he had to squeeze past numerous boxes. Evidently the contents of the house had been packed up ready to be loaded onto a removals van. He came out in a cold sweat, thinking that if he had not read Sam's note for another few days he would have been too late to confront Ava.

'Answer me, damn it,' he said harshly.

Ava was cornered in the cramped room and she grabbed a heavy-based frying pan from one of the packing boxes. 'Stay away from me,' she said fiercely, waving the frying pan in the air. 'I'll defend myself if I have to.'

Giannis forced himself to control his temper when he heard real fear in her voice. 'I'm not going to harm you,' he growled. 'All I want is your honesty. I have a right to know if you had conceived my child.'

After several tense seconds she slowly lowered her arm and dropped the frying pan back into the box. Her teeth gnawed on her bottom lip. 'All right...*yes*. I had just found out that I was pregnant when I flew back to London.'

Giannis stared at her slender figure in dark jeans and a loose white sweater. Her honey-gold hair was tied in a ponytail and her peaches-and-cream skin glowed with health. She looked even more beautiful than he remembered. But she did not look pregnant. Surely there would be some sign by now? When his PA in Greece had been expecting, her stomach had seemed to grow bigger daily.

He shoved his hands into his coat pockets and clenched his fingers so tightly that his nails bit into his palms. 'You said that you *were* pregnant,' he said stiltedly, fighting to hold back the volcanic mass of his emotions from spewing out. 'Does it mean that either by accident or design there is no longer a baby?'

Now she stared back at him and her eyes were as dark as storm clouds. 'Accident or design? I don't think I understand.'

'Your brother said in the Christmas card that it was a shame about the baby. And before you left Athens you told me you wanted to focus on your career. Did you terminate the pregnancy?'

She reeled backwards and knocked over a box of Christmas decorations, sending gaudy baubles rolling across the carpet. '*No*, I did not.'

Giannis snatched a breath. He needed her to spell it out for him. 'So you are carrying my child?'

'Yes.' Her voice was a whisper of sound, as if she was reluctant to confirm the news that blew him away. 'Sam thought it was a shame that we had broken up when I am expecting your baby,' she muttered.

Euphoria swept through Giannis but it was swiftly replaced with anger. 'Why the hell did you try to keep it a secret from me? I had a right to know that I am to be a father.'

'Don't take that moral tone with me. You have no rights to this baby, Giannis.' Colour flared on Ava's pale cheeks and her eyes flashed with temper. 'I know what you are. I've heard the rumour that you are involved with the Greek mafia.'

'What?' Shock ricocheted through Giannis. He wondered if Ava was joking, even if the joke was in very poor taste. But as they faced each other across the room full of packing boxes and spilt shiny baubles he realised that she was serious.

'No doubt you will deny it. But I didn't tell you about my pregnancy because I won't take the risk of my baby having a criminal for a father.' She crossed her arms defensively in front of her and glared at him.

He kept his hands in his pockets in case he was tempted to shake some sense into her. Not that he would ever lay a finger on a woman in anger, and certainly not the mother of his child. Giannis's heart lurched as the astounding reality sank in that Ava was expecting his baby.

Five years ago he had lost his unborn child, but by a miracle he had been given another chance to be a father. A chance perhaps of redemption. He wanted to be a good father, as his own father had been, and he would love his child as deeply as his father had loved him. Emotions that he had buried for the last fifteen years threatened to overwhelm him. But he had to deal with Ava's shocking accusation and somehow defuse the volatile situation.

'Of course I deny that I belong to a criminal organisation because it's not true. Who told you the rumour about me?'

'I'm not prepared to say.'

'It must have been at Stefanos's party.' Giannis knew he had guessed correctly when Ava dropped her gaze. He remembered that her attitude towards him had changed when they had spent the night on Gaia. She had left the party early, saying she had a headache. When she had been sick the next morning she had blamed it on a migraine, but she must have known then that she was pregnant.

Fury swirled, black and bitter, inside him at the realisation that Ava had tried to hide his child from him because she had believed an unfounded rumour. A memory flashed into his mind.

'I saw you talking to Petros Spyriou at the party while I was with Stefanos. Did he tell you the ridiculous story that I am a criminal?'

'I don't know the name of the man who spoke to me.'

'So you believed the words of a stranger without question and without giving me a chance to refute his slanderous allegations?' When she bit her lip but said nothing, Giannis continued, 'We had been lovers for a month before we went to Gaia, yet what we shared clearly meant nothing to you.'

'What did we share, Giannis, other than sex and lies? You blackmailed me to be your fake fiancée so that you could trick Stefanos to sell his company to you.' Her voice faltered. 'When I heard a rumour that you use TGE as a cover for your criminal activities I didn't know what to believe.'

'So you ran away,' he said scathingly. The savage satisfaction he felt when colour flared on her face did not lessen his unexpected sense of betrayal, of hurt, *damn it*, that she had so little faith in him.

When they had stayed on Spetses he had spent more time with her than he'd done with any other woman. Even when he had dated Caroline for nearly a year, their relationship had amounted to meeting for dinner a couple of times a week and occasional weekends together when their work schedules had aligned.

'Petros Spyriou is Stefanos's nephew,' he told Ava. 'Petros believes that his uncle should have put him in charge of Markou Shipping instead of selling the company to me. He is jealous of me, which is why he made up disgusting lies about me.' Giannis gave a grim laugh. 'Petros succeeded in scaring you away but he'll find himself in court facing charges of slander and defamation of character.'

'He said that a few years ago a journalist tried to investigate you but was dissuaded from publishing information that he'd discovered about you.'

Inside his coat pockets, Giannis curled his hands into fists and wished that Stefanos's weasel of a nephew was standing in front of him. His criminal record had been expunged ten years after he'd served his prison sentence, which was standard procedure in Greek law. But somehow a journalist had found out about it and demanded money to keep quiet. Giannis had been loath to give in to blackmail, but coming soon after he'd broken up with Caroline, and the loss of his first child, his emotions had been raw and he'd been desperate to keep the details of his father's death out of the media spotlight.

He had no idea how Stefanos's nephew had found out about the journalist, and he guessed that Petros did not know what information the journalist had discovered. But the suggestion that there were secrets Giannis wanted to keep hidden must have been useful to Petros when he'd told Ava lies about him being involved with the Greek mafia. The story was so crazy it was laughable—yet Ava had believed Petros and as a result she had hidden her pregnancy, Giannis thought bitterly.

His jaw clenched as he remembered that while they had lived together at Villa Delphine he had been tempted to confess to Ava that he had been responsible for his father's untimely death. Thank God he had not bared his soul to her. He certainly would not tell her the truth now. He could imagine her horrified reaction and he dared not risk her disappearing again with his baby.

'Everything Petros told you was pure fabrication.' He shrugged. 'Believe me, or don't believe me. I don't give a damn. But you won't keep my child from me. If you attempt to, I will seek custody and I will win because I have money and power and you have neither.'

'No court ruling would allow a baby to be separated from its mother,' Ava snapped, but she had paled.

Giannis flicked his eyes over her, his emotions once more under control. 'Are you willing to take the risk?'

His black gaze was so cold. Ava gave a shiver. It seemed impossible that Giannis's eyes had ever gleamed with warmth and laughter. Or that they had once been friends as well as lovers. But their wild passion had resulted in the baby that was growing bigger in her belly every day. Giannis's child. It was strange how emotive those two words were, and even stranger that when she had seen him standing on the doorstep her body had quivered in response to his potent masculinity.

She must be the weakest woman in the world, she thought bleakly. He had barged his way into her home and threatened to try to take her baby from her, yet her heart ached as she roamed her eyes over his silky hair and the sculpted perfection of his features. She had thought about him constantly for the last three months but, standing in the chaotic sitting room, he was taller than she remembered and his shoulders were so broad beneath the black wool coat he wore.

He was like a dark avenging angel, but was his anger justified? Had she been too ready to believe the rumour that he was a criminal because of her father's criminality? Ava wondered. Supposing Stefanos's jealous nephew *had* lied? If she hadn't had that devastating conversation with Petros, she would have told Giannis as soon as she'd done the test that she was pregnant, and perhaps he would not be looking down his nose at her as if she were something unpleasant that he had scraped off the bottom of his shoe.

A loud knock on the front door broke the tense silence in the sitting room. She glanced towards the window and saw a lorry parked outside the house. 'We'll have to continue this conversation another time,' she told Giannis. 'The removals firm are here to take my mother's furniture into storage now that she has sold the house.'

He frowned. 'I thought this house belonged to you, and you had sold it because you planned to move away so that I couldn't find you.'

'I lived here with my family before we moved to Cyprus. My father had registered the deeds of the house in my mother's name. After my dad...' she hesitated '...after my parents divorced, Mum, Sam and I came back to live here, although I went away to university. My mother and her new partner have bought a bed and breakfast business in the Peak District.'

'So where will you live? I assume you will need to stay in the East End to be near to your work. At least while you are able to continue working until the baby is born,' Giannis said, the groove between his brows deepening.

She looked away from him. 'I was made redundant from my job when the victim support charity I worked for couldn't continue to fund my role. I've arranged to rent a room in a friend's house, but I'm thinking of moving back to Scotland where property is cheaper and I will be nearer to Sam and Mum.'

She would need help from her family after she became a single mother, Ava thought as she hurried down the hallway to open the front door. The removals team trooped in and it quickly became clear that she and Giannis were in the way, when the men started to carry furniture and boxes out to the van.

'You had better go,' she told him. 'My friend Becky, who I am going to stay with, offered to come over later to collect my things as I don't have a car.'

'I'll put whatever you want to take with you in my car and drive you to her house.' Giannis's crisp tone brooked no argument. 'Which boxes are yours?'

She pointed to two packing boxes by the window and when his brows rose she said defensively, 'I don't like clutter, or see the point in having too many clothes.'

'Is that why you left the dresses that I'd bought

for you during our engagement back at the apartment in Athens?'

'I left the clothes and the engagement ring behind because you did not buy me, Giannis.' The idea that he had paid for the designer dresses and the beautiful pink sapphire ring with money he might have made illegally was repugnant to Ava, and a painful reminder of her privileged childhood which she'd later discovered had been funded by her father's crimes.

Giannis's eyes narrowed but he said nothing as he picked up one of the boxes which contained her worldly possessions. But when Ava bent down to pick up the second box he said sharply, 'Put it down. You should not be lifting heavy things in your condition.'

'Who do you think packed all the boxes and lugged them down the stairs?' she said drily. 'Mum is busy getting her new house ready and I have spent weeks clearing this place, ready for the new owners to move in.'

'From now on you will not do any strenuous activity that could harm my baby,' Giannis growled. His accent was suddenly thicker and he sounded very Greek and *very* possessive. Ava supposed she should feel furious that he was being so bossy, but her stupid heart softened at his concern for his child. Since she'd left Athens she had debated endlessly with herself about whether she should tell him she was pregnant. One reason for not doing so was that she had assumed he would be angry at having fatherhood foisted on him. She was surprised by his determination to be involved with the baby.

She had already given the house keys to the estate agent and when she walked down the front path for the last time Ava realised that she was severing the final link with her father. Number fifty-one Arthur Close was where Terry McKay had plotted his armed robberies and controlled his turf. He had been a ruthless gangland boss, but to Ava he had been a fun person who had built her a treehouse in the garden. She had been utterly taken in by her father's charming manner but finding out the truth about him had left her deeply untrusting.

After the bitterly cold wind whipping down Arthur Close, the interior of Giannis's car was a warm and luxurious haven. Ava sank deep into the leather upholstery and gave him the postcode of Becky's house.

'Put your seat belt on,' he reminded her. But, before she could reach for it, he leaned across her and she breathed in the spicy scent of his aftershave. He smelled divine, and for a moment his face was close to hers and she hated herself for wanting to press her lips to the dark stubble that shaded his jaw.

He secured her seat belt and she released a shaky breath when he moved away from her and put the car into gear. Did her body respond to Giannis because it instinctively recognised that he was the father of her child? How could she still desire him when she did not know if she could trust him? she wondered despairingly. The sight of his tanned hands on the steering wheel evoked memories of how he had pleasured her with his wickedly inventive fingers. *Stop it,* she told herself, and closed her eyes so that she was not tempted to look at him.

He switched the radio onto a station playing easy listening music, and the smooth motion of the car had a soporific effect on Ava. She'd been lucky that she'd had few pregnancy symptoms and the sickness she had experienced in the first weeks had gone. But the bone-deep tiredness she felt these days was quite normal, the midwife had told her at her check-up. It was nature's way of making her rest so that the baby could grow.

When she opened her eyes she wondered for a moment where she was, before she remembered that Giannis had offered to take her across town to Becky's house. So why were they driving along the motorway? The clock on the dashboard showed that she had been asleep for nearly an hour.

She jerked her gaze to Giannis. 'This isn't the way to Fulham. Where are you taking me?' Panic flared and she unconsciously placed her hand on her stomach to protect the fragile new life inside her.

'We are going to my house in St Albans. We'll be there in about ten minutes.' He glanced at her. 'We need to talk.'

'I don't want to talk to you.' She reached for the door handle and Giannis swore.

'It's locked. Are you really crazy enough to want to throw yourself out of the car travelling at seventy miles an hour?'

His words brought her to her senses. 'I have nothing to say to you. You...threatened to take my baby from me.' Her voice shook and she sensed that he sent her another glance.

'I was angry,' he said roughly.

'That doesn't make it okay to speak to me the way you did.'

'I know.' He exhaled heavily. 'I don't want to fight with you, Ava. But I want what is best for the baby, and I do not believe that being brought up in a bedsit and being dumped in a nursery for hours every day while you go to work is anywhere near the best start in life that we can give to our child.' He paused for a heartbeat and said quietly, 'Do you?'

Unable to think of an answer, she turned her head to look out of the window so that he would not see the tears that had filled her eyes when he'd said *our child*. For the first time since she had stared in disbelief at the positive sign on the pregnancy test, she felt that she wasn't alone. It made her realise how scared she had been at the prospect of having a baby on her own, with no one to share the worry and responsibility with. Her mother was busy with her new life and part-

ner, and her brother thankfully seemed to be sort-
ing himself and enjoyed working on their aunt
and uncle's farm. There was no one she could
rely on apart from Giannis. But, despite his assurance that he wasn't a criminal, she did not
know if she believed him.

They left the motorway and drove through
a small village before Giannis turned the car
through some wrought iron gates which bore a
sign saying 'Milton Grange'. At the end of the
winding driveway stood a charming Georgian
house built on four storeys, with mullioned windows and ivy growing over the walls.

Snow had been falling lightly for the last half
an hour and the bay trees in front of the house
were dusted with white frosting. But, although
the snow looked pretty, Ava was glad to step into
the warm hallway where they were greeted by
Giannis's housekeeper.

'The fire is lit in the drawing room and lunch
will be in half an hour,' the woman, whom Giannis introduced as Joan, said when she had
taken their coats.

'What a beautiful house,' Ava murmured as she
looked around the comfortably furnished draw-

ing room, decorated in soft neutral shades so that the effect was calming and homely.

'I bought it as an investment,' Giannis told her. 'But it's too big, especially as I do not live here permanently. I arranged for a charity which provides help to parents and families of disabled children to use the top two floors as a respite centre. Builders reconfigured the upper floors and in effect turned one large house into two separate properties.'

Ava sat down in an armchair close to the fire and furthest away from the sofa where Giannis took a seat. He gave her a sardonic look but said evenly, 'Would you like tea or coffee?' A tray on the low table in front of him held a cafetière and a teapot.

'Tea, please. I should only drink decaffeinated coffee, but actually I've gone off coffee completely since I've been pregnant. Just the smell of it made me sick at first.'

He frowned. 'Do you suffer very badly with morning sickness? It can't be good for the baby if you are unable to keep food down. Are you eating well?'

'I'm fine now, and I'm eating too well.' She

gave a rueful sigh. 'If I'm not careful I'll be the size of a house.'

'You look beautiful,' he said gruffly. Ava swallowed as her eyes met his and she felt a familiar tug deep in her pelvis. He was *so* handsome and she suddenly wished that the situation between them was different, and instead of offering her a cup of tea he would whisk her upstairs and make long, slow and very satisfying love to her.

'How far along is your pregnancy?'

'I'm eighteen weeks. At twenty weeks I am due to have another ultrasound scan to check the baby's development and I'll be able to find out the sex.' She bit her lip. 'It's possible that I conceived the first time we slept together in London.'

'As I recall, neither of us slept much that night,' he drawled in that arrogant way of his which Ava found infuriating.

'But now we must deal with the consequences of our actions,' she said flatly.

He took a sip of his coffee and said abruptly, 'I would like to come to your scan appointment. Do you want to find out the baby's sex?'

'I think I do. I suppose you hope it's a boy.' If the baby was a girl, perhaps Giannis would lose interest in his child. Her hand shook slightly as she placed the delicate bone china teacup and saucer down on the table.

'I will be equally happy to have a daughter or a son. All that matters is that the child is born safe and well.'

His words echoed Ava's own feelings and her emotions threatened to overwhelm her. She was too warm sitting by the fire, but she did not want to move nearer to Giannis. Instead she pulled off her jumper and only then remembered that the strap-top she was wearing beneath it was too small. The material was stretched over her breasts, which had grown two bra sizes bigger. She hoped he would assume that the flush she could feel spreading across her face was due to the warmth of the fire and not because she'd glimpsed a raw hunger in his eyes that evoked a molten heat inside her. She tensed when he stood up and strolled over to where she was sitting.

'You said that you are currently without a job, so how were you planning to manage financially?'

'My old job in Glasgow is still available. Working as a VCO is not a popular or well-paid career,' she said ruefully. 'I will be entitled to maternity pay for a few months after the baby is born, but then I'll have to go back to work to support both of us.'

'I want to be involved with my child,' Giannis told her in a determined voice. 'And of course I will provide financial support for you and the baby.'

'I don't want your money,' she said stubbornly. She could not bear for him to think that she had trapped him with her pregnancy because he was wealthy.

'What you want and what I want is not important. The only thing that matters is that we do the right thing for our child, who was unplanned but not unwanted—am I right that we at least agree on that?' he said softly.

His voice was like rough velvet and Ava nodded, not trusting herself to speak when she felt so vulnerable. 'What do you suggest then?' she asked helplessly.

He hesitated for a heartbeat. 'I think we should get married.'

CHAPTER NINE

FOR A FEW seconds Ava could not breathe, and there was an odd rushing sensation in her ears. Giannis had not said that he *wanted* to marry her, she noted. And why would he? All he wanted was the baby she carried, and she was simply a necessary part of the equation.

'You're crazy,' she said flatly. 'It wouldn't work.'

He pulled up a footstool and sat down in front of her, so close that it would be easy to stretch out her hand and touch the silken darkness of his hair—easy and yet impossible.

'What is the alternative?' he asked levelly. 'Even if we came to an amicable agreement about shared custody, a child needs stability, which I can provide in Greece at Villa Delphine. I could buy a house for you in England and we could send our child back and forth between us like a ping-pong ball—Christmas with you, first birthday with me, and so on. But that wouldn't make me happy, I don't think it would make you happy and I'm certain it would not be a happy childhood for our son or daughter.'

Ava couldn't argue with his logic. Everything Giannis said made sense. But her emotions weren't logical or sensible; they were all over the place. She tensed when he took hold of her hand and rubbed his thumb lightly over the pulse thudding in her wrist.

'Like it or not, you and the baby are my responsibility and I want to take care of both of you.' He met her gaze and the gleam in his dark eyes sent a quiver of reaction through her. 'Our relationship worked very well for the month that we pretended to be engaged,' he murmured.

It would be too easy to be seduced by his charisma and fall under his spell, but if she was going to survive him she had to be strong and in control. 'We did not have a relationship—we had sex,' she reminded him tartly.

The word hung in the air between them, taunting Ava with memories of their wild passion and Giannis's body claiming hers with powerful thrusts.

'Don't knock it, *glykiá mou*,' he drawled. 'You enjoyed it as much as I did.'

Hot-faced with embarrassment, she dropped her gaze from his amused expression and wondered what he was thinking. Her pregnancy was not really showing yet, but she was conscious of her thickening waistline which meant that she had to leave the button on her jeans undone. Before Giannis had met her, he had slept with some of the world's most beautiful women—and she doubted his bed had been empty for the past months that they had been apart.

'So, do you expect it to be a proper marriage?' she said stiffly.

His eyes narrowed. 'I do not expect anything, certainly not intimacy, unless you decide it is what you want.'

She should feel relieved by Giannis's assurance that he would not put pressure on her to consummate their marriage, but Ava felt even more confused. He was a red-blooded male and celibacy would not be a natural state for him. But perhaps he intended to find pleasure elsewhere. For her own protection she needed to ignore the chemistry between them while she was still unsure if she could believe his insistence that he was not a criminal.

Giannis stood up and offered her his hand to help her to her feet. 'What is your answer?'

She ignored his hand. 'I need time to consider my options.' Her tone was as cool as his. They could have been discussing a business deal instead of a decision which would affect the rest of their lives. But her pregnancy had already had a fundamental effect, and it occurred to her that, whether or not she accepted his proposal, they would be linked for ever by the child they had created between them.

'Do not consider them for too long,' he said as he ushered her out of the drawing room and across the hall to the dining room. 'I intend for us to be married well before the baby is born.' The implacable note in Giannis's voice warned Ava that the only option he would accept was her agreement to become his wife.

'The gel will feel cold, I'm afraid,' the sonographer said cheerfully before she squirted a dollop of thick, clear lubricant onto Ava's stomach.

Ava tried to suck her tummy in as the sonographer smeared the gel over her bump. She was intensely conscious of Giannis sitting beside the hospital bed where she was lying for the ultrasound scan. Her top was tucked up under her breasts and her trousers were pushed down low on her hips, leaving her stomach bare. From her angle, looking down her body, her stomach seemed huge, which was hardly surprising after she had spent the past couple of weeks enjoying Giannis's housekeeper's wonderful cooking, she thought ruefully.

'I understand you need to eat for two,' Joan had said cheerfully when Giannis announced that he and Ava would be getting married as soon as it could be arranged. The wedding could not take place until twenty-eight days after they had given notice at the local register office.

The bright lights in the scanning room made the pink sapphire ring on Ava's finger sparkle. This time her engagement was real, and her heart lurched at the thought that very soon she would be Giannis's wife.

She had accepted his proposal the day after he had asked her to marry him—following a sleepless night when she'd faced the stark choice of having to believe him or Stefanos Markou's nephew. On a practical level she knew that Giannis was determined to be a father to his baby and she concluded that she would be in a better position to safeguard herself and her child if she was married to him.

'You can choose a different ring if you would prefer not to wear this one,' he'd said when he had returned the pink sapphire heart to her.

Ava had slid the ring onto her finger and told herself that she hadn't missed it being there for the past few months. 'It seems fitting to keep the ring that you gave me while I was your fake fiancée, seeing as our marriage will be one of convenience,' she'd said stubbornly, determined he would not know how much she had missed him.

His eyes had gleamed dangerously but he'd said evenly, 'Whatever you wish, *glykiá mou.*'

What she had wished was for him to pull her into his arms and kiss her senseless so that she could pretend they were lovers back on Spetses—before rumours, doubts and her pregnancy had driven a wedge between them. But Giannis had walked out of the room and she'd felt too vulnerable to go after him and make the first move to try to break the stalemate in their relationship.

She pulled her mind back to the present as the sonographer moved the probe over her stomach. 'If you look on the screen, here is Baby's heart— you can see it beating. And this here is one of Baby's hands…and just here is the other hand…' The sonographer pointed to the grey image on the screen. 'You can make out Baby's face quite clearly.'

Ava caught her breath as she stared at her baby's tiny features. She felt Giannis squeeze her fingers. She'd already had a scan at twelve weeks, to accurately date her pregnancy, but this was his first experience of seeing his child and she wondered how he felt now that the baby was a tangible reality rather than something they had spoken about.

The sonographer spent several minutes studying the baby's vital organs and taking measurements. 'Everything looks absolutely as it should do,' she said at last. 'I understand that you have decided to find out the baby's sex.'

'Yes,' they both replied at the same time.

The sonographer smiled. 'You are going to have a little boy. Congratulations.'

Ava tore her eyes from the image of her son— *her son*! Blinking back tears of pride and joy, she glanced at Giannis. Her heart turned over when she saw a tear slide down his cheek as he stared intently at the screen. He dashed his hand over his face and when he turned to her he showed no sign of the fierce emotion she had witnessed although, when she looked closely, his eyes were suspiciously bright.

'Now we know what colour to paint the nursery,' he murmured.

She nodded, unable to speak past the lump that had formed in her throat. Whatever happened between them, she knew now, without doubt, that Giannis would love his son and would never be parted from him. Which meant that somehow they would have to make their unconventional marriage work.

Another thought slid insidiously into her mind as she remembered her ex's scathing comments when she had admitted to him that her father was the infamous East End gangster, Terry McKay. Craig had decided against marrying her for fear that their children might grow up to be criminals like their grandfather.

Of course there was not a 'criminal' gene, Ava tried to reassure herself. But she couldn't forget what Stefanos's nephew had told her about Giannis being involved in organised crime. If the rumour about him was true, and if there was such a thing as a 'criminal' gene, what would the future hold for the baby?

In the car on the way back to Milton Grange neither of them spoke much. Ava's thoughts were going round and round in her head and she did not have the energy to try to breach the emotional distance that existed between her and Giannis. His playboy reputation when she had first met him had made her believe that he was not capable of feeling strong emotions, but that was patently not true, she realised as she remembered the tears on his face when he had seen the scan images of his baby son.

When they arrived at the house he went straight to his study, citing an important business phone call that he needed to make. The cold, grey weather at the end of January did not encourage Ava to go out for a walk, and instead she made use of the heated swimming pool in the conservatory.

She hadn't got round to buying a maternity swimsuit, and the bikini that she'd bought from a boutique on Spetses barely fitted over her fuller breasts. But no one was going to see her, and the midwife had said that swimming was a good form of exercise during pregnancy. The water was warm and she swam several laps before she climbed out of the pool and wrung her dripping-wet hair between her hands. A sudden blast of cold air rushed into the conservatory as the door opened, and her heart gave a jolt when Giannis strode in wearing a towelling robe.

'You said you would be working all afternoon,' she muttered, feeling heat spread over her face as he stared at her ridiculously small bikini that revealed much more of her body than she was comfortable with. She was tempted to run across to the lounger where she had left her towel, but she couldn't risk slipping on the wet tiles.

'I was bored of working and decided to come and swim with you.' He shrugged off his robe and Ava roamed her gaze hungrily over his muscular chest covered in black hairs that arrowed down his taut abdomen and disappeared beneath the waistband of his swim-shorts.

'Well, I've got out of the pool now.' Her flush deepened when she realised the inanity of her statement.

'I can see that,' he mocked her softly. But as he walked towards her his smile faded and his dark eyes glittered with a feral hunger that confused her.

'Stop staring at me.' She tried to cover the gentle swell of her stomach with her hands but could do nothing to disguise the fact that her breasts were almost spilling out of her bikini top. She felt exposed, knowing she looked fat, and sure that Giannis must be comparing her to all the gorgeous women who had shared his bed in the past.

He halted in front of her and she noticed a nerve jump in his cheek. 'How can I take my eyes from you when you take my breath away?' he said thickly.

Ava bit her lip. 'I was slim the last time you saw me in a bikini.' She had nearly said naked, but memories of when they had lain together, skin on skin, their limbs entwined and their bodies joined would only add fuel to the fire burning inside her.

'You look incredible.' Dark colour winged along his cheekbones. 'Can you feel the baby move?'

'I've felt flutters rather than kicks at this stage but the midwife said that the baby's movements will become stronger as he grows bigger.'

Giannis was focused on her bump. 'May I touch you?'

She gave a hesitant nod. It was his baby too, and she could not deny him the chance to be involved in her pregnancy. But when he placed his hand on her stomach and stretched his fingers wide over its swell she trembled and hoped he had no idea of the molten heat that pooled between her thighs.

'There, did you feel that?' She caught hold of his hand and moved it slightly lower on her stomach just as a fluttering sensation inside her happened again.

He drew an audible breath. *'Theos,'* he said in an oddly gruff voice. 'Between us we have created a miracle, *glykiá mou.'*

Standing this close to him was creating havoc

with her emotions. She needed to move away from him and break the spell that he always cast on her. But it was too late, and she watched helplessly as his dark head descended.

'Giannis,' she whispered, but it was a plea rather than a protest and the fierce gleam in his eyes told her that he knew it. His breath warmed her lips before he covered her mouth with his and kissed her the way she had longed for him to kiss her, the way she had dreamed about him kissing her every night since she had left Greece.

She couldn't resist him. It did not even occur to her to try. He was the father of her unborn child, the man she was going to marry, and she wanted him to make love to her. Even the knowledge that *love* played no part in their relationship did not matter at that moment, as desire swept like wildfire through her veins. She had been starved of him and she pressed her body up against his, closing her eyes as she sank into the sensual pleasure of his kiss.

His hand was still resting on her stomach, and she held her breath when he moved lower and ran his fingers over the strip of bare skin above the waistband of her bikini bottoms. She willed him to slip his fingers beneath the stretchy material and touch her where she ached to be touched. She wanted him to push his fingers inside her, and incredibly she felt the first ripples of an orgasm start to build deep in her pelvis before he had even caressed her intimately.

Tension of a different kind ran through her as she faced up to where this was leading. How could she give herself to Giannis when she had doubts about him? In many ways, it had been easier to have sex with him while she had pretended to be his fiancée because she'd assumed that their relationship would end at the same time as their fake engagement. But now she was going to be Giannis's wife—if not for ever then certainly until their child was old enough to be able to cope with them separating. If she made love with Giannis she would reveal her vulnerability that she was desperate to hide from him.

But then suddenly it was over as he wrenched his mouth from hers. She swayed on her feet when he abruptly snatched his arm from around her waist. He swore as he swung away from her and dived into the water.

Ava watched him swim to the far end of the

pool and wondered if he had somehow been aware of her doubts. A more likely explanation for his rejection was that he found her pregnant shape a turn-off. Giannis had been attentive because she was carrying his child, but he'd made it clear that he did not want her.

At least she knew where she stood with him, Ava told herself as she dragged her towel around her unsatisfied body to hide the shaming hard peaks of her nipples. He was marrying her to claim his baby. And she had agreed to be his wife because she feared that he would seek custody of their son—not immediately perhaps, but she couldn't bear to live with the threat hanging over her.

Why the hell had he come on to Ava like a clumsy adolescent on a first date? Giannis asked himself furiously as he powered through the water. He heard the conservatory door bang, signalling her departure, but he kept on swimming lap after lap, punishing himself for his loss of control.

Since he had seen the grainy scan images of his child he'd felt as if he were on an emotional rollercoaster. Ava's pregnancy had seemed unreal until the moment the sonographer had pointed out on the screen the baby's tiny heart beating strongly. In that instant he'd realised that nothing—not money or possessions or power—were important compared to his son.

Back at the house he'd paced restlessly around his study. unable to concentrate on a financial report he was supposed to be reading. Work had always been his favourite mistress, the area of his life where he knew he excelled, but—just as when he had taken Ava to Spetses—he had wanted to be with her instead of sitting at his desk.

Walking into the pool house and seeing her in a tiny bikini had blown him away. Pregnancy had turned her into a goddess and he had been transfixed by her generous curves—her breasts like ripe peaches and the lush swell of her belly where his child lay. He'd wanted to touch her and feel a connection with his baby, and when he'd felt the faint movements of a fragile new life a sense cf awed wonder had brought a lump to his throat. Something utterly primal had stirred in his chest. His child. His woman. He would die to protec: both of them, he acknowledged.

Had he kissed Ava to stake his claim? With savage self-derision he admitted that he'd felt a basic need to pull her down onto a lounger and possess her in the most fundamental way. Desire had drummed an insistent beat in his blood and in his loins. He had forgotten that she did not trust him—although he should not be surprised by her wariness after he had threatened to take her child, he thought grimly.

He had kissed her for the simple reason that he could not resist her, but when he'd felt her stiffen in rejection he knew he had no one to blame but himself. When he'd persuaded her—or pressurised her, his conscience pricked—to marry him, he had promised himself that he would be patient and wait for her to come to him. Instead he'd behaved like a jerk, and in truth he was shocked that she had got under his skin to the degree that she dominated his thoughts and disturbed his dreams.

It would not happen again, Giannis vowed as he climbed out of the pool. He would control his desire for Ava because too much was at stake. He had discovered that he wanted more from her than sex. He wanted everything—her soft smile and infectious laughter, her cool, incisive intelligence and her fiery passion. And he wanted his child. Even if he failed to win all that he hoped for, he *would* have his son.

By the middle of February a thaw had turned the winter wonderland of snow and ice to grey slush, just in time for the wedding which was to take place in the private chapel in the grounds of Milton Grange. Not that Ava cared about the weather when her marriage to Giannis would be as fake as their engagement five months earlier had been.

Since the incident by the pool they had maintained an emotional and physical distance from each other. The closest contact they'd had was when their hands had accidentally brushed as they'd passed each other on the landing, on the way to their separate bedrooms.

She was thankful that the wedding would be a small affair. It had been arranged at short notice, and both her mother and Giannis's mother were on holiday in the warmer climes of the southern hemisphere and could not attend. Her best friend Becky was coming, and Sam had promised to be there. Ava was looking forward to seeing him—although if her brother had not been partly responsible for damaging Giannis's boat she would not now be pregnant and about to marry a man who had become so remote that sometimes she wondered if the close bond she had felt between them on Spetses had been in her imagination.

But the problem was not only Giannis, she acknowledged. Her trust issues meant that she found it difficult to lower her guard. And now her father was once more in the forefront of her mind.

It had started with an email she'd received from an author who was writing a book about East End gangs and had discovered that Ava was Terry McKay's daughter. The author wanted to ask her about her childhood growing up with her notorious gangster father.

She sent a message back saying that she never discussed her father. But Ava knew she could not stop the book being published. People were fascinated by crime, and even though she had changed her name to Sheridan there was always a chance that she would be revealed as Terry McKay's daughter.

It would be unfair for Giannis to find out about her father in a newspaper article or book review, her conscience nagged. She ought to tell him the truth about her background before she married him. Especially as she had come to believe that Stefanos's nephew had lied about Giannis having links to a criminal organisation.

But she could not forget Craig's suggestion that her children might take after her criminal father, and she was fearful of Giannis's reaction. Would he reject her and his son? Maybe she should just keep quiet and hope that he never discovered her real identity. Tormented by indecision, she withdrew into herself—which did not go unnoticed by Giannis.

'You're very pale, and you have barely spoken a word all day,' he commented during dinner on the evening before their wedding. He frowned. 'Do you feel unwell? The baby...'

'I feel fine, and I've felt the baby kicking and I'm sure he is fine too,' she was quick to re-assure him. She knew that Giannis's obsessive concern about her health was because he cared about his child. But how would he feel if he was to learn that his son's genes came from a very murky pool? She pushed her food around her plate, her appetite non-existent. 'It's just pre-wedding nerves.'

He gave her a brooding look from across the table. 'There is no reason for you to feel nervous. I have told you that I will not make demands on you,' he said tersely.

If only he would! Ava wished he would whip off the tablecloth, plates and all, and make hot, urgent love to her on the polished mahogany dining table. Sex would at least be some sort of communication between them, rather than the current state of simmering tension and words unspoken.

There had been times over the past weeks when she had caught Giannis looking at her with a hungry gleam in his dark eyes that made her think he still desired her. But then she remembered how he had wrenched his mouth from hers that day by the pool, and her pride would not risk another humiliating rejection if she made the first move.

She went to bed early, giving the excuse that she was tired, and ignored his sardonic expression as he glanced at the clock which showed that it was eight o'clock. Surprisingly she fell asleep, but woke with a start from a dream where she was standing in the church with Giannis and someone in the congregation halted the wedding and denounced her as a gangster's daughter. The look of disgust on Giannis's face stayed in her mind after she had opened her eyes and her stomach gave a sickening lurch as she jumped out of bed and, without stopping to pull on her robe, ran down the hall to his room.

'Ava.' Giannis was sitting up in bed, leaning against the pillows. The black-rimmed reading glasses he wore only added to his rampant sex appeal and in the soft light from the bedside lamp his bare chest gleamed like bronze, covered with whorls of dark hairs. He dropped the documents that he had been studying onto the sheet and sat bolt upright, concern stamped on his handsome face. 'What's wrong?'

'I can't marry you,' she blurted out.

CHAPTER TEN

GIANNIS'S BREATH WHISTLED between his teeth. It was not the first time that Ava had made him feel as if he had been punched in his gut. Her accusation that he was involved in criminal activities had made him furious and her lack of faith in him had hurt more than he cared to admit. Did she still believe Petros's lies, or was there another problem? He racked his brain for something he might have done which had caused her to want to call off the wedding.

'I have done my best to reassure you I do not expect anything from our marriage that you are not willing to give,' he said curtly.

The way she bit her lower lip had a predictable effect on his body and he was grateful that the sheet concealed his uncomfortably hard arousal. She looked mouth-wateringly sexy in a peach-coloured silk negligee that showed off the creamy upper slopes of her breasts—so round and firm, separated by the deep vee of her cleavage where he longed to press his face. He forced himself to concentrate when she spoke.

'I am well aware that you find me sexually unattractive,' she snapped, but her voice shook a little and Giannis had the crazy idea that she sounded hurt. 'That isn't the issue.'

'What is the issue?' He was too tempted to pull her down onto the bed and clear up the misunderstanding about his sexual feelings for her to give a damn about an 'issue'. But Ava was clearly distraught and he resolved to be patient. 'Come, *glykiá mou*,' he murmured. 'Tell me what is troubling you.'

She stopped pacing up and down the room and swung round to face him. 'I haven't been honest with you.'

For one heart-stopping second Giannis wondered if the child she carried was his. She had told him it was likely that she'd conceived the first time they'd had sex, but could she have already been pregnant when he'd met her? If that was so, why would she have hidden her pregnancy from him after she'd left Greece? his mind pointed out.

'When you asked if I wanted to invite my father to the wedding, I told you that I am not in contact with him,' Ava said in a low tone. 'What I failed to say is that my father is serving a fifteen-year prison sentence for armed robbery.'

Giannis released his breath slowly as the tension seeped from him. He felt guilty that he had doubted her. Of course the baby was his. But it occurred to him that there would be no harm in following his lawyer's advice and arranging for a paternity test when the baby was born.

'Do you mean you do not want to get married without your father being present?' It was the only reason he could think of that might explain why she was so upset.

'I mean that I am the daughter of Terry McKay, who once had the dubious honour of being Britain's most wanted criminal.' She buried her face in her hands and gave a sob. 'I'm so ashamed. My father carried out a string of jewellery raids in Hatton Garden and he was involved in drug smuggling and extortion. We—my mum, Sam and I—knew nothing about his secret life as a criminal until he was arrested and sent to prison.'

Giannis slid out from beneath the sheet and

quickly donned a pair of sweatpants before he walked over to Ava and gently pulled her hands down from her face. The sight of tears on her cheeks tugged on his heart. 'Why do you feel ashamed? You were not responsible for your father's behaviour,' he said softly.

'I loved my dad and trusted him. I had no idea that he was a ruthless gangland boss.' She gave another sob. 'The man I thought I knew had fooled me all my life. I find it hard to trust people,' she admitted. 'I was desperate to prevent my brother from turning to a life of crime.'

'I can understand why you were so anxious to save Sam from being sent to a young offenders' institution. And why you believed Petros's lies about me,' Giannis said slowly. He drew Ava into his arms and his heart gave a jolt when she did not resist and sank against him while he lifted his hand and smoothed her hair back from her face. Oddly, he felt as though a weight had been lifted from him now that he knew why she had listened to Stefanos's nephew.

'I'm sorry,' she said huskily. 'I should have known that you are a million times a better man

than Petros tried to convince me when he said
you were involved in criminal activities.'

A better man? Giannis rested his chin on the
top of her head so that he did not have to look into
her eyes. What would Ava say if he told her that
he had killed his father? Not deliberately—but
his stupidity and arrogance when he was nineteen had led to him making a terrible mistake
that he would regret for the rest of his life. His
conscience insisted that he *should* tell her what
he had done. But then she might refuse to marry
him or allow him to see his child. His jaw hardened. It was a risk he was not prepared to take.

'I was afraid to tell you about my dad because
of how it might make you feel for the baby.'

Puzzled by her words, he eased away from her
a fraction and stared at her unhappy face.

'My ex-boyfriend decided not to marry me in
case our children inherited a criminality gene.
What if our child—?' She broke off, choked by
tears.

'Your ex was clearly an idiot.' Giannis drew
her close once more. 'Children learn from their
environment and our son will have the security
of being loved and nurtured by his parents. The

things we teach him when he is a child will shape the man he'll grow up to be.'

'I suppose you're right,' she said shakily. Giannis felt her body relax against him as he stroked his hand down the length of her silky golden hair. Hearing that her father was a criminal explained a lot of things and he admired her determination to protect her brother.

He could not pinpoint the exact moment that his desire to comfort her turned to desire of a very different kind. Perhaps she picked up the subtle signals his body sent out—the uneven rise and fall of his chest as his breathing quickened and the hard thud of his heart.

He looked into her eyes and saw her pupils dilate. She licked her tongue over her lips in an unconscious invitation and the ache in his gut became unbearable.

'I know you want me,' he said thickly, and watched a flush of heat spread down from her face to her throat and across her breasts. 'Why did you reject me when we were in the pool house?'

'It was *you* who rejected me. You dived into

the swimming pool because you couldn't bear to be near me.'

'You froze when I put my hands on you, and I assumed that you did not like me touching you.'

Ava's blush deepened. 'I liked it too much. But I wasn't sure if I could trust you.' She hesitated and said huskily, 'I'm sorry I listened to Petros.'

'So, do you like it when I touch you here?' Giannis murmured as he slid his hand over the swell of her stomach. He felt a fierce pride knowing that his baby was nestled inside her. He moved his hand lower and heard her give a soft gasp when he lifted up the hem of her negligee and stroked his fingers lightly over the silky panel of her panties between her legs.

'Don't tease me,' she whispered. 'My body has changed from when we first met. I don't want pity sex.'

He made a sound somewhere between a laugh and a groan as he pulled off his sweatpants and pressed the hard length of his arousal against her stomach. 'Does this feel like pity sex, *glykiá mou*?'

His hands shook when he tugged her nightgown over her head and cupped her bounteous breasts in his palms. 'It's true that your body has changed with pregnancy and you are even more beautiful. Have you any idea how gorgeous you are with your erotic curves that I want to explore with my hands and lips? Do you know how it makes me feel when I look at your body, so ripe and full with my child? I feel like I am the king of the world,' he told her rawly. 'And I want to make love to you more than I have ever wanted anything in my life.'

'Then stop talking and make love to me,' she demanded, her fierce voice making him smile before he claimed her mouth and kissed her as if the world was about to end and this was the last time he would taste her sweet lips. He was so hungry. Never in his life had he felt such an overwhelming need for a woman. But Ava was not any other woman—she was *his*, insisted a primal beast inside him, and the possessiveness he felt was shockingly new.

Despite their mutual impatience, Giannis was determined to take the time to savour every delicious dip and curve of Ava's body. Her breasts, he discovered, were incredibly sensitive, so that when he stroked his hands over the creamy globes and flicked his tongue across one dusky pink nipple and then the other she gave a thin cry that evoked an answering growl deep in his throat.

He lifted her and laid her on the bed, but when she tried to pull him down on top of her he evaded her hands and moved down her body, hooking her legs over his shoulders before he lowered his mouth to her slick feminine heat.

The taste of her almost sent him over the edge, but he ruthlessly controlled his own desire and devoted himself to his self-appointed task of pleasuring her. And he was rewarded when she arched her hips and dug her fingers into his shoulders. Her honey-gold hair was spread across the pillows and Giannis had never seen a more beautiful sight than Ava's rose-flushed face in the throes of her climax.

Only then, when she was still shuddering, did he spread her legs wide and position himself above her, entering her with exquisite care until he was buried deep within her velvet softness.

'I won't break,' she whispered in his ear, as if she guessed that he was afraid to let go of his iron self-control. She moved with him, matching his rhythm as they climbed to the peak together, and when he shattered, she shattered around him. And beneath his ribs the ice surrounding Giannis's heart cracked a little.

The following day, pale sunshine burst through the clouds and danced over the carpet of snowdrops in the churchyard when Ava posed on the chapel steps with Giannis for the wedding photographer. On her finger was the simple gold band he had put there, and next to it the pink sapphire heart ring that had been his unexpected choice when she'd been his fake fiancée, a lifetime ago, it seemed.

And in a way it was a lifetime. Her name was no longer Sheridan, or McKay. She was Ava Gekas, Giannis's wife, and in a scarily few months she would be a mother.

'Your bump barely shows,' Becky—whom Ava had chosen to be her maid of honour—whispered when the two of them had entered the private chapel where the other guests were assembled and Giannis was waiting for her at the altar. The ivory silk coat-dress Ava had chosen instead of a full-length bridal gown was cleverly cut to disguise her pregnancy, and her bouquet of palest pink roses, white baby's breath and trailing ivy made a pretty focal point.

Giannis was devastatingly handsome in a charcoal-grey suit that emphasised his lean, honed physique. Ava found she was trembling when she stood beside him, ready for the ceremony to begin.

'Are you cold, *glykiá mou*?' he murmured as he took her unsteady hand in his firm grasp. 'I'll warm you later.' The wicked glint in his eyes brought soft colour to her pale cheeks. He might not love her, but their wild passion the previous night was proof that he desired her and gave her hope that they could make something of their marriage. For their child's sake they would have to, Ava mused, and decided that the burst of winter sunshine was a good omen.

The wedding reception was held at a hotel in the village, and afterwards a car drove them to the airfield where Giannis's private jet was waiting to fly them to Greece.

'We will come back after the baby is born,' he said when the plane took off and Ava gave a wistful sigh. 'If you would prefer to live at Milton Grange, I can move my work base to England.'

She stared at him in surprise. 'Would you really do that? I thought you wanted our son to grow up in Greece.'

'We'll make a safe and secure home for him wherever we live, but I want you to be happy, *glykiá mou.*'

Hope unfurled like a fragile bud inside Ava. She had been worried that Giannis might want everything his way, but it sounded as if he was willing to make compromises. She smiled at him. 'I'll be happy living at Villa Delphine. Spetses is a beautiful place to bring up a child, and thankfully it's warmer than England,' she said ruefully. 'I'm looking forward to swimming in the sea.'

He laughed. 'You won't be able to do that for another few months. The sea temperature doesn't warm up until about June.'

'When the baby is due.' She felt butterflies in her stomach at the prospect of giving birth. 'It will be good to take the baby swimming when he is a few months old.'

'And I'll teach him how to sail when he is old enough. I was five when my father first took me sailing, and I loved the excitement of skimming over the waves in Patera's yacht.'

Giannis rarely mentioned his father. Ava looked at him curiously. 'Did your interest in boating have anything to do with your decision to run a cruise line company?'

He nodded. 'My father ran a business giving chartered cruises around the Greek islands. The *Nerissa* was his first motor yacht. There was a lot of competition from other charter operators but, instead of getting into a price war, Patera's idea was to offer a high standard of luxury on the boats, aimed at attracting wealthy clients.' A shadow crossed his face. 'After my father died, I continued to offer exclusivity rather than cheap cruises. The Gekas Experience was my father's brainchild and I was determined to make it successful in his honour.'

'You must miss him,' she said softly.

'I think about him every day. He was a wonderful man and a kind and patient father, as I hope I will be to our son.' Giannis hesitated and Ava sensed that he was about to say something else, but he turned his head and looked out of the window and she felt his barriers go up.

The idea that he was hiding something from her was not an auspicious start to their marriage.

But when they arrived on Spetses just as the sun was setting, Giannis insisted on carrying her over the threshold of Villa Delphine as if she were a proper bride and their marriage a true romance, as his staff who were waiting in the entrance hall to greet them clearly believed.

'I have a surprise for you,' he said as he took her hand and led her upstairs. He opened the door on the landing next to the master bedroom. 'What do you think?'

Ava looked around the room that had been turned into a nursery, with pale blue walls and a frieze of farmyard animals. There was a white-painted cot that at the moment was filled with a collection of soft toys, but soon it was where their baby would sleep.

'We can change anything that you don't like,' Giannis said when she remained silent.

She swallowed the lump in her throat. 'It's beautiful and I don't want to change a thing.'

'I asked the builders to create a connecting door into our room,' he explained.

'Our room' had a nice sound, Ava thought as she followed him through the new doorway into the bedroom and went unresistingly into his arms when he drew her towards him.

'I love the nursery.' *I love you.* She kept the words in her heart. Giannis did not love her and that made her feel vulnerable. She felt guilty that she had not trusted him at the beginning of her pregnancy, and it was understandable that it might take him a while to forgive her. But last night had proved that he desired her, and it was a start. She wound her arms around his neck, smiling at his impatient curse when he discovered the dozens of tiny buttons that fastened her dress.

'Patience is a virtue,' she reminded him sweetly, and he punished her by ravishing her mouth with his before he trailed his lips down her throat and tormented her nipples with his tongue until she pleaded for mercy. 'I want you,' she told him when they were both naked and he pulled her down onto the bed.

He grinned as he lounged back against the pillows like an indolent Sultan and beckoned her by crooking his finger. 'Then take me,' he invited. And she did, with a fierce passion that made him groan when she took him deep inside her and made love to him with her body, her heart and her soul.

Afterwards, when he held her in his arms and stroked her hair, Ava pressed her lips against his shoulder and silently whispered the secret in her heart. Give it time, she told herself when he kissed the tip of her nose and settled her against him.

'Go to sleep, *glykiá mou*. You've had a tiring day,' he murmured. They were not the words she longed for him to say, but she thought that he cared for her a little. For the first time since she had learned the truth about her father when she was seventeen, Ava finally relaxed her guard and allowed hope and happiness to fill her heart.

Springtime in Greece arrived earlier than in the UK and the countryside on Spetses was a riot of colourful red poppies and white rock roses with their bright orange centres. Pink daisies bobbed their heads in the breeze and the scents of chamomile and thyme filled the air.

Ava loved the island and quickly grew to think of it as her home. It helped that she spoke Greek, and she chatted with the locals in the market and the little cafés where she stopped for coffee when she went shopping in the pretty town around the old harbour. Some days Giannis travelled to his office in Athens by helicopter, but more often he worked in his study and joined her for lunch on the terrace.

He introduced her to his friends who lived on the island and Ava was surprised that some of them were married couples with children. She had been worried that he would miss his playboy lifestyle and she was heartened that he seemed comfortable and relaxed when they met up with other families.

The weeks slipped by and it seemed that every day the sun shone in the azure sky. The only black cloud to darken Ava's sunny mood was Giannis's mother. Filia had been away, staying with relatives in Rhodes, but when she returned to Spetses Giannis invited her to dinner at Villa Delphine.

Her sharp gaze flew to Ava's baby bump. 'I wondered why the wedding was arranged so quickly,' she said with a sniff. 'Giannis did not do me the courtesy of telling me that I am to be a grandmother.'

Ava shot him a startled glance. It was strange that he hadn't announced her pregnancy to his mother. During dinner she was aware of an undercurrent of tension that her attempts at conversation could not disguise. 'Did you enjoy your trip?' she asked Filia in a desperate bid to break the strained silence between mother and son.

Filia shrugged. 'Loneliness travels with me wherever I go,' she said as her black eyes rested on Giannis. Ava was glad when the uncomfortable evening came to an end. Filia gathered up her shawl and purse. 'I hope you will act more responsibly when *you* are a father than you did with your own father,' she told Giannis.

'Do not doubt it. I will take the greatest care of my son,' he replied curtly.

Later, Ava found him standing outside on the terrace. The night was dark, the moon obscured by clouds, but it emerged briefly and cast a cold gleam over Giannis's hard profile. He looked remote and austere and she did not know how to reach him.

'Your mother is an unhappy woman,' she observed quietly.

He stiffened when she placed her hand over his

on the balustrade. His reaction felt like a very definite rejection that stirred up her old feelings of vulnerability. 'I was the cause of her unhappiness,' he said in a clipped voice, but he did not offer any further explanation and Ava was too uncertain of their tenuous relationship to ask him what he meant.

'I'm going to bed,' she murmured. 'Are you coming too?' When they made love she felt closer to him, emotionally as well as physically, and maybe she would find out what was on his mind.

'I have some paperwork to read through and I'll be up in a while.' He brushed his lips over hers but lifted his head without giving her a chance to respond, leaving her longing for him to kiss her properly. 'Don't wait up for me.'

Giannis watched Ava walk back inside the house and swore beneath his breath as he pictured her hurt expression. He knew he should go after her, scoop her into his arms and carry her up to their bedroom, as he knew she had wanted him to do. Of course he wanted to make love to her. Sex wasn't the problem. She was in the third trimester of her pregnancy and he found her curvaceous figure intensely desirable. Their hunger for one another was as urgent as it had always been—although she did not have quite so much energy and often fell asleep in his arms before he'd even withdrawn from her body.

He felt an odd sensation as if his heart was being crushed in a vice when he thought of her curled up beside him, her face flushed from passion and her honey-gold hair spread across the pillows. He loved to stroke his hands over the swell of her stomach where his son was nestled inside her. Sometimes when the baby moved, Giannis could actually see the outline of a tiny hand or foot. It would not be long now before the baby was here, but his excitement was mixed with trepidation. What did he know about fatherhood and caring for a baby? What if he made a mistake and harmed his son, as he had made a tragic mistake years ago?

Tonight, his mother's reference to what he had done had reminded him of the fragility of life. As if he needed reminding, he thought grimly. He could never forget the consequences of his irresponsibility when he was nineteen, or forgive himself, as quite clearly his mother was unable to do. Now, as he awaited the birth of his baby, he missed his father more than ever. It tore at his heart to know that his son would not meet his grandfather, and would never know the affection and kindness that his *patera* had showered on Giannis. But he would love his own son as deeply as his father had loved him, he vowed.

He gripped the balustrade rail and stared across the beach at the black sea, dappled with silver moonlight. His father had loved the sea, and Giannis felt closest to him on Spetses. That was why he wanted his son to grow up on the island, and thankfully Ava seemed happy living at Villa Delphine. But would she be happy to live in Greece with him if he admitted that he had caused his father's death and been sent to prison for driving after he'd drunk alcohol, which the coroner had suggested had been a likely reason for the fatal car crash?

She might decide that he was not fit to be a father and take his son back to England. The memory of Caroline's reaction to his confession five years earlier haunted him. He could not risk losing his baby, and with a sudden flash of insight he realised that he did not want to lose Ava. He had married her so that he could claim his child, but over the past months since their wedding she had slipped beneath his guard.

His jaw clenched. If he wasn't careful he would find himself falling in love with Ava, which had never been part of his plan. He had been in love with Caroline—at least he'd be certain at the time that he loved her, and her rejection had hurt. But the loss of his first child had hurt him far more. A voice inside him whispered that what he had felt for Caroline had been insignificant compared to the riot of feeling that swept through him when he thought of his wife.

Theos, what a mess. Giannis strode across the terrace and entered the house. He hesitated at the foot of the stairs before he turned and walked resolutely into his study, acknowledging self-derisively that work offered a safety net and a hiding place from his complicated emotions.

But when he switched on his laptop and read the email that pinged into his inbox from the journalist who had tried to blackmail him five years ago he felt a hard knot of fear in the pit of his stomach, knowing that he could never escape from his past.

CHAPTER ELEVEN

AVA HAD NO idea what time Giannis had come to bed the previous night. With only six weeks to go until her due date, she often felt a bone-deep tiredness and, despite her efforts to remain awake and talk to him, she had fallen asleep. In the morning she had seen an indent on the pillow next to her where his head had lain, and when she'd gone downstairs he was already working in his study.

But at least his black mood seemed to have lifted and he greeted her with a smile when she reminded him that she had a routine check-up with the midwife. In a couple more weeks they would move into the apartment in Athens so that she would be near to the private maternity hospital where the baby would be born.

'I'll come to your appointment with you,' he offered. 'But it's too far for you to walk into town. Thomas can take us in the horse and carriage.'

His phone rang, and his smile faded and was replaced with a disturbingly harsh expression when he glanced at the screen. 'I'm sorry, *glykiá mou*, I need to take the call. What time is your appointment?'

'In half an hour, but I want to do some shopping first. Thomas will take me to the town, and I'll see you later.'

Cars were not allowed in Spetses Town, and Ava enjoyed the novelty of travelling in an open-topped carriage, shaded from the hot sun by a parasol and listening to the sound of the horse's hooves clipping along the road. She gave a soft sigh of contentment. Her life at Villa Delphine was idyllic and Giannis's tenderness towards her lately made her feel cherished in a way she had never felt before. For some reason he had a difficult relationship with his mother, hence his tense mood last night. But Ava was focused on becoming a mother herself and pregnancy cocooned her from the real world.

At the clinic, the midwife listened to the baby's heartbeat and was satisfied that all was well. 'I'll give you your medical notes so that you can take them to the maternity hospital on the mainland when you go into labour,' the midwife explained as she handed Ava a folder.

Out of idle curiosity Ava skimmed through her notes. She spoke Greek fluently but she was not so good at reading the language, and she assumed she must have misunderstood the last sentence on the page.

'Does it say that a blood sample will be taken from the baby when he is born?' Her confusion grew when the midwife nodded. 'Is it standard procedure in Greece?'

'Only when a paternity test has been requested by the parents,' the midwife told her.

Ava's heart juddered to a standstill. She certainly had not requested a test to prove the baby's paternity. But Giannis must have done so—which meant he must have doubts that the child she was carrying was his.

Somehow she managed to walk calmly out of the clinic and smiled at Thomas when he helped her into the carriage. But she felt numb with shock. Since she'd married Giannis, she had believed that all the misunderstandings between them had been resolved and they did not have secrets. But all this time he had suspected her of trying to foist another man's child on him. She felt sick. So hurt that there was a physical pain in her chest.

When she arrived back at the villa and heard the helicopter's engine—an indication that Giannis was about to leave the island—anger surged like scalding lava through her veins. She almost collided with him in the entrance hall as she ran into the house, and he was on his way out.

He looked tense and distracted, and he frowned when she thrust the folder containing her medical notes at him. 'I need to talk to you.'

Concern flashed in his eyes. 'Is there a problem with the baby?'

'The baby is fine. The problem is *you*.' As she spoke, Ava asked herself why Giannis would be so anxious about the baby's welfare if he really believed it wasn't his child.

'Why did you ask for a paternity test to be carried out when our son is born?' she demanded. 'Don't try to deny it,' she said furiously when his eyes narrowed. 'The request for a blood test is written in my notes. Do you think that when I left you after we had been to Stefanos Markou's party, I immediately hooked up with some other guy?'

'No,' he said tersely. 'But at the time I asked for the paternity test I thought it was possible that you had already been pregnant before we slept together in London.'

She shook her head. 'How could you doubt my integrity like that?'

'Like you doubted me when you believed a jealous man's lies about me being a criminal?' he shot back. He raked his hand through his hair, and Ava noted that he avoided making eye contact with her. 'Look, something important has come up and I have to go to Athens.'

'You're *leaving*? Am I not important enough for you to want to stay and discuss a major issue with our relationship? Clearly I'm not,' she said dully when he picked up his briefcase and strode across the hall.

He paused in the doorway and turned to look at her. 'I realise that we need to talk, and we will as soon as I have dealt with a...problem at the office.' His voice sounded oddly strained. 'To tell you the truth I had forgotten about the paternity test. And it could not have been carried out without your consent.'

'The truth is that you don't care about me and I was stupid to hope that you would ever fall in love with me, as I…' She broke off and stared at his granite-hard features.

'As you…what?'

'It doesn't matter,' she said wearily. 'You're in too much of a hurry to talk to me, remember?'

Giannis looked as though he was about to speak, but he shook his head. 'Something arrived for you while you were out. Look in the bedroom,' he told her before he walked out of the villa.

A few minutes later, Ava heard the helicopter take off while she was climbing the stairs up to the second floor. She pushed open the door of the master bedroom and stopped dead, the tears that she had held back until then filling her eyes. On her dressing table was the biggest bouquet of red roses she had ever seen. At least three dozen perfect scarlet blooms arranged in a crystal vase and exuding a heavenly fragrance that filled the room. Propped up against the vase was a card and she recognised Giannis's bold handwriting.

For my beautiful wife. You are everything I could ever want or hope for. Giannis

There was no mention of love, but surely the roses were a statement that he felt something for her? Ava's fingers trembled as she touched the velvety rose petals. She sank down onto the edge of the bed and gave a shaky sigh. If the roses had been delivered before she had gone to her ante-natal appointment and discovered that Giannis had asked for a paternity test on their baby she would have taken his romantic gesture as a sign that he loved her and she would have told him how she felt about him.

Now that she had calmed down, she could understand why he had requested the test. They had been strangers when they had slept together for the first time. Not only had she believed Stefanos's nephew's lies about Giannis, but she had kept it secret that her father was a criminal. They had both hidden things from each other, but if their marriage was going to work—and the roses were an indication that Giannis wanted her to be his wife—then they must be honest about their feelings.

He had promised that they would talk when he

returned home. But the prospect of waiting for him at the villa did not appeal to Ava, and she picked up the phone and asked Thomas to take her to Athens on the speedboat that Giannis kept moored at Villa Delphine's private jetty.

By the time she reached TGE's offices in the city it was lunchtime and most of the staff were away from their desks. Giannis's PA, Sofia, greeted Ava with a smile. 'He's still in a meeting. I'm just off to lunch but I'll let him know that you are here.'

'No, don't disturb him,' Ava said quickly. 'I'll wait until he has finished.' It would give her a chance to prepare what she wanted to say to him. How hard could it be to say the three little words *I love you*?

But as the minutes ticked by while she waited in his secretary's office, she felt increasingly nervous. Maybe he had given her the red roses simply because he knew that she liked flowers, and wishful thinking had made her read more into his gift?

From inside Giannis's office, Ava could hear voices. She stiffened when one voice suddenly became louder and distinctly aggressive. 'I'm warning you, Gekas. Give me one million pounds or I'll go public with the story that you spent a year in prison for killing your father when you were drunk. I can't imagine that TGE's shareholders will be so keen to support Greece's golden boy when they hear that you are an ex-convict,' the voice sneered.

'And I'm warning you that I will not tolerate your blackmail attempt,' Giannis snarled. His eyes narrowed on the lowlife journalist who had called him that morning and demanded to see him. Demetrios Kofidis was the reason he'd had to leave Ava and come to Athens, and he was impatient to deal with the scumbag so that he could hurry back to Spetses and reassure his wife that he trusted her implicitly.

He cursed himself for ever thinking of having a paternity test when he knew in his heart that the baby was his. It was a pity he had not listened to his heart, he thought grimly. He could only hope that he hadn't left it too late to tell Ava in words what he had tried to say with the roses.

'You paid me to keep quiet about your past five years ago,' the journalist said. 'Pay up again,

Gekas, or I'll sell the story to every tabloid in Europe and beyond.'

Giannis pushed back his chair and stood up. 'You think you're clever, Kofidis, but I recorded our conversation and before you arrived I alerted the police about you. If you publish anything about me you will be arrested for attempted blackmail quicker than you can blink. Now get out of my sight.'

He kept his gaze fixed on the journalist when he heard the faint click of the office door opening. 'I told you that I don't want to be disturbed, Sofia.'

'Giannis.' Ava's voice was a whisper, but it sliced through Giannis's heart like a knife as he jerked his eyes across the room and saw her standing in the doorway. One hand rested protectively on the burgeoning swell of her stomach. Her honey-blonde hair was loose, tumbling around her shoulders, and she was so beautiful that his breath became trapped in his throat.

'What are you doing here, *glykiá mou*?' he began, trying to sound normal, trying to hide the fear that churned in his gut as he wondered how much she had heard of his conversation with the journalist. 'Sweetheart…'

'You went to prison, and you didn't tell me.'

'I can explain. It was an accident… I drove my father home from a restaurant and…'

'You didn't tell me,' she repeated slowly. 'I thought there were no more secrets between us, but all this time you held something back from me—because you don't trust me.'

'I *do* trust you.' Giannis crashed his hip bone against the corner of the desk in his hurry to reach Ava, but as he strode across the room she stepped back into the outer office.

'There have been too many secrets and lies between us—and that is the biggest lie of all,' she choked, before she spun round and ran over to the door.

'Ava, wait.' Giannis cursed as he followed her into the lobby. His offices were on the ground floor and the lobby was bustling with staff returning from their lunch break. He apologised when he knocked into someone. Ahead of him Ava had reached the front entrance. The glass doors slid open and she walked out. Moments later he followed her outside.

'*Ava.*'

She was hurrying down the flight of concrete steps in front of the building and glanced over her shoulder at him. In that instant she stumbled, and Giannis watched in horror as she lost her footing and fell down the remaining steps. It seemed to happen in slow motion and, just as when he had taken a bend in the road too fast sixteen years earlier, he felt shock, disbelief and a sense of terror that made him gag.

He was still at the top of the steps and there was nothing he could do to save Ava. She gave a startled cry and landed on the pavement with a sickening thud. And then she was silent. Motionless.

Giannis heard a rushing noise in his ears and a voice shouting, '*No! No!*' Much later he realised that it had been his voice shouting, pleading. *No!* He couldn't lose Ava and his baby.

He raced down the steps and dropped onto his knees beside her, carefully rolling her onto her back. Her eyes were closed and her face was deathly pale. A purple bruise was already darkening on her brow.

'Ava *mou*, wake up.' He felt for her pulse and

detected a faint beat. Glancing up, he saw a crowd of people had gathered. 'Call an ambulance,' he shouted. 'Quickly.'

Someone must have already done so, and he heard the wail of a siren. But Ava did not open her eyes, and when Giannis looked down her body he saw blood seeping through her dress.

His heart stopped. *Theos*, if she lost the baby she would never forgive him and he would never forgive himself. If he lost both of them… A constriction in his throat prevented him from swallowing. He brushed his hand over his wet eyes. He could not contemplate his life without Ava. It would be a joyless, pointless existence, and nothing more than he deserved, he thought bleakly.

From then on everything became a blur when the ambulance arrived and the paramedics took charge and carefully lifted Ava onto a stretcher. As the ambulance raced to the hospital her eyelids fluttered on her cheeks, but she slipped in and out of consciousness and her dress was soaked with blood.

'My wife *will* be all right, won't she?' Giannis asked hoarsely.

'We will soon be at the hospital,' the paramedic

replied evasively. 'The doctors will do everything they can to save her life and the child's.'

The last time Giannis had cried had been at his father's funeral, but his throat burned and his eyes ached with tears as he lifted Ava's cold, limp hand to his lips. 'Don't leave me, *agápi mou*,' he begged. 'I should have told you about my father, and I wish I had told you that I love you, my angel. I'm sorry that I didn't, and I promise I will tell you how much you mean to me every day for the rest of our lives, if only you will stay with me.'

He thought he might have imagined that he felt her fingers move in his hand. And he needed every ounce of hope when they arrived at the hospital and Ava was rushed into Theatre. 'A condition called placental abruption occurred as a result of your wife's fall,' the doctor explained to Giannis. 'It means that the placenta has become detached from the wall of the uterus and she has lost a lot of blood. The baby must be delivered as soon as possible to save the lives of both the child and the mother.'

For the second time in his life he had maybe left it too late to say what was in his heart, Giannis thought when a nurse showed him into a waiting room. Pain ripped through him as he remembered how he had stood at his father's graveside and wished he had told his *patera* how much he loved and respected him, and how one day he hoped to be as good a father to his own child.

Now his baby's and Ava's lives were in the balance. They were both so precious to him but he was unable to help them. All he could do was pace up and down the waiting room and pray.

Ava opened her eyes, and for the first time in three days her head did not feel as if a pneumatic drill was driving into her skull. In fact the concussion she'd suffered after falling down the steps had been unimportant compared to nearly losing her baby. Of course she had no memory of the emergency Caesarean section she'd undergone or, sadly, of the moment her son had been born.

When she'd come round from the anaesthetic Giannis had told her that, despite the baby's abrupt entry into the world six weeks early, he weighed a healthy five pounds. They had settled on the name Andreas during her pregnancy and, although she had still felt woozy when she had been taken in a wheelchair to the special care baby unit, she had been able to hold her tiny dark haired son in her arms and she'd wept tears of joy and relief that he was safe and well.

Now, seventy-two hours after the shocking events that had preceded the baby's early arrival, she looked across the room and her heart skipped a beat when she saw Giannis sitting in a chair, cradling Andreas against his shoulder. The tender look on his face as he held the baby was something Ava would never forget, and the unguarded expression in Giannis's eyes as he looked over at her filled her with hope and longing.

'You're still here,' she murmured. 'I thought you might go back to the apartment for a few hours. The nurses will look after Andreas in the nursery now that he has been moved from the special care ward.'

'I'm not going anywhere until the two of you are ready to be discharged from hospital.' His gentle smile stole Ava's breath. 'How are you feeling?'

'Much better.' She'd had a blood transfusion, stitches and she was pumped full of drugs to fight infection and relieve pain, but her son was worth everything she'd been through. She sat up carefully and held out her arms to take the baby. 'He's so perfect,' she said softly. Her heart ached with love as she studied Andreas's silky-soft black hair and his eyes that were as dark as his daddy's eyes.

'He is a miracle. You both are.' Giannis's voice thickened. '*Theos*, when I saw you fall down those steps and I feared I had lost both of you...' His jaw clenched. 'I didn't know what I would do without you,' he said rawly.

It was the first time that either of them had mentioned what had happened, and the deep grooves on either side of Giannis's mouth were an indication of what he must have felt, believing he might lose the baby he had been so desperate for. Ava handed Andreas to him. 'He's fallen asleep. Will you put him in the crib?'

She rested her head against the pillows and thought how gorgeous Giannis looked in faded jeans and a casual cream cotton shirt. She was glad that a nurse had helped her into the shower earlier and she had managed to wash her hair.

He came back and sat down on the chair next to her bed. Suddenly she felt stupidly shy and afraid, and a whole host of other emotions that made her pleat the sheet between her fingers rather than meet his gaze. 'What happened to your father?' she asked in a low tone.

Giannis exhaled slowly. 'I was nineteen and had just set up TGE with my father. We'd gone to a restaurant for dinner and during the meal I drank a glass of wine. I certainly did not feel drunk, but even a small amount of alcohol can impair your judgement. Driving home, I took a steep bend in the road too fast and the car over-turned. I escaped with a few cuts and bruises, but my father sustained serious injuries.'

His eyes darkened with pain. 'I held him in my arms while we waited for the ambulance, and he made it to the hospital but died soon afterwards. I have never touched alcohol since that night, even though I've often wished that I could numb my grief and guilt.'

'Why didn't you tell me?' Ava could not disguise her hurt. 'It wasn't overhearing what you had done that upset me, but realising that you had kept such a huge secret from me. I trusted you when I told you about my father being a criminal, but you only ever shut me out, Giannis.'

'I was afraid to admit what I had done,' he said heavily. 'A few years ago I fell in love.'

Jealousy stabbed Ava through her heart. 'What happened?'

'Caroline fell pregnant. Her father was an American senator who was campaigning in the Presidential elections, and when I admitted that I had served a prison sentence Caroline refused to marry me because—in her words—having an ex-convict as a son-in-law might have damaged her father's political ambitions. She told me she had suffered a miscarriage, but I'm fairly certain that she chose not to go ahead with the pregnancy. I overheard her on the phone telling a friend that she had dealt with the pregnancy problem,' he answered Ava's unspoken question.

'So when you found out that I had conceived your baby, you were worried that I might do the same as your ex-girlfriend?'

He grimaced. 'I was determined to have my child, and I treated you unforgivably when I forced you to marry me.'

She stared at his handsome face and her heart turned over when she saw that his eyelashes were wet. This was a different Giannis—a broken Giannis, she thought painfully. His vulnerability hurt her more than anything else. 'You didn't force me,' she said huskily. 'I chose to marry you, knowing that you had asked me to be your wife because you wanted your son.'

'No, Ava *mou*. That was not the reason I proposed marriage.'

She dared not believe the expression in his eyes, the softening of his hard features as he stared at her intently. 'I need to tell you something,' she said shakily. 'I heard the things you said in the ambulance. At least, I think I heard you, but maybe I dreamed it...' She broke off and bit her lip, aware of her heart thudding in her chest. 'Why did you ask me to marry you?'

'I love you.'

The three little words hovered in the air, but were they a tantalising dream? Ava wondered. Did she have the courage to give her absolute trust to Giannis?

'Don't!' Her voice shook and tears trembled on her eyelashes. 'Don't say it if you don't mean it.'

'But I do mean it, *agápi mou,*' he said gently. 'I love you with all my heart and soul.' Suddenly his restraint left him and he leapt to his feet, sending his chair clattering onto the floor. He sat on the edge of the bed and captured her hands in his.

'I adore you, Ava. I never knew I could feel like this, to love so utterly and completely that I cannot contemplate my life without you.' He stroked her hair back from her face with a trembling hand. 'When you left Athens I couldn't understand why I was so miserable until my head accepted what my heart had been telling me. I missed you, and I decided to ask you if we could start again. But then I read the Christmas card from your brother and discovered you were pregnant with my child.'

'And you were angry,' Ava said quietly.

'I was scared. I don't deserve you or our son.' He swallowed convulsively. 'I destroyed my family with my reckless behaviour, and I'm terrified that I might somehow hurt you and Andreas. *Theos*...' His face twisted in pain. 'It is my fault that you fell down those damned steps and you and the baby could have died. I should have been honest with you about what happened to my father. And of course I don't want a paternity test. I know Andreas is mine. But I've made so many mistakes and I have to let you and my son go.

If you want to take Andreas to live in England I won't stop you. All I ask is that you allow me to be part of his life.'

Ava listened to the torrent of emotion that spilled from Giannis. It was as if a dam had burst and his feelings—his love for her—poured out, healing her hurt and filling her with joy.

'Oh, Giannis. Darling Giannis.' She wrapped her arms around his neck and clung to him. 'The only way you could ever hurt me is if you stop loving me. The only place I want to be is with you, because I love you so much.'

'Really?' The uncertainty in his voice tore Ava's heart. She put her hands on either side of his face. 'You have to learn to forgive yourself and believe me when I say that you deserve to be happy and loved by me and your son and the family that we will create together.'

'Ava,' he groaned as he pulled her into his heat and fire and held her so close that she felt the thunderous beat of his heart. '*S'agapó, kardiá mou.* I love you, my heart. My sweet love.'

He kissed her then—wondrously, as if she was everything he had ever wanted or would ever need. And she kissed him with all the love in her heart and her tears of happiness mingled with his as he threaded his fingers through her hair and gently eased her back against the pillows.

'We will never have secrets,' Giannis murmured between kisses.

Ava smiled. '*Did* I hear you say in the ambulance that you would tell me every day how much you love me, or did I dream it?'

'It was no dream, *kardiá mou*. It was a promise that I intend to keep for ever.'

EPILOGUE

THEY TOOK ANDREAS to Spetses when he was four weeks old. Despite his traumatic birth he was a strong and healthy baby with a good set of lungs, his father noted ruefully at two o'clock one morning. Ava recovered remarkably quickly and was delighted to be able to fit into her jeans two months after her son's birth. Her confidence in Giannis's love grew stronger with every day, and the first time they made love again was deeply emotional as they showed with their bodies their adoration for each other.

Life could not be better, Ava thought one afternoon as she pushed Andreas in his pram around the garden of Villa Delphine. Giannis had reluctantly gone to his office in Athens, but he'd called her a while ago to say that he was on his way home. 'Your *patera* will be here soon,' she said to Andreas and when he gave her a gummy smile she told him that both the Gekas males in her life had stolen her heart.

Her spirits dipped when she saw Giannis's mother walking across the lawn. Filia's waspish expression softened as she looked in the pram. 'My grandson grows bigger every time I see him,' she commented, and Ava felt guilty that she did not invite her mother-in-law to Villa Delphine as often as she should. The visits were always strained and she knew that Giannis found his mother difficult.

'Where is my son?' Filia demanded. 'Giannis promised weeks ago that he would arrange for his private jet to fly me to Italy so I can visit my daughter, but I still have not heard when the trip will be. I suppose he has forgotten about me.'

'Giannis has been busy at work lately, and he spends as much time as he can with Andreas, but I'm sure he hasn't forgotten about your trip,' Ava explained.

'No doubt he expects me to take a commercial flight. He is so wealthy, but he gives me nothing.'

Ava nearly choked. She knew that Giannis had bought his mother the beautiful house she lived in on Spetses, and he paid for her living expenses and her numerous holidays. 'I don't think you are being fair to him,' she murmured.

Filia snorted. 'It isn't fair that I have spent the last fifteen years a widow, thanks to Giannis.' She gave Ava a sharp look. 'I suppose he has told you that he was responsible for his father's death?'

Giannis froze with his hand on the gate which led into the garden. He knew that the tall hedge screened him from Ava and his mother, who were standing some way across the lawn. But he could see them and he could hear their voices.

'Giannis told me what happened sixteen years ago.' Ava's voice was as cool and clear as a mountain stream. 'I know that he loved his father very much, and his grief has been made worse by his feelings of guilt. It breaks my heart to know that he can't forgive himself,' she said softly.

Hidden behind the hedge, Giannis brushed a hand over his wet eyes.

'Why do you defend him?' he heard his mother ask.

'Because he made a terrible mistake that I know he has regretted every day since the accident. It was an accident with devastating consequences, but it was an *accident*. I know that the man I love is a good and honourable man.'

'So you do love him?' Filia said with a snort. 'You did not marry him because he is rich?'

'I married Giannis because I love him with all my heart, and I'd love him if he didn't have a penny to his name.' Ava's fierce voice carried across the garden. 'What happened in the past was tragic, but it is also a tragedy that you have not forgiven your own son.' She put her hands on her hips. 'Your constant criticism of Giannis has to stop, or I am afraid that you will no longer be welcome at Villa Delphine to visit Andreas.'

His wife was a warrior, Giannis thought, shaken to his core by Ava's defence of him. She was amazing. He opened the gate and strode across the garden. His footsteps were noiseless on the soft grass, but his mother was facing him and she immediately appealed to him.

'I hope you will not allow your wife to threaten to withhold my grandson from me? Say something to her, Giannis.'

'There are many things I want to say to Ava. But I will speak to her alone. Leave us, please,' he told his mother curtly. She opened her mouth to argue but, after looking at his expression, she clearly thought better of it and without another word she turned and walked out of the garden.

'I'm sorry if I upset your mother,' Ava said ruefully. 'But I meant what I said. I won't let her upset you. What are you doing?' she asked as Giannis pushed the pram across the garden and into the summer house.

'The bedroom is too far away for what I have in mind,' he murmured as he pulled her into his arms.

Her eyes widened when he pressed his aching arousal against her pelvis. 'Mmm—what exactly do you have in mind?'

'I want to make love to you, darling heart,' Giannis said thickly. 'But first I need to tell you how much I love you, and thank you for loving me and for giving me our gorgeous son.' He tugged the straps of her sundress down and roamed his hands over her body.

'You are so beautiful, so perfect. Mine, for eternity.' He threw the cushions from the garden furniture onto the floor and laid her down before covering her body with his. And there he made love to her with fierce passion and a tenderness that made Ava realise that dreams could come true.

'Eternity sounds perfect,' she agreed.

* * * * *

LET'S TALK
Romance

For exclusive extracts, competitions
and special offers, find us online:

f facebook.com/millsandboon

⬤ @millsandboonuk

🐦 @millsandboon

Or get in touch on 0844 844 1351*

For all the latest titles coming soon,
visit millsandboon.co.uk/nextmonth